C000067722

RoomHates

Life in the Brohouse | Book 1

Carmen Black

SCARLET LANTERN
Publishing

Scarlet Lantern Publishing

Chapter 1

RACHEL

It's a bright, uncharacteristically warm day in late September. The plastic grip of my camera is hot beneath my fingertips as I squint into the viewfinder.

In the view of my lens is the University of Aurora.

It's a pretty campus, pretty in that Colorado way. The mountains loom in the distance, the very tips of them painted white. Large, tan buildings surround me, square and flat-roofed, the glass of each window covered with a marine reflective film. The blue-silver shine is too blindingly bright to look at. The quad's lawn is perfectly manicured, but it barely matters; the grass is drowned in red and orange leaves, flying from the trees that surround the lawn. The breeze turns direction and blows directly at me. It's freezing cold compared to the blazing sun overhead and a small flood of red-gold leaves drift around my sneakers, crackling like fire.

My head is hot from the sun. I tilt the camera this way and that, trying to find my image. The buildings, the trees, the mountains, the leaves; they're all very pretty, all very Colorado, but I can't find the way to make it all work together. *Trees in the foreground, mountains in the background? Buildings foreground, trees background? Leaves foreground, quad background?* It's like trying to complete a puzzle without an image of the final result. I know it goes together somehow, but I can't see what should connect where.

The windows of the buildings are starting to dazzle me. I sigh and lower the camera with no photos taken. I can't find my angle today, it seems.

Like most days.

I deposit the camera back in its case, put the case in my overfull backpack, and heft it over my shoulders, wheeling my suitcase behind me. It's getting toward midday anyway and I've been travelling since five this morning. I need to get to my new home.

Every route I take I can see new students, just like me, wandering in the same direction toward the dorms. I'm pretty much the only one walking in the opposite direction. A suitcase bumps against mine, sending them both skittering. I wrench mine back under control and wheel it closer to me only to have the same thing happening again. Trying to walk against the tide is humiliating. It practically screams: 'Hey, look who got a late acceptance!' 'Hey, guess who got in too late to get a dorm room!'

In truth, I hadn't wanted to go to the University of Aurora. Beautiful as it was, it wasn't an art school. I had one of those vision boards on my wall, all the pictures tacked on neatly among fairy lights and washi tape. I liked the idea of going to art school surrounded by artists and great thinkers, who could by increments nudge me to greatness. When I slept, I dreamed of art school. When I was awake, I daydreamed of art school.

But I couldn't make the art come.

I had always been artistic. *Talented*, even. Art school was the natural next step, but I had never really found that 'thing'. Call it a niche, an inspiration, a reason to be. Whatever it was, I didn't have it. I had, in the end, settled on photography for my portfolio only because there was no time left for anything else. It was so rushed that I received rejection after rejection. Finally, I applied to Aurora's underfunded and poorly considered art department, and I only did it because Colorado was as far as I could get from my disappointed New York family.

No, Aurora isn't an art school. If anything, it's a sport school. Getting a sports scholarship to Aurora U is basically a ticket to greatness. I'd seen on the website that a quarter of their sports teams went on to become professional *whatevers* at the sport they did. And they seem to outnumber anyone else here—half of the students shoulder-checking me as I walk through the mass look as though they live at the gym. Sweatpants, polo shirts, and varsity jackets are practically the uniform here. The girls all have practical, high-scraped ponytails, perfect smiles on perfect bodies as they heft overstuffed carryalls like they weigh nothing. The guys wear shirts

way too small at the bicep—*or maybe their biceps really* are *that big?*
I squint at them against the glare of the noonday sun, all these
perfect silhouettes and beautiful bodies...

Something crashes into my back, hard and fast, and I go
sprawling, my suitcase clattering to the ground behind me. The
oncoming students walk around me, not bothering to look down.
Thanks, assholes!

I turn around. Above me loom two of the tallest guys I've seen on
campus.

One of them has to be at least 6'2", his bright blond hair glinting
where it just brushes his shoulders; and those are the broadest
shoulders I've ever seen on an actual human being. Under one arm,
he's carrying what must have knocked into me; a long set of Kayak
paddles. Under his other arm, he's holding some football shoulder
pads.

The other guy is even taller than that, maybe 6'6", and he's not
got the Thor-like build of the blonde guy, but his biceps are *huge*,
practically bursting out of his navy polo shirt. He's scowling down
at me, his dark hair falling in strands across his eyes.

"Watch where you're going," Tallest Guy says, face screwed up in
disdain, before walking fully around me and my suitcase. I splutter
in infuriation—*you should be looking where you're going, your friend
knocked me over with his dumb paddle!*—and turn where I'm
sprawled on the ground to yell after him, but a large, strong hand
yanks me up by my arm. I turn, now unceremoniously standing,
back to Broad Shoulder Guy.

"Keep a look out, yeah?" he says, before hefting the shoulder pads
a little higher under his arm, picking up his kayak paddle where he'd
put it on the ground, and walking past me as well. I'm so shocked I
don't even yell after him. *He picked me up like I weighed nothing.*

When I pick up my suitcase from the ground, the hard plastic is
scuffed all over. I grimace.

What a welcome to Aurora.

The students thin out the further I get from campus, wandering
the wide sidewalks with my phone open in my hand. I'm getting
close. This had been the only affordable place I had found in
Aurora, and I'm kind of surprised it was so cheap to rent. Sure, I'm
getting one room of four, and I'll apparently have to live with three
guys, but even then. I've seen the pictures on the website; it's a really

nice apartment, big windows and modern furnishings, and it's barely a fifteen-minute walk from the campus.

Or, it *should* be. The phone dings to tell me I've arrived, but the block I'm stopped by is one building with no doors. I circle the block, and the only places with doors are businesses, not apartments. I grimace down at my phone, and zoom out to check the map properly. I really am at the right place, as far as I can tell, but how do I get in? I circle the block twice more before admitting defeat and opening up the email chain with the guy who had advertised the room on the student bulletin board.

sethgarcia@uofauroratrackandfield.edu
To: *rachelmiller@destansa.com*
Subject: Room for Rent
Cool! Looking forward to meeting you tomorrow. Give me a call if anything goes wrong.
303-555-0195

I dial the number. It rings for a really long time, so long I almost consider hanging up, before clicking through.

"Yeah?" a voice says. He sounds like he just woke up.

"Hi, Seth?"

"*Yeah?*"

"It's, uh, Rachel. Rachel Miller."

"Who?"

I blink.

"Rachel Miller, I'm moving in today."

"Oh, shit. That's today?"

"...Yeah, uh, I'm outside, but I can't find the entrance. Could you help me—"

"*Urgh.* I knew this would happen. Fuckin'...hang on."

The line goes silent. I check to make sure he hasn't hung up. He hasn't, but I can't hear anything at all.

"Hello?"

No answer. I'm about to hang up myself and ask random strangers for help when I hear a voice yell from overhead.

"*RACHEL!*"

I jolt and look up. Three floors above me, a guy with scrubbed-up hair like he's only just got out of bed is leaning out from his balcony yelling down at me. He's wearing a varsity jacket, boxers, and beneath the jacket, nothing else. He's slim, he's not some giant football player or something, but his muscles look like I photoshopped them on.

Wait, did he sleep in his varsity jacket?

Seth points directly underneath the balcony he's standing on.

"It's through there, dipshit!"

A few passers-by look over. My head fizzles for a moment with shock and rage. I stare at him, shirtless but for his varsity jacket, barefoot, his muscular legs dusted with thick, dark hair, his expression of impatient distaste. He had been so *polite* over email.

I look where he's pointing; there's a concealed entryway at the side entrance of the optician's office. I don't look at or thank Seth; I walk for the doorway. Head still buzzing with anger, I locate the right button on the list of apartments and press it for one long, angry tone until the door clicks open. There are three long, narrow sets of stairs that I heft my suitcase up. The door is open wide, but Seth's not exactly there to welcome me. Not that he hasn't given me one hell of a welcome already, along with the rest of Aurora's asshole student populace. I roll the suitcase along the entryway. A long, wide and airy corridor, with two rooms on the side, leading down to the kitchen. A staircase between the two rooms, presumably leading to the next two. The walls are clean and freshly painted in a neat grey, but the floor is disgusting; you would think a dozen people lived here rather than three. Shoes of all kinds litter the hallway, mixed with random trash and unopened letters. One or two pairs of shoes are neat and paired, tucked into the corner next to the door, but most of them represent enough of a trip hazard that I have to lift my suitcase again and pick through them.

The first bedroom door I pass opens. It's Seth again, this time with his hair slightly less sticky-up, and with jeans and a shirt on. I find myself missing the view. *If he's going to be an unmitigated asshole to live with, he could at least walk around with the washboard abs on show.*

"That one," he says, pointing to the next bedroom door along, and then slams his door in my face. I blink. *Even the abs might not be enough. How long did I sign this lease for?*

I trip along the shoe-filled corridor and push open my bedroom door, my new apartment keys jingling in its lock. It's a relief to snatch the keys out and lock the door behind me. I push my head against the cool wood a moment, breathing deep to try and restrain myself from fist fighting a guy who would definitely win, and then turn to take in my new home.

It's furnished, barely. The walls are painted off-white and are scuffed almost everywhere that a leg can reach. There's a long, wide piece of wood bolted to the wall, and above that several smaller planks bolted higher; these, presumably, represent my desk and bookshelves. The desk chair is missing one of its wheels; if I sit on it, I'll basically fall off. The wardrobe is no better than some painted plywood screwed together, and will fit maybe half of my clothes if I folded them small. It has a dingy, fingerprint-covered mirror glued to one of its doors. The bed is a single and it's covered in sheets that, when I brush my fingers over them, feel like they were made of recycled paper. There's no bedside table; instead, there's a mildewed windowsill just by the head of the bed, and a frosted-glass window above it that is maybe four inches high, but stretches from one side of the wall to the next.

There are no pillows. I did not pack any. I can foresee this being one of the many problems with living here.

I sigh and knead my temples, willing myself to calm down. *It'll be fine. Sure, it's not exactly the nicest place in the world, it's not those pretty dorm rooms you saw on the website or washi taped to your vision board, but you have keys that lock the door, and windows nobody can see into, and a bed you can sleep in. It's yours.*

Plus, you can always just drench the place in fairy lights and posters.

I put the suitcase on the bed and the bed sheets crinkle in a very un-fabric way. I put my backpack down next to it, *crinkle*, and put my arms above my head, relishing how my aching back is finally free of its load. As I stretch, I catch a glimpse of myself in the dingy mirror on the wardrobe.

I look tired. My eyes, green-grey depending on how the light catches them, have dark circles under them from the early start. I usually wear at least a little makeup, but today I had to get on a plane, so nothing on earth sounded worse than makeup. As a result, the freckles that are usually hidden by foundation are dusting my cheeks; it's almost like looking at a stranger. My hair is unusual for me too; long, blonde and thick, it's one of the few things I take pride in. I usually have it curled and carefully styled, but today necessitated a fishtail braid just to keep it out of my face. I didn't really succeed at that; little strands have escaped and they're falling flat against my forehead. I blow them out of my face, staring at mirror-me, and they flop right back. Unbelievable. I sigh, shrug my shoulders up and down to loosen them up from all the backpack wearing, and unpack.

It's going to be too much for that lame excuse of a desk. My lenses, DSLRs, analogue cameras, the film canisters, the memory cards, the huge foam cases they all live in, and my (honestly unnecessary) darkroom kit would already be stretching the desk's capacity. Add all the other art supplies, from the sketchbooks to the oils, and the thing's going to pop right out of the wall. That's leaving aside notebooks, planners, pens, post-it notes... *and where am I going to put makeup?* I have maybe *half* of the space I need. I pile all the stationery and a few sketchbooks on the left side of the desk, the makeup on the right, and it creaks ominously but doesn't fall. I pull all the clothes out of the suitcase, put all the arty stuff apart from my favorite camera back in there, and tuck the suitcase under the bed. *That'll do for the first week or so.*

My favorite camera, a beautiful Retinette built in an era that made film cameras unbreakable, goes right back in my backpack, and the backpack goes on a hook on the bedroom door. I assess the clothes, give up, stuff them all on the floor of the wardrobe, and wedge the door shut with some of my shoes. *That'll do for at least the first semester.*

I take stock of the room. I need pillows, mostly. Good sheets. Maybe some posters, to cover the walls. Fairy lights, because I'm pretty sure you're supposed to have those in college.

I wrinkle my nose. *And some scented candles, or a diffuser or something. I can smell those nasty corridor shoes from behind the door.*

I pull out my phone and check my bank account. With my deposit and first two months of rent paid, plus the plane tickets, and a trip to the airport sandwich place that was absolutely not necessary at all, the money that's left isn't going to stretch for all of what I want. I can start with some pillows and bed sheets, and also *maybe* some food.

I need a job, I think miserably. I'd made an informal clientele for wedding and party photography at home that had been pretty lucrative, but home was now hundreds of miles away and this was a town full of students that didn't have the money to spend on photography they didn't need.

I should probably find a store that sells what I need before they all shut for the evening, but I'm parched and my water bottle is long since empty. I take the risk: I unlock my bedroom door and go further down the corridor to the apartment kitchen.

It's *filthy*. If I didn't think three guys lived here before, I definitely do now. There's already a mound of dirty dishes, despite the semester only starting tomorrow. There was definitely some sort of party here recently because there are empty bottles on every available surface and the floor tiles are sticky. There are also shoes in here. One of them, a giant sneaker that's dripping *water*, is on the breakfast bar, next to some Band-Aids that I *really* hope aren't used. No sign of food, but a ton of protein powder, gumming up the surfaces and half-empty in giant plastic tubs. Seth looks like he goes to the gym, but he surely can't be using all of this himself. *Are there more weird jocks in this house? Are they all weird jocks?*

The microwave looks like its seen better days, like maybe Vietnam, but the oven looks weirdly clean as if it hasn't been used. Behind the protein powder-infused breakfast bar, there's an expensive-looking couch with some worrying stains on it, and a giant television on the wall that, like the oven, looks beautifully and suspiciously clean. Leaning against the television on the wall is some kind of kayak. I try not to think about the kayak and the damage it could do, and may already be doing, to a TV that expensive. Beyond that, there's the balcony, where Seth had yelled at me to welcome me home.

The sink has some sort of grey matter in it. I decide I'd rather die of dehydration.

As I walk back down the corridor, tripping over shoes as I go, Seth's opening bedroom door sends me darting for my own, closing it behind me just in time. I can hear a woman laughing, Seth hushing her, and a whispered discussion that's slightly too quiet to make out. I hear the front door open, then close. Then I hear Seth's door close.

I take out my phone and scroll my texts until two minutes pass, and then I quietly open my door, step out into the corridor, and lock the bedroom door behind me. My keys jangle in my hand and I quickly close them into a fist to silence them, but the damage is done. Seth's bedroom door opens and I straighten up while forcing on a neutral smile.

"Gymnastics team," Seth says proudly, jerking his thumb behind him to the front door. His sneer is making me nauseous. "*Really flexible.*"

In this moment, two parts of me have a fight in my head. One part of me, the bit I got from Mom, wants to drag him by the ear to the kitchen and make him clean the floor with his tongue until he learns how to talk to and about women. The other part, the peacemaker part, wants to laugh awkwardly and pelt it for the door, just like my dad at all social functions that last longer than an hour.

Unfortunately, the *me* part, that traitorous *Rachel* part, doesn't make a decision between them, and so I stand there staring at him until he blinks, rolls his eyes theatrically, and goes back in his room. I realize after the fact that, in the twenty minutes since I entered the apartment, Seth had once again taken his shirt off.

I can't leave the place fast enough.

Shopping for bed sheets and pillows isn't what I wanted to be doing just an hour after I got to Aurora, but I'm getting the feeling that the apartment isn't going to feel like home anytime soon. I'll need to find ways of avoiding these guys. Even if the other two roommates aren't as asshole-ish as Seth, they're still contributing to a kitchen that's growing new life forms.

My phone rings and I tuck it between my ear and my shoulder while I sort through various pillows at the store for the cheapest option.

"Rachey, you promised to call when you got there."

"Hey Mom. I got here, by the way."

"How was the taxi from the airport? You checked on GPS that they weren't taking you the long way round and ripping you off?"

The taxi from the airport had been an hour and a half, and I had only had 15% battery left that I wasn't going to waste fact-checking a nice old man in a Buick. *Come to think of it, what am I on?* I put a random pillow in my cart and check the screen. 4%. *At least this'll be a quick conversation.*

"He didn't, Mom, it's fine."

"And your new friends, are they okay?"

"New friends?"

"The girls you're living with!"

Okay, so, Mom would have flipped if she had heard her little girl would be living in an apartment with three men. If she knew, I would have to barricade the door to prevent her dragging me home.

"They're fine, Mom," I lie. "They're not *friends* with me yet, it's only been a few hours."

"Give them time, Rachey."

"*Rachel*, Mom, *Rachel*, I'm not five."

"No, you're not," Mom muses sadly. "All grown up, eighteen years old."

"Nineteen in a month."

"No fishing for presents, Rachel Aubrey Miller."

"Not even a little?"

"Anyway, you can't expect handouts all your life. You need to get a job."

That one smarts. I screw up my nose a little as I throw the first bed sheets I see into the cart. "I'm *getting* one, Mom, *again*, only been here a few hours, *remember*?"

"Don't take that t—"

The phone dies. That's the worst possible time for it to die. I have a momentary thrill of fear that I'm going to have to go home and explain myself to her, but then I realize... I don't have to go home. I live on my own now. I'm an *adult*.

An adult who's living in a place that the health department would probably burn down, with at *least* one and potentially *three* asshole jock roommates, but an adult nonetheless. In celebration, I add a very unnecessary and very vanilla-scented candle to the cart, and smile. Nobody can tell me what to do. I could add six hundred candles to the cart if I wanted. I'm an *adult*.

The enthusiasm wanes a little as I grimace at the receipt a few minutes later. I *will* need a job for six hundred candles. *How can one three-wick vanilla-pod-and-sandalwood candle cost this much? Why did I buy it? Why did I contemplate buying two?*

The sheets, the pillows, and the way too expensive candles are weighing down my backpack horribly as I walk back. I didn't buy food; I can't find the energy to go anywhere else with this heavy a bag, this tired a body, and this empty a bank account. I have a few granola bars that Mom packed in my suitcase despite my insistence I wouldn't need them, and I'm never going to tell her exactly how much I now regret complaining about them. With each step I take up the stairs to the apartment, I hunger for granola.

At the front door, I tiredly contemplate the keys in my hand. One of them definitely opens the apartment door; the others presumably lead to my room, the balcony, and, judging by the number of extra keys, four secret balconies I haven't discovered yet. I don't want to get it wrong on the first try; Seth's room is right by the front door, and ending the day by once again having a jock call me a dipshit would be altogether too much. As I look at each key in turn, comparing them to the lock thoughtfully, I hear a voice that's *way* too close behind me.

"You're here early."

I yelp and wheel around, keys held in my hand ready to poke in someone's eye. I'm not sure I could reach his eyes, now that I look at him. They're way above my head. They're also attached to a tall man with blonde Thor hair brushing his impossibly wide shoulders, and unless he has an equally muscular twin, this is unmistakably the asshole who whacked me with his kayak paddle.

"Oh shit," he says, blinking down at me, "*You're* the gym girl?"

"The *what?*" I sputter. Does he think I fell over earlier because I was going for a cartwheel?

At this point, the door opens. Seth still does not have a shirt on. I'm starting to get a negative Pavlovian reaction to toned abs. Seth has to look up at Thor guy as well; Seth's taller than me, and his hair kind of defies gravity in places so it makes him taller still, but he's got at least four inches between him and Thor dude, who's probably 6′2″.

"Hey, Hunter," he says affably to Thor guy. "I thought you were at practice tonight."

"Got your text," blond asshole (*Hunter*) says. "'Besides, tonight's more of a hazing thing than a practice thing, I'll be back in time for drinks. Is this the girl? You said she had bigger tits."

I interject before either of them can continue to ruin my evening.

"I'm coming through," I say, and walk through with my keys at the perfect height to key Seth's nipples like a car if he doesn't move. He has the common sense to move. It takes me an awkward few seconds to find the right key for my bedroom door, and I can feel their eyes on me from across the corridor as I fumble into my room and lock the door behind me, before immediately pressing my head against the jamb to listen in. They talk a damn sight louder than Seth and his mystery woman did earlier as they wander upstairs. My room is right next to the stairs; I can hear each creaking step up.

"If it *had* been the girl," Seth says, his voice clipped and sardonic, "What about 'you said her tits would be bigger' was going to fly?"

"We'd already met, it wasn't gonna fly anyway."

"What?"

Hunter makes a grunting noise. "She was the girl I told you about, got in the way of my kayak paddle."

Got in the way? I got in the way of your precious paddle, asshole?

Seth laughs. They're starting to get quieter now that I'm having to listen in from overhead and not from the doorway.

"Sounds like it," he says. "This bitch can't go in a straight line without getting lost."

Hunter says something back, but they're now too quiet to hear. I *thunk* my head against the door, breathing heavily, and the hollow plywood reverberates with the force. My head hurts, but it's a welcome distraction from how upset I am. I close my eyes. My cheeks are warm and my eyes are fizzing with the effort not to cry.

Two out of three roommates, and they're already discussing my tits and arguing about their what, sexual conquests? I've never been around guys like this; I'm an art girl, I hung around the arty guys at high school. They could be self-obsessed, but they were usually okay. I've never been within earshot of this many jock sports guys, and it's gone exactly as I would have feared. The University of Aurora isn't a place for arty guys, it's a place for jocks, and I'm stuck in a house with them. I breathe deep and my breath hitches with a sob. I cover my mouth to keep it quiet. Bet they wouldn't be assholes to me if I was whatever big-boobed gym girl Hunter was talking about trying to score with...

Wait.

I wipe my eyes and frown up at the ceiling. *Gym girl?* Seth had escorted some girl out earlier, he had said she was from the gymnastics team, that she was flexible.... Hunter had come back, asked if I was 'the girl', the *gym* girl that he had got Seth's text to come back to the house...

Oh my god. Oh my god. Do they share girls between them?

I have no idea how to react, so I go straight to the stash of granola bars and unwrap one tearfully, jamming it in my mouth in the hopes that some food might help me process this insanity. Hunter and Seth, who were already setting records for the fastest I've ever grown to hate someone, had just added the most insane of wrenches to my already fragile first day at college. Would they be bringing in a woman and fucking her, what, one at a time? Would they fuck her as a *group*?

I think about Seth's washboard abs, rippling with effort, and Hunter's blonde hair glinting in a low light, and then guiltily take another bite of the granola bar. I do it so hard my teeth click together. *That's gross,* I tell myself. *That's so gross.*

I hear the front door open, then close. Footsteps down the corridor and past my room, toward the kitchen. I quietly unlock the door and peek my head out.

Walking into the kitchen is Hunter's friend, the pissed-off guy who had told me to 'watch where you're going' when Hunter had whacked me with the kayak paddle. He's unmistakable; he's so tall that his coiffed brown hair almost brushes the doorframe, and his biceps are still straining the sleeves of his polo shirt. He turns, and I catch a glimpse of him—high cheekbones, angry grey eyes—before I immediately shut the door again and re-lock it. I hear him go upstairs, taking the steps two at a time. I hear the guys upstairs talking; they say 'Hey, Lucas!' and then subside back into voices too quiet to hear.

All three roommates. They're *all* asshole jocks.

I sit on the floor and light my new candle, the scent of vanilla filling the room. I close my eyes tight.

Going to college in Aurora is off to a rocky start, I think, *but I won't let some shitty roommates stop me. I'm going to do great in class. I'm going to—*

An inner voice that sounds kind of like my mom pitches in unhelpfully.

Going to what? What are *you going to do with your life?*

I stare at the candle, the firelight flickering in the glass and melted wax. I cup my hands around the warm glass and let it calm me.

I'll figure it out.

Chapter 2

SETH

When I wake up, my mouth is dry. Lucas and Hunter had been determined to go to the football team hazing last night. They'd invited me, but I turned them down on two grounds. One, I'm not on the football team. Lucas, asshole number one, pointed out that he isn't either. Two, I have practice this morning. Hunter, asshole number two, pointed out that so did he.

I only had one way of getting out of an evening of watching giant-shouldered football idiots cry like babies while Hunter and Lucas got them to do weird shit—get them so drunk before they left that they forgot they'd ever invited me along. Unfortunately, that had involved some significant drinking of my own.

Hence the dry mouth. And also the headache and why I feel like death warmed up in a microwave.

I still have lectures this morning.

God damn it.

I drag myself out of bed. I don't enjoy how my brain feels like it's tilting in my skull. I grimace against the pale sunlight filtering through the blinds and, eyes closed, grope on the ground for the pile I keep clean clothes in.

I run through a checklist as I stumble through the apartment: *Shoes, water, keys, watch.* I pick up at least three pairs of shoes that aren't mine before finding any that belong to me. Water is a hard one: I have one water bottle and I keep it *clean.* Lucas, whose water bottles all smell like swamp water, has his ever-expanding collection in a pile in, near, or below the sink. There's one on the floor too. Hunter only drinks protein shakes, but he seems to only want to keep the containers wherever I last put my one and *only* water bottle. After about a minute of glaring at the piles of things that can hold liquid, I grab a water bottle from Lucas' pile, fill it with some of Hunter's protein shake and hope it's a hangover cure. I don't mix it well enough and it's clumped-up and chalky, but it's at least a liquid, and also kind of a food. My keys are where I left them last night when I saw Lucas and Hunter out; still in the door, which is closed but not actually locked. I decide I'd rather die than try to find my goddamn watch, and stumble out of the door, locking it behind me.

It's five in the morning and Aurora is beautiful. Nobody's up but me and the sun, which hasn't yet crested over the distant mountains. There's a mist in the air, hanging in clouds of fog around the university campus, clinging in humid waves to my skin. I breathe the cool air in, out, and squint against the dawning sun. I wish, briefly, that I was dead so that I wouldn't have to do this. Then I start running.

It's never enjoyable at first. I'm still hungover and bone tired. My limbs don't want to move and my gait is all over the place. It takes a few minutes for my legs to warm up. My head starts to clear and my eyes adjust to the sun. My hair is whipping about my forehead, and the air is cool and clean.

This is the part of running that I love. It's why I do track.

My first year at Aurora U had been insane. I had gone here on a track and field scholarship—it was the only way I was going to afford college. Thankfully for me, I'm pretty fucking good at track. I'm best at long distance running, but I'll give most of the guys who do the long jump a run for their money and I can throw a javelin a long fucking way. I've only been here one year, but I place higher than most of the guys here and I know they know it. Probably why I'm not great friends with any of them. I know I intimidate them. Thankfully, I've at least got Hunter and Lucas watching my back. They might not be track, but they'd probably be better at it than my teammates anyway. I know they feel the same about their teammates, too.

I've made it a few miles, and my legs are burning nicely now. I relish the feeling of it, the lactic acid buildup in my thighs and calves. The morning run isn't for anyone but me. I'll have lectures in an hour, and after my lectures I'll have to go to practice, but nobody gets to tell me what to do with my time before that. Right now, the mist sticking my hair to my forehead, the ground moving faster and faster beneath my feet... this is my moment of freedom. Just to prove it, I gun it harder until I'm going past the Aurora U dorm blocks, and let out a yell, loud enough to wake all the lazy assholes who aren't up yet. They ought to thank me, really, I bet half the guys in the dorms don't have alarms set. I'm a one-man public service.

I turn for home, and I force myself to up the pace as I go; faster and faster even though I want nothing more than to go slow. The most important part of a race is the last hundred meters: the rest is just pace-setting to get you there. You need to reserve just enough in the tank to be able to sprint to the finish line. I practically barrel into my apartment door, bouncing back just in time to avoid collision. I gasp for breath up the three flights of steps, and go right for the kitchen the second I get in. Protein shakes are fine but right now I need water.

Lucas is already up and around. He's microwaving egg whites, and it smells fucking disgusting.

"That smells like ass," I inform him, turning the faucet on and jamming my head under to drink from it. Lucas glares at me.

"Have you tried drinking out of a glass?" I don't reply, as I'm drinking, and Lucas' mouth twitches. "Or maybe a sippy cup?"

Sated, I remove myself from under the faucet. I gesture around the kitchen.

"Find me one not full of swamp water, Lukie, I'll use it right now. It's been a week and a half and this place is already gross as shit. I'm not cleaning up for you two."

Lucas rolls his eyes and takes out his egg whites from the microwave. He douses it in hot sauce, like that'll do anything to make it taste better, and carries it over to the couch, flipping on the TV. I drop down beside him, looking up at the TV, which I notice something about at the same time he does.

"You put your fucking kayak against the TV again."

Lucas shrugs unrepentantly. "You hate it so much, you move it."

"I just ran a fucking 5K and then some, *you* move it."

"Asshole."

"Asshole."

The mop's under the couch, so I pull it out. An empty beer bottle, dislodged, clinks across the tile. I hold out the mop and knock it against the kayak until the kayak tips over, crashing on top of Hunter's DVD pile. He never watches them anyway, so it's his fault really. Lucas hasn't brought any cutlery with him to the couch: he rolls up the egg white-and-hot sauce omelet like a burrito and eats it with his fingers. I make a retching sound and he ignores me. We watch ESPN in silence for a couple minutes before I say anything.

"You go to the hazing?"

Lucas grunts an affirmative around his egg whites before speaking with his mouth full. "Mm-hm. Hunter bailed 'cause that girl texted him."

"Which girl?"

"The one you banged yesterday."

"Oh, *that* girl." I grimace, trying to remember her name. "... Mitzi."

"Millie."

"Dumb name either way. Great ass, though. Gymnast."

"Flexible, I know, I got the text." Lucas takes a last bite of the omelet—stretched-out giant freak that he is, he's already finished the whole thing.

"How was the hazing?"

Lucas shrugs. "It was dull. They got all the new guys drunk, stripped them, and handcuffed them to each other. Left them in the park."

I snort. That's pretty funny. Lucas lost his sense of humor in the womb, so he doesn't look so stoked, but it's his fault for bothering to go even after Hunter bailed. Lucas does rowing; why does he even care about going to Hunter's football hazing?

There's a click from the corridor. I crane my head forward, and Lucas follows suit. It's the new girl. Her hair's different from yesterday; it's down instead of up. She's already halfway out the front door when she spots us. Her eyes widen, and she slams the front door so hard it shudders in the jamb.

"Swear to god," Lucas says, "I've seen her before."

"Hunter didn't tell you? You have," I say. "She's the ditz that knocked into him."

"No kidding." Lucas frowns after her. "So that's the gymnast? She fell over like a sack of bricks."

"She's not the *gymnast*," I say. "She's the *psycho roommate*. I told you this, asshole. You know, dumb bitch who can't follow directions and tries to walk her keys into my neck? That one."

"Too late to get rid of her?" Lucas asks. I bang the handle of the mop into his head.

"No, dipshit, you could have tried *helping* with the fucking *roommate search*, though." I'm pissed he's complaining about this: I busted my balls advertising the empty room and I only got one response. Lucas and Hunter didn't even try to help. "That way we wouldn't have ended up with some frigid bitch next door to my room."

Lucas' expression sours. "I really thought Matt would come back."

I sigh. "Yeah, me too."

Matt used to have the new girl's bedroom. He was one of the team; Hunter, Matt, Seth, Lucas. Basically the dream team. He'd ended up getting feelings for one of the girls we were passing around, fucked us all over the rent for this place, and more importantly fucked over the bro code for the house.

When we all moved in, all sports guys, we'd ended up fighting a lot over the same girls. Matt had come up with a bro code for the house: every girl we fucked, we'd send her number to the other guys afterwards. There's no fighting over a girl when we're all getting a piece. Hell, after a while we even started leaving reviews for the other guys to know who was worth it or not. Gymnast girl, Mitzi or Millie or whatever, had gotten five out of five.

Then Matt had gone and kept one for himself and he was living with her like a happy fuckin' family. And now instead of it being a bro house, we have to live with some weirdo bitch.

More sounds in the corridor; it's Mitzi, or Millie. Flexible girl. She's wearing a dress she wasn't wearing yesterday. I lean forward and watch her as she leaves. The fabric's low-cut: her boobs look great. She glances over at the kitchen as she closes the door, sees me, does a half-salute, and closes the door behind her. Class act. Some girls get weird about the bro code.

Lucas has been watching too. He raises an appreciative eyebrow.

"*That's* Millie," he says.

"Yup."

"Psycho roommate has a better ass," Lucas decides, "But Millie has the better tits."

"You're crazy," I say. I think back to psycho roommate. Had I checked out her ass? Maybe I should, just to get something out of the experience. She wasn't bad to look at, in general. The freckles were cute enough.

"What's psycho's name, anyway?"

"Rachel."

"Huh," Lucas says. He's looking back to ESPN, but he's clearly not giving an opinion on the football. I turn to face him properly.

"What?"

Lucas' mouth twitches up, just a little. "Nah, it's just... you don't *usually* remember their names."

For some reason, this really gets me riled. I glare at him. "Well, yeah! I've been the one emailing the bitch all week about the fucking rent agreements! Bills!" This does nothing to make Lucas' infuriating smirk lessen, and I up the ante. "*Money*, Lucas! Not that you give a shit, leaving your sneakers on the counter, kayak on the *very expensive* TV! Moneyed rowing asshole!" I flop back a little into the couch, anger dissipating. I'm not sure why that got me so mad.

Lucas leaves his plate on the couch as he stands up and wanders around the kitchen, looking for, presumably, a cup that isn't full of swamp water.

"I bought the TV," Lucas says. "And I bought the kayak. I like keeping my stuff together."

"That's a new one," I comment as I watch him now hunt around the room for two matching shoes. Lucas is just careless with all of his stuff. He doesn't worry about anything that isn't the next conquest. Get on his wrong side, and he can be scary, but anything that doesn't stand between him and his next rowing match, or his next girl, he's the Dalai Lama about it.

Lucas finds two shoes that match and hops around the floor pulling them on. Lanky fuck. I'm not short, I'm 5'10", which is *statistically average*, thank you, but Lucas is 6'6" and his hair, when he gels it up, is practically an extra two. I know you need to be tall for rowing, but he's being excessive about it.

"You gonna lie around here and act like a bitch all morning?" Lucas asks, smirking over at me. "You didn't even go out last night."

"I just ran a 5K! What have *you* done this morning?"

"Gotten some *sleep*, Seth, try it sometime." Lucas seems uncharacteristically bothered about something when he looks over at me. "How early were you up?"

"Five," I say, and I follow it up quickly because I know he's about to point out that I was still awake when they left the house at two in the morning. "What do you care how my sleep schedule is? Are you my coach now?"

"I just think you'd be less of an asshole if you slept consistently. It's like the first rule of college athletics," Lucas says, before pausing and gesturing at himself. "Look at me."

I sputter. "You're *not* an asshole? Was that a *joke*, Lukie? Did you just make a *joke*?"

Hunter comes into the kitchen just too late to have witnessed, effectively, a miracle. I point wildly at Lucas.

"Hunter! He made a joke! He's finally done it!"

Hunter, who, to his credit, is funnier than I am, immediately grabs Lucas and slaps him on the back. "You did it! Your parents are gonna be so proud, bro, *so* proud!"

Lucas pushes Hunter away, rolling his eyes, and walks for the front door. He yells over his shoulder as he picks up the backpack he'd left there. "I have class, you do too, go do something productive!"

"This is a turning point for you, Lukie!" Hunter calls after him, grinning wide. Lucas slams the door even harder than Rach-*psycho roommate* had. Hunter snorts, brushing hair out of his eyes.

If Lucas is our humorless tall rowing freak, and I'm the smart and handsome track and field guy, Hunter's the muscle-bound quarterback. That is to say, he's not just the quarterback stereotype, he really is the quarterback. Works hard and plays hard. I've never seen him go to any of his classes, but he doesn't get kicked out because he's too much of a campus icon to be touched. Everyone knows he's going places once he's done playing college football.

He's clearly just got out of the shower; Hunter's usually crazy about his hair looking Thor-like and shiny, but right now it's wet and hanging in strands over his face. He's also only wearing a towel, which has helped me with the shower deduction. I think he must have lost the feeling in his feet or something, because he's wandering around the kitchen barefoot—I would want a whole other shower if I stepped on this sticky-ass floor. Hunter makes himself a PB&J while glancing over his shoulder at ESPN, and I try to pretend that I'm not going to be late for the first lecture of the day if I don't leave.

Hunter breaks the silence.

"So," he says, "Millie was definitely a good call, bro."

"Yeah?"

"Yeah, I'm giving her ten outta ten. Whole package. Plus she's really cool about the bro code."

Millie (see, I'm getting it now) had indeed been really cool about the bro code. Some girls you bang aren't into the idea of coming back to the same place to get with the next guy in the house, then the next; they want to be in a relationship, they think it's gross to be just there for fun. Some girls, like Millie, figure out they're getting a three-for-one deal and get with the program pretty enthusiastically.

And then there's some girls like Ra— *psycho roommate*, who are cute enough to get on my radar, but enough of an asshole to drop right off it again.

Cute? I frown at myself. I need to get this train of thought back to the other girl. The one I actually fucked.

"Great boobs," I say, stretching and standing up, checking my keys are still in my pocket.

"Fantastic tits," Hunter agrees. "You gonna go work for a living?"

"Someone's gotta. You gonna go to *any* classes this year?"

Hunter laughs. "They gonna cancel football this season?"

"Alright, alright. Hey, clean some of your dishes while we're out."

"Nah."

That's no surprise. Hunter's not cleaned a single dirty dish he's ever made. I shrug my shoulders, make a point of kicking one of Hunter's shoes across the kitchen, pick up my varsity jacket off the floor of the corridor, and make my way to the front door.

"And move your shoes! It's like a goddamn maze in here!"

"Nah!"

"Asshole!"

With that loving farewell, I'm on my way to class. I take it at a slow jog; I've got practice later, after all. The air has lost that clean, crisp quality I love to run in. It's warming up and it smells of exhaust fumes instead of mountains and leaves. Of the colleges to do track and field in, this had the most rural setting, but, unfortunately, it's still more urban than I'd want. Every day I consider moving out of the bro house and setting up in a shack in the woods. More so now that the bro house is now the 'bro house plus Rachel'.

I make it to class with less than a minute to spare, and drop down in the front row. Most people have shit with them to take notes, but Seth Garcia doesn't walk around with a backpack, because Seth Garcia doesn't go to kindergarten anymore. What I can't remember, I won't put in the assignment. I'm not the best in the class, but I'm good at bullshitting essays at the last minute, and that's good enough to keep me at Aurora U while I do the whole varsity athletics gig. The jacket's basically a badge of "I'm not here to be asked questions, I'm thinking about how to improve my ten mile pacing, don't bother me." I settle in and put on my 'don't talk to me' face, bouncing one leg up and down impatiently.

It works every time. I'm the best it gets at being an asshole.

Chapter 3

RACHEL

Most of Aurora, and anything outside of Aurora like Denver, will be easier to get to if I had a car, but thankfully it's only a half-mile walk to campus. It's a pretty walk, too. I pass by no less than three candle stores on my way (*oh God, I need a job so bad*), and the air is really clean and sharp compared to New York. Plus, no matter where you look, the low-built beige buildings are towered over by the nearby mountains, topped with picture-perfect snow. I can already sense how much film I'm going to waste on getting the perfect picture of those mountains. *In fact, why wait?*

I take out my camera—today, to not look like a tourist or a dumb junior, I'm not carrying one around my neck, I've got my smallest camera perched precariously in my jacket pocket. I always have my Retinette ready in the backpack, but this is just a quick snap for experimenting with angles and composition, not an award-winning photo or anything. I pull it out and have a look through the viewfinder.

The sun has already crested above the mountains, and the mountain top is lit so brightly that I'm not sure how to take this image without it getting washed out. Plus, no matter which way I place the camera, there's someone in the way: I'm part of a slow-but-steady stampede of students going to campus, and they're not going to stop for some photography student. I give up, pocket the camera without a single photo taken, and keep walking.

If I keep this up, I muse fatalistically, *I can fail out of Aurora U in probably a record time. What kind of art student can't even get enough inspiration to hit the shutter button on their stupid camera?*

The campus is still as pretty as it was the day before; the wide brown buildings, the billowing spray of red-gold leaves over the quad, and a sea of students. Today, though, there's a kind of energy there wasn't the day before; everyone's *excited*. A lot of my excitement for college had kind of been dampened by my unfortunate living situation and unfortunate (if good-looking) jock roommates, but I'm actually getting excited just by being around all my fellow brand new students.

Yesterday meant nothing, I remind myself. *Today is when I really get started with my new life at Aurora U.* For the first time today, I smile, *really* smile, and take everything in. It's not a big art school; hell, it's a sports college if anything but I can make it my own. I can find friends in the art department, maybe even a guy, and move in with them as soon as possible. It'll be a little Aurora art commune where people keep the kitchen clean and don't call me a bitch. It'll be heaven.

Not as much musculature on show, something traitorous comments. *Those three are practically anatomy models. You strip them down, you could do a life study, see where it goes...*

This time, I don't punish that traitorous part of my brain. If I'm going to suffer these guys, I can at least have fun imagining them.

After the nightmare of locating the apartment yesterday, I basically memorized the route to the art department. It's not exactly the nicest building on campus; it looks like it was built in the seventies and hasn't seen much funding since then. Still, there's something about that battered façade, the grey-beige walls, the walls buried in ivy, the strange statuary tucked up against its walls and the posters in the windows... it's kind of romantic, in its own 'faded glory' kind of way.

There are things at the Aurora U art department that aren't familiar; the sheer size of the place, room after room after room of kilns and darkrooms and studios. But there are things that are, like the hum of students arguing about proportions and reference use and whether Gentileschi was better than Sirani or not. More than anything, the smell grounds me in the place; the chemicals of the darkroom and the earthiness of the clay, the sharp stench of turpentine like it's soaked into the walls. It all mixes together into that unchanging smell of 'art department'.

It smells like home. I had no idea how much I needed something so familiar until it makes me well up a little. I have to pretend to yawn, so I can discreetly wipe my eyes without my fellow students staring at me weird. I can't be seen crying on campus before I've even declared my major.

I shrug my bag onto my shoulders and move to find my class, winding through the tide of art students standing in clumps outside classrooms. I find Photography 101 in the far right hallway, passing a group of students dressed in black from the tips of their hair to their toes. They eye me up and down before continuing with their conversation. *I guess the art community here is small.* It makes absolute sense given the number of jocks I passed to get to the art department.

I enter the small room, finding rows of available seats and contemplate for a moment whether I'm the sort of keen student to sit in the front, or lobby for the back. Sitting in the front, I would be prompted to take notes and my notebooks wouldn't dissolve into doodles of bored mini characters and hearts. Still, the back seat is calling my name and I answer it with one step after another until I plop my butt into the metal contraption and wait dutifully for my fellow art colleagues to enter.

A group of classmates enter, one boy and two girls, who stare at me curiously. They are your typical artsy group dressed impeccably in a combination of blacks, stripes, and spots. The boy, currently smiling at me shyly, has short black hair and black rimmed glasses. Unlike my jock roommates, he is thin and lean with hardly any muscle, high structured cheekbones, and pouty lips. His skin is like porcelain, as if he's never seen sunlight, and his blue eyes continue to glance in my general direction. I look behind me, briefly wondering if someone is standing behind me, and quickly realizing they are indeed staring at me. Especially the boy who, I decide frankly, is very easy on the eyes. Maybe he isn't a muscled God, but he can definitely stare at me whenever he wants.

He turns his attention to the two other girls hovering around him, a blonde with bobbed hair and perfect makeup dressed in a yellow and black polka dotted dress and a brunette wearing a long nineties looking overcoat and pinstriped pants. They nod to each other, before striding toward me, sitting down in the chairs surrounding me and staring at me with wide interested eyes.

"You're obviously new," the blonde says as she leans in conspiratorially toward me.

"Yeah," I say, looking around nervously and wondering if I should have sat in the front seat instead. I really do not need more enemies at this school. I don't think I could take hating my roommates and hating my classmates.

"We know because you're sitting in our spot," says the brunette, nodding to my seat.

"Oh." I grab my bag and begin to stand. "I didn't know we had assigned seats. Sorry." "No, sit." The blond takes my bag and puts it back next to my desk. "I'm Charlie."

"And I'm Josh," the boy adds quickly with a wink. My face heats and I quickly turn away, hoping he doesn't notice my face becoming as red as a strawberry.

I turn to the brunette, who smiles and says, "I'm Lauren."

"Oh, I'm Rachel."

"Rachel," Charlie holds out her hand and I shake it lightly with a dead fish grip that would shame my father. "You're late in the game."

I chuckle nervously. "Yeah, I was a late register. Aurora wasn't—"

"Your first choice," Lauren finishes and nods. "Yeah, same here. Sport colleges aren't really the best for us artsy folk."

"Which is why we need to stick together," says Charlie. "It's a good thing you found us, Rachel."

"Good indeed," adds Josh, nodding his approval.

"Who knows what other ruffians you could have met?"

"Possibly those weirdoes who sit in the front seat," says Lauren, grimacing at the front row.

"I guess it's a good thing I sat in the back, then," I say, twiddling my fingers under the table. I'm never so nervous when it comes to meeting new people, however that was back in New York. This is Aurora, where everyone loves sports, goes running together, probably plays a daily game of tennis and holds hands while they puke their brains out after an intense drinking game, all in the name of P-I-G. "So, how do you like it here so far?"

"Parties are great," says Charlie while looking at her black fingernails. "But everyone here is a meat head. If you aren't interested in intramural sports or weight training, then you're pretty much doomed."

Josh and Lauren nod their approval.

"So I guess you guys aren't the type to go to a football game here?"

Lauren shrugs. "Only if there's free booze involved."

"Or free food," adds Josh.

"But I think we can all agree our sport of choice is debating the finer points of post-production," says Charlie.

Josh rolls his eyes. "I still think it's cheating."

Charlie and Lauren scowl at Josh and I cover my mouth to keep myself from bursting into laughter. "I think that's a sport I can do," I say through a fit of giggles. "That and yoga."

"Ah, yes, yoga," says Lauren, staring off dreamily through the window. "Sadly, that's not a sport here."

"Really?" I raise an eyebrow.

Charlie shrugs. "If you can't make a team of it, then it's not a sport."

I roll my eyes. "That's stupid."

Lauren looks at Charlie and nods. "I like her." She turns back to me and grabs my hand. "Can we keep you?"

I chuckle. "Please do."

"So, where do you hail from, Rachel?" Josh leans back in his chair and crosses his legs, giving me a hint of his yellow bicycle printed socks under his black skinny jeans. "I doubt it's anywhere around here."

I bite my bottom lip. "Your suspicions would be correct." I smile, holding his gaze and hoping I'm not blushing as much as I suspect. "I hail from the great New York City."

"Oh, you don't say." Charlie claps her hands. "But what are you doing here? Why aren't you in Juilliard or Columbia University?"

I sigh. "That's a long story that I really don't want to get into."

"You must have had classes outside all throughout high school and weird hippie teachers," says Lauren.

I burst into laughter again, this time clamping down on my stomach to keep it from aching. "Not at all. I went to a normal school like you."

"Ah, too bad."

"And where are you living now?" asks Charlie.

I look at the ceiling, taking a deep breath. *Ah, yes, my wonderful living arrangements.*

Lauren, Charlie, and Josh all share a look before Lauren asks, "Is your living situation all good? You're not living in the streets, are you?"

"Ugh," I groan. "I wish I was. I think the streets are cleaner than my current living conditions."

"Really?" asks Josh.

I nod. "My roommates aren't the greatest." I grimace. "Actually, they are assholes. Complete and utter assholes. Maybe I should be happy I don't live that far away from campus, or that I even have a place after registering late and coming when everything was already taken, but I don't really feel so lucky and I feel like absolute crap." I look between the shocked expressions surrounding me and wince. "Sorry, maybe I shouldn't have opened my mouth."

"No," said Charlie, patting my hand. "You have found us and we are here for you, Rachel. Consider us your new friend group and we won't take no for an answer." She winks and I instantly feel better. "Now, who do you live with? Maybe we can pound some respect into their sorry asses." Charlie punches her fist in emphasis, erupting another fit of giggles out of me.

I inhale deeply, calming myself before I finally answer, "I live with some jocks. The one on the track team, his name is Seth and—"

"Let me guess," Lauren interrupts, her expression worrying me as she glances back at Josh and Charlie. "Your other roommates are Hunter and Lucas."

I nod slowly. "Yeah, how did you know?"

Charlie groans and runs her hands through her hair. "Those boys are famous on this campus."

"Really?" I lean back in my chair as Charlie and Lauren lean closer, nearly popping my personal space bubble. Josh grimaces, which does nothing to ease my worry.

"Yeah, really," says Lauren. "They are total sex gods."

"Really?" I ignore the shrill in my voice.

Charlie closes her eyes and nods. "Yep."

"And they throw huge, crazy parties," adds Lauren.

"They also share their women," says Josh.

Lauren and Charlie whirl around to face him, leaning in close. Josh holds up his hands, as if they are shields to fend them off. "Really?" Both girls shout, drawing looks from other classmates entering the room.

Josh slowly nods. "There's been some talk. Some fights as well." He shrugs and quickly looks away. "Some girls are totally cool with it, I guess. Others not so much." Josh glances at me, holding my gaze with those beautiful blue eyes. "But those guys definitely share."

I groan and rest my face in my hands. "Last night they were talking about some girl." I rub my face. "I thought it was just her, but they share all of them?" I look between the three. "Please tell me this isn't true."

Silence greets me in response.

"Don't worry," says Charlie, patting my shoulder. "I'm sure something will become available at the end of this semester."

"I don't know if I can hold out that long," I whimper. "Those guys are brutal."

"Well, until then you can hang out with us," says Lauren, patting my hand. "It's just a place to sleep and store your shit. You don't have to hang out there."

"Yeah, you can hang out with us at the coffee shop," says Charlie, punching the air like she is some sort of artsy superhero.

I chuckle and my eyes lock on Josh. He gives me a shy smile that meets his intense blue eyes. *Oh, yes, I can definitely spend a bunch of my free time with you.*

"Alright class," says a grey-haired woman with round spectacles while kicking the door closed. "I don't want to hear it, I know I'm late. Let's just begin."

Josh turns around in his seat and I straighten in my chair, happy to know there is one less thing for me to worry about with my new life in Aurora.

After my last class of the day, I find myself standing in front of the bulletin board outside of my Finite Math classroom with flyers hanging from each inch of the display. There are dance callouts, Capture the Flag Sundays, Football Leagues, running groups, Intramural Volleyball, but nothing much on job openings. Nothing, except for a retail opening at the Fleet Feet Aurora running store just on the edge of campus heading into the small college town. *And it isn't far from home.*

I snatch the flier and walk through the hallway, reading the contents on the paper. Part time position with minimum wage, flexible hours, discount on running goods *(which I'll never use)*, and the possibility for growth. Sounds perfect. I hold the paper to my chest, walking down the steps and toward the small kiosk at the bottom floor.

I'm absolutely starving after only eating granola bars for dinner the night before and staving off breakfast for a late lunch. I look at the time. 4:00 in the afternoon. That is quite a late lunch, but looking at the prices and remembering the very few dollars I have in my bank account reminds me that I couldn't just splurge on a giant mocha and a piece of cheesecake. My stomach grumbles and I look at the flier again. *If they hired me tomorrow I would have money in my bank by next Saturday. Then I could get all the candles and giant mochas a girl could ever need.*

But I don't like running. I'm not an athlete. I've never worked in retail and even if I did, I wouldn't have any idea on how to sell running shoes to wealthy jocks. *But you need money, Rachel. Money makes the world go round, Rachel. Especially your world.* And it would be so easy. I wouldn't have to wait tables and deal with low tips. I could sit at the desk and smile while ringing up socks and tennis shoes. Maybe there wouldn't be too many customers either.

I buy myself a small peanut butter and jelly sandwich and shove it in my mouth while walking through the quad and toward the quaint college town in the distance bordering it. The bright yellow Fleet Feet Sports flag flaps in the wind in front of the small opening to the store, making it easy to spot. I push through the door, the bell ringing, but no one comes to answer its call. There are several students surrounding the shoes, a stack of them piling next to one customer in particular. Thin girls in yoga pants walk around in bright yellow and pink shoes, one running on a treadmill next to the wall.

I go to the desk, waiting for whomever it is taking their sweet time to come on the floor. *I guess they are busy. Probably won't be spending too much time at the desk, but still. Money is money.*

In the mean time I stare at the assortment of gels in front of me. The name on the packaging spells out GU. *Now is that GU as in goo? Or is it just the letters GU?* They are all different flavors ranging from chocolate, peanut butter, strawberry-banana, cucumber mint. I pick up one, smooshing the package in-between my fingers and inwardly gag. *Why would anyone ever eat this crap?* I drop it down into the box on the table and turn to the assortment of Fitbit and Garmin watches locked behind a glass door.

$500 for a sports watch? I grimace. *That's crazy. How can I sell this stuff? All of it is crazy.*

"Sorry to keep you waiting," I hear a familiar voice behind me.

No.

I don't want to turn around. In fact, I outright refuse to turn around. *It better not be him.* I grind my teeth and hiss at the feeling of my nails digging into my palms. *That better not be who I think it is.*

I chance a glance over my shoulder and inwardly groan. *It is him.*

I watch Seth Garcia bring out several boxes to the blonde girl sitting next to the pile of already opened shoe boxes. His brown hair is sticking up in tufts and he wears a grey Fleet Feet shirt tight enough to expose his lean chest muscles under his varsity jacket. *He has a nice smile,* a sneaky little thought whispers in the back of my head and I scowl, wanting to smack myself out of whatever spell he put over me. *He is a complete asshole.*

I sigh and with slumped shoulders I begin my gloomy exit toward the door. *There is no way I can live and work with him.* My stomach grumbles and I close my eyes at its reminder of my lack and need of money. I stare at the exit, longing to walk through it. I really, really, really do not want to go up to him and ask for an application. Actually, I don't want to talk to him at all except for at the end of the school year when I return my keys and wish him a nice life. But I take a deep breath and remind myself of the giant mochas, the fairy lights, and the scented candles.

I turn myself around, roll back my shoulders, and take the few steps toward the cash register, where he is currently ringing up the blonde girl purchasing two pairs of shoes. *You can do this, Rachel. Do it for the candles.*

Chapter 4

SETH

"Alright, you're all set," I say, my smile breaking my face while I hand the bag to the hot looking bitch with the see-through pink tank top. No bra and her tits are completely visible. She leans them over the table, giving me an ample view of her cleavage. *Nice.* "Have a nice day..." I look at her meaningfully. I already gave her my number on the Fleet Feet card I stashed in her bag. Not that I really need her name, but bitches sometimes need a little effort in order to get them into bed. Or up against a window. Outside bent over a bench. Whatever it takes to get my dick wet.

"Lisa," she giggles.

"Lisa," I repeat.

She gives me one last smile, before turning on her heel and making her way to the door. Her ass sways magically back and forth and I can't help my thoughts drifting to whether or not she is wearing any underwear under those tight pink leggings. What's-her-name turns back around at the door and gives me one last wave before leaving. I raise my hand, licking my lips while imagining my cock pounding into that tight ass.

Yeah, she'll definitely call.

"And how can I help you—" I stop, words leaving me as Rach-psycho bitch steps forward. *What the fuck? Is she stalking me now?*

"What the hell are you doing here?"

She doesn't bother answering me and instead sets a piece of paper down in front of me, which I don't even bother to look at. Since when does she know where I work? I look around, noticing there are at least four other customers in the shop so it's not like she can key me in the neck without witnesses. *Not like that would stop her.*

"I saw you have a job opening," she says, twiddling her fingers while staring back at me.

I blink and finally look down at the flier. It says Fleet Feet all over it. We have been looking for a replacement for a while, ever since Lindsay graduated and left. *Ahh Lindsay.* Lindsay was great. Great body, nice ass, big tits, and completely lesbian. We would check out girls together and she would smack me around and call me a dog. It was a love-hate relationship. Maybe leaning more toward hate, but at least she wasn't completely psychotic. Like this bitch Rachel.

She stands in front of me, staring at me expectantly, driving me crazy with those annoying mutant green eyes. I mean really. Who had green eyes that green? "What?" I ask angrily when she tilts her head to the side and crosses her arms in front of her barely there chest. It doesn't help that she's covered her girls with a baggy green plaid jacket that simply hangs off her body as if saying, *don't even think about looking at my not-even-there breasts.*

"I was hoping you'd give me a job application."

I scoff and look her up and down. Nothing about her reads runner, with her white cropped top exposing a slim bit of skin above her high waisted patched-up pants. She isn't even wearing tennis shoes, instead opting for brown ankle boots. "You want to work here?" *Do you even play sports?* My guess would have to be a resounding no.

She nods. "Right on, Sherlock. You've solved the case."

I glare down at her, tempted to send her back to whatever hell hole she came from, but we do need another sales assistant and by the looks of the growing customers coming in now from the end of their classes, we need one now. I sigh and yank open the drawer, grabbing an application and tossing it in her general direction before leaving the register and greeting the next customer. Let her figure it out. I'm in no mood to play mommy to an idiotic freshman with no tits.

"Welcome to Fleet Feet Sports, can I help you find a pair of new running shoes?" I ask the muscled man in front of me. "Or are you interested in our running assessment program?"

"I just want to look around, man."

I nod, glancing over my shoulder and getting a wonderful view of psycho bitch's ass. "Fine with me."

I cross my arms, frowning while I watch her fill out the form at the counter. Her ass is better than Mitzie—or whatever hell her name is, which is shocking since it's not like she's the sporty type whatsoever. *Surprising indeed.* Her hair falls over her shoulder, shrouding her pretty face. The thought has me scowling. *Nothing about her is pretty. She's crazy. She's a complete idiot.*

She looks over her shoulder and rage bubbles within me when she catches my stare. I scowl when she raises an eyebrow and waves the application back and forth. "I'm done," she says, handing me the application before shrugging on her bag and heading for the door.

"Where do you think you're going?"

She glances at the door again. "I thought—"

"Well, you thought wrong. Interview begins now."

She looks around pathetically. "Shouldn't I meet with your supervisor?"

"I am the supervisor, numb nuts."

She swallows, glances toward the door for the second time and I nearly laugh as a slew of emotions tumble through her, like she's really dug herself a hole. *Well, duh.* Honestly, I don't understand how stupid little girls like her even get accepted in Aurora University. She rests her bag gently on the floor and leans against the cashier's desk. "Alright, I guess I'm ready."

I take a moment to scan the contents written there, finding some freelance photography, but nothing more than that. Just some weddings and graduations, too. Nothing of substance that could actually be beneficial to a running store. Wonderful. She isn't just an idiot. She's a complete moron. "I see you haven't worked in retail before," I start, feeling already bored of this. *Why do I even bother?*

She nods. "Not at all."

"So, given your lack of experience, what can you really add to Fleet Feet?"

"I have worked in customer service before and I know how to sell goods."

My eyes narrow and I stop myself from groaning. *Like what does she mean by that? Completely useless and I don't have time for uselessness.* "You know how to sell goods? What goods?"

"Well, I..." she pauses, grimacing for a moment.

"Well, I what?" I do not have time for this. Someone needs to be watching the customer on the treadmill and there are two people eyeing some shoes on the wall. One customer is already going for the door.

"Well, I sold my photography skills in New York and discussed with clients their wants and needs."

I roll my eyes. "And how possibly would that work here?"

Rachel scowls up at me and rests her hands on her hips. "I can take pictures of your products and post them online. Do some advertisement for you. That sort of thing."

"But you don't have any experience in that," I point at her application. "All you've done is taken some pretty pictures for mommies and daddies."

"But I know how to take a good picture," she hisses, and I can tell she's trying not to raise her voice. I look around and see a few stares in our direction. "Can you say the same about yourself, Mr. Running Man?"

I purse my lips and grip the paper in my hands. I really do not like the fact that she found something useful. The boss would love the idea of having photographs for social media. In fact, he is always searching for someone in the art department, yet they always steer clear of anything to do with movement. The weirdoes always remain in their own closed off pacts and frankly I'm surprised to see psycho bitch not doing the same.

"Do you even run?" I ask, knowing the answer wouldn't even matter at this point.

"Don't think I could even if there was a zombie apocalypse."

I roll my eyes. Just great. Most likely she'll quit this gig after a day and I will have wasted all my efforts for nothing. "Fine. Hired." I stalk to the storage room, already pushing the curtain to the side when I turn around and see her still hovering by the cash register. "Well, are you coming or what?"

She looks around and I nearly stomp my foot. The door clangs shut with one customer having left and I see more glancing at the door with the same idea. I really do not need to explain to the boss why we lost so many customers today, especially when I'm looking for a raise. "Job starts now."

"Oh," she breathes. "Do you want me to—"

"I want you to get your ass here," I snap, pointing at the ground I'm standing on.

She, thankfully, hurries toward me, slinging her bag over her shoulder and follows me behind the curtain into the cluttered stock room. I roll my eyes when I glance over my shoulder, finding her looking around at the metal shelving filled with Nikes, ASICS, Brooks, Saucony as well as running belts, compression socks, GU energy gels, and a plethora of other running products I love testing out.

This job is amazing. The store discount is amazing and every time there's a new product, the employees get to test it out, talk to the company reps, and sometimes receive free samples. It is definitely a perk, especially being a track star and all.

And sharing it with someone like her, who doesn't give a rat's ass about over pronating, arch support, and running rhythm is like a punch in the gut. Samples are going to be completely wasted on her. She's not even going to know how things work. How is she ever going to sell anything?

Seriously, I bet she lasts one day.

I dig through one of the boxes, finding several employee shirts, but all of them are XL until I finally find a small blue shirt. I chuck it in her general direction. "Put that on." I look her up and down again. "And next time dress a bit more..." I wave at her and grimace, "sporty. You know. Tennis shoes. Running pants."

"Will yoga pants work?"

I bite my tongue from saying something even ruder. There's nothing wrong with yoga, but the question is stupid. Absolutely, freaking stupid. Most people don't even realize the difference between yoga pants and workout pants. It's simply the flexibility of the fabric is all, which is why it's so stupid.

I inhale deeply, letting it out slowly. "Sure, yoga pants work fine."

She smiles brightly and I feel my heart plummet. "Perfect."

I grimace. "Whatever."

I turn around, striding back toward the entrance to the floor and praying there are still customers to sell to. I really need some more money. I stop, peaking around the shelving unit and watching with something I ascertain to be curiosity as she pulls her crop top over her shoulders. She's wearing a nude bra, her freckly breasts peeking out at the tops. They aren't the largest I've ever seen. There's a little pudge in her stomach, but I wouldn't necessarily say her body is bad. *Quite cute actually.*

I grimace and shake my head, stalking out of the storage room. *Don't even go there.* I scowl, looking around at the shop and seeing at least six customers all waiting to be helped. Great, six new customers and I have a newbie who knows absolutely nothing about sports. I smile wickedly as a thought enters. A terrible, wonderful little thought. I glance back at the storage room. *Let's see how long you last, psycho bitch.*

"Welcome to Fleet Feet Sports," I say to a tall, lanky man staring at the shoe rack. He's the sort of guy who plays basketball and looking at his thick socks stuffed inside his tight tennis shoes, I would surmise he has some pretty stinky feet. "Would you like to try anything on?"

Chapter 5

RACHEL

This whole retail thing, I'm quickly discovering, is not easy. Not easy at all. And Seth is being a complete jackass about it. As soon as I flung on my shirt and met the bastard on the floor, he gave me a customer to size, didn't bother to explain the whole storage room and searching for shoes concept, and just sat at the cash register, happily charging customers and wishing them a pleasant day.

Currently, I'm helping a customer put on a shoe. His stinky socks nearly swallowing me whole and I have to stop myself from gagging. *Get a job. It'll be easy. I can buy candles and drink mochas in my fairy lit room.* I scowl up at Seth, leaning over the table while he smiles at another female customer. His gaze dipping down and glimpsing her giant cleavage. *Wasn't the whole point of a sports bra to keep the girls in?* And why do people walk around like that? Just walking around in sportswear as if advertising: *Hi, I go for long runs and can lift my body weight over my head, but can I have a conversation about the historical analyses of modern-day technology and its effects on youth? No. No I cannot.*

The blonde girl takes her bag and leaves. I scowl at Seth, hoping with my magical telepathic powers he hears my struggles and moves to assist me. Instead, he grabs his jacket and bag and heads for the door.

"Excuse me, just for a moment," I say to the gentleman above me, before bounding toward Seth and blocking his exit. "Where do you think you're going?"

He sighs, tugging at the doorknob. "Out. I have practice."

I smack his hand away and cross my arms. "But you're leaving me alone."

Seth has the audacity to shrug. "So?"

"So? I don't know anything. I don't know how to handle the cash register." I motion toward the terrifying device at the desk. "I barely understand the storage system."

Seth rolls his eyes and shakes his head. "You'll figure it out."

"But," I watch him walk through the door, not bothering to look back. I stand there, waiting, praying he'll return, but after several minutes and no sign of him, I will myself back to my customer. I can't believe I ever talked myself into this. When I saw that asshole, I should have just left. I should have looked around more, scoped out the cafes. Working at a lovely hip and fresh cafe would've been nice. I could invite the girls and Josh to visit, possibly share a cup of coffee with Josh and have him look over my photos. I could be getting discounted giant mochas.

But no. Instead I settled for a running store, working with an asshole who wants to make my life complete hell.

"I think I'll get these," says the man while walking around the store in the shoes I just shoved onto his sweaty, stinky feet.

I paste on a smile, feeling fear dig into me while I stride over toward the cash register. "Wonderful."

My first sale. *Take that, stupid Seth Garcia.* The cash register stares back at me and for a split second I hear the theme of the The Good, The Bad, and The Ugly playing in the background. This is a piece of cake. Everyone does this. No big deal. I grab the box and scan the barcode. At least I know I'm supposed to do that.

See. Easy.

I stare at the buttons, waiting for something to happen. But there's nothing. Nothing is happening.

"Something wrong?" asks the man in front of me, tapping his credit card on the desk.

"No," I say in a pitch too high. "No, no, no. Everything's perfectly fine."

I stare at the computer, willing it to tell me what more it wanted from me. My hands hover above the keyboard, wondering if I should press enter, or type in FINISHED. Anything. The clang of the door opening and the, "Who the hell are you?" makes me stop from doing anything more and I nearly burst into tears when I am met with a girl, her brunette hair in a high pony tail while wearing a pink Fleet Feet Sports shirt.

"Oh, thank God," I run to her and grab her hand, ushering her toward the computer. "I'm new and I have no clue what I am doing."

"Obviously," she says, clicking the mouse a couple times before pressing enter. "You can scan your card," she smiles at the customer and with another click the receipt prints. "Have a lovely day," she calls after him.

I lean against the table, throwing back my head and looking heavenward.

"Alright newbie, what's your name and why are you at the register by yourself?" Asked the brunette looking me up and down.

"I'm Rachel, and Seth, the bastard, just left me here for practice."

The brunette turns to the door, her lips pursing and her eyebrows furrowing. "Seth left you all alone?"

I nod, wanting to explain more; that the bastard actually hates me and wants to make my life miserable. But I keep my mouth shut. I don't want her to hate me, too. She might actually save me from having to lock up the store all by myself.

"What's your name?" I smile and ask instead. "And can you please teach me everything I need to know about the scary cash register?"

The brunette laughs. "Sweetie, a monkey could do this work."

I frown. "Sadly, I am not a monkey."

That earns another laugh and the brunette pats me on the back. "I'm Kristen and don't you worry. I'll get you all sorted." She winks at me and goes on to explain the register and the storage room system to me. I sigh in relief, realizing not all my coworkers are complete assholes.

***

I stand outside the apartment, staring at the door and wondering if it was worth returning home at all after helping Kristen lock up the shop. I hear muffled voices inside and grimace, knowing I would have to go past them in order to get to my room. *Might as well get it over with,* I tell myself while shoving my key into the door and pushing it open. I'm immediately welcomed by the sight of Seth and Lucas watching some game on the television while Hunter stands in the disgusting kitchen, sniffing through the glasses before opening the cabinets. His grimace alerts me to the fact that there are no clean glasses awaiting him, or anyone of us.

Lucas turns in my general direction, eyeing me up and down while I kick the door closed. I shrug on my bag, which keeps slipping off, and keep my head down, hoping to get to my room before the boys get any funny ideas. The hallway is still littered with shoes and I pick through them. Unfortunately, I'm not as adept at skipping over a littered hallway and my toe snags on one, sending me tumbling face forward into the sticky floor. No one bothers to ask if I'm okay while I groan, lifting my head and wondering what I did in my past life to earn me such terrible karma. I roll over and grab my bag, unzipping it and taking out my camera. I check for any damage, but it seems the only thing damaged was my ego. *I'll take it,* I think while trying to stand amidst the shoes.

"Geez," says Lucas, shaking his head. "Psycho roommate sure is clumsy."

Psycho roommate? Rage boils deep within me and I grind my teeth to keep myself from saying something I know I'll regret. Three on one isn't quite a good number to be fighting with, but psycho roommate? *He dares say that as if I'm not even in the room? How was I the psycho roommate when the whole lot of you live in a pigsty and trade girls around like they are baseball cards?*

I sigh and throw the shoes around me to the side, making a little room so I can stand. "Watch it with those." Hunter scowls at me. "Those are expensive."

Then why do you leave them all over the apartment if they are so expensive? Once again, I bite my tongue. I continue to stand, eyeing my room like the safe haven it is. Just a few steps more and I will be home and safe away from these freaks of nature. I grab my bag and take a step toward the door.

"How was Betsy?" Hunter asks, leaning against the cluttered counter.

"Ugh. Two stars," says Seth, not bothering to turn around and answer. "She just laid there like a dead fish."

"She's hot though," adds Lucas, as if that's the only thing important.

Seth shakes his head. "Yeah, but that's not everything. At some point you gotta move, moan, do something. She just did absolutely nothing. Even after I ran there from work and everything."

"Good to know," says Lucas.

Hunter chuckles. "That's what you get for being too needy."

Seth groans. "I guess."

Something catches my attention with this conversation. And it isn't the fact that these assholes are speaking about a woman as if they are rating a campus restaurant. No. I already know these jerks are misogynist pigs. I tell myself it's nothing and I should just get to my room and drown out their muffled sounds with some indie rock music. But sadly, I remain in my place. Shoulders shaking. *No,* a little whisper whimpers in the back of my mind. *It's nothing. Just go.*

Instead, I turn around and open my stupid mouth. "I thought you said you had practice, Seth."

Seth glances over his shoulder, his eyes narrowing on me. "Did I?"

I cross my arms and nod. *It's not a big deal, just go. You were saved by Kristen earlier. Why do you have to confront him on this? No good will come of it.* But I ignore that little voice. Maybe I shouldn't, but something inside me snaps. This jerk-off left me completely alone in a store full of customers and didn't even bother explaining shit to me. And now I return and have to listen to him give a two-star rating to a girl who is probably nice deep down inside.

"You did," I finally say, jutting out my chin while keeping eye contact. I am not going to bow down to him. I am a strong, independent woman and I deserve some explanation.

Seth shrugs and turns around. "Huh." He doesn't bother to elaborate.

The boiling sensation returns to me, like I'm a volcano about to explode. I look around at the room, at the growing mess. The shoes littering the hallway, the mildew crusting the sink, the glasses filled with yellowish nearly green water, and the stench of sweat and rotten eggs permeating the air around us.

And the bathroom.

I grimace, remembering my shower from this morning and the sink covered with various toothpastes, socks slipped over the sink, swimming trunks hanging from the shower door and hairs (*I don't even want to know where they came from*) stuck in the shower drain.

And that's when I just have to open my stupid mouth again. Why I can't be a good girl and just go back to my room is completely beyond me. I'm only two steps away from my door. Two steps away from my little sanctuary and my mouth opens, and what comes out is, "I think we should have a roommate meeting."

Seth and Lucas turn fully around in the couch. All three pairs of eyes are on me, staring at me as if my hair has suddenly grown snakes and frozen them in this catatonic frustrated look. It takes a moment for anyone to say anything. Whatever game on the television is still blaring in the background. I take a look at the screen and realize it's football. *Of course. I should have known.*

Seth finally blinks and turns to both Lucas and Hunter, with a look that still reads 'what the hell is going on?'.

"What?" he nearly shouts.

Lucas and Hunter shake their heads.

"I don't know, bro," says Hunter. "You were the one who brought it here. You get rid of it."

"Because you fuckers didn't bother to help." Seth massages his temples and rolls his neck. He groans before making eye contact with me again. "Why the fuck do you want a meeting?"

I point at the three boys, my fingering quivering slightly, but I am not backing down from this. "This place is a mess."

Lucas chuckles and turns back around in his spot on the couch.

"So?" Hunter says, crossing his arms.

"So?" I motion toward the shoes and the kitchen. "We can't live like this. It's absolutely disgusting."

"And what do you want us to do about it?" Seth asks, standing up and walking toward me like a wolf stalking a deer. "You want us to clean?" he asks in a mockingly sweet tone.

"Ha!" shouts Lucas. "Fat chance."

"Why don't we clean it together?" Even though I wasn't the one to make the mess, I can help. I would do anything to not live in this pigsty. Anything. "I can do the bathroom, someone can take the kitchen, and another can do the floors. It could be a bonding moment." I grimace as the words come out. *Bonding moment. Ha! Like we could ever bond over anything.*

"Bonding moment," Lucas laughs. "Did you hear that, Seth?"

Seth rolls his eyes. "Yeah, yeah, I heard."

"I don't have time for this," says Hunter. "I've got things to do."

"Yeah, coming from the one who makes the most mess," says Seth.

Hunter shrugs. "I'm a busy man."

"I'm sure if we all help out, it can be done in a couple hours."

Hunter groans. "Seth, make it stop speaking."

"Well, do you have a better idea?" I rest my hands on my hips. "I mean, I didn't even make the mess and I'm willing to help out."

That earns me a scowl from both Seth and Hunter. "How kind of you," Hunter nearly growls.

A terrible smile curls Seth's lips and that small voice in my head returns. *Go back to your room and forget you said anything.* He stalks toward me, towering over me, but I am not going to be scared. I hold my ground, frowning up at him and waiting for whatever stupid nonsense he's about to utter.

"I have an idea," he says, and with his tone of voice I feel another tug toward my door. "The one who does the least push-ups cleans the apartment."

"I can definitely get down with that," says Hunter.

"Sounds good," says Lucas.

I shake my head. "That's ridiculous." Not to mention I'm not even sure I can do one push-up let alone the hundreds I would need to stay in the game with these idiots.

"Shall we have a vote?" Seth turns on his heal and waltzes back to the couch. "All for push-up challenge raise your hand."

All three bastards raise their stupid hands.

"All for not?"

I don't raise my hand, scowling at the three in front of me.

Seth pouts mockingly. "That's three against one, roomie."

"You have to be freaking kidding me." I stomp my foot, knowing I look childish yet not giving two shits. "I'm not doing this."

"But you have to," says Seth. "We had a vote and everything. You did call a roommate meeting, right?"

I pinch my nose and look skyward. "But it's not fair! I can't even do one push-up."

Seth shrugs. "Me neither. I'm a track athlete, not a muscle head like Hunter. Who knows, maybe you beat me and I'll have to clean up the mess."

I glare at him. "Yeah, sure. Like that's likely."

"Whatever, psycho roommate," says Seth. "But you were the one who wanted a meeting," he points at me, looking annoyed. "You were the one who couldn't live with the mess. And now we are offering you a solution and you're snubbing your nose, looking down on us like we're the pieces of shits when everything was fine and dandy before."

"Fine!" I shout, my hands fisting to keep from strangling his stupid neck. "Let's do this. Who wants to go first?" My scowl darkens when I see Mr. Bigshot Muscles Hunter raise his hand, smirking as he drops from his huge height down onto the sticky floor and quickly pumps out at least a thousand push-ups right there and then.

"101, 102, 103," calls Seth, crouched down low while counting.

Lucas leans against the couch, crossing his arms and watching Hunter with a smirk. He looks up at me briefly and I feel his eyes raking up and down my body, as if undressing me right there. I scowl back at him, crossing my arms over my chest. *This is ridiculous. Why did I even agree? Am I freaking stupid?*

"200," calls Seth and Hunter jumps up, flexing his muscles ridiculously.

"I could probably do more, but what's the point?" He stalks over to the couch and then it's Lucas's turn, jumping down into a plank and continuing with this stupid show of meat headedness.

"105, 106," Hunter and Seth yell out together.

Yep, I'm going to lose. I'm totally going to lose and they will force me to clean the whole apartment and then what? I will become their slave? Just great. Just great, Rachel. I shouldn't have said anything. I should've kept my mouth shut and just gone to my room, but noooooo. I just had to call them out on their disgusting lifestyle. I scowl at Seth, still calling out numbers while Lucas completes push-up after push-up. If he hadn't just left me at the shop, then none of this would've happened. If he was just a nice human being I wouldn't be stuck in this mess. Why? Why wasn't he nice to me? What did I do wrong to deserve this?

My gaze falls on his arms, looking at the biceps stretching the thin fabric of the Fleet Feet Sports shirt. Yep, those look like they can do at least fifty push-ups. I'm out of the game. Screwed. I wonder what those arms would feel like wrapped around me. *Or pinning me down to the bed.*

"250," call Seth and Hunter while Lucas stands. He takes a moment to straighten his hair and wink at Hunter.

"Show off," mutters Hunter.

Seth pouts. "Ahh, poor Rachel. Getting nervous? Should I go easy on you?" He rests his palms on the floor and grimaces. "Ugh, this floor is nasty. Good luck to the loser."

Lucas and Hunter chuckle.

"1," calls out Lucas.

"2," says Hunter.

I look away and shake my head, fighting back the stupid tears. I got myself into this mess.

"5," says Lucas.

To my surprise Seth jumps up and shakes out his arms.

"That's it?" asks Hunter.

"You must be joking," says Lucas, looking him up and down.

"Think you can beat that, roomy?" Seth leans over, his face mere inches from mine. My breath hitches, for a minute thinking he's going to press those lips against me. His gaze dips down, my face heats at the thought of him closing the gap between us. "All you need is six," his voice is soft and low.

I yank off my jacket and toss it at Lucas and Hunter, who both barely avoid it. It winds up hitting the couch and I roll up my sleeves, walking to the center of the kitchen. "Game on," I mutter, planting my palms on the sticky floor and ignoring the shudder rippling down my spine at the feeling. *Just don't think about what's been on this floor.* I move my body into a plank easily. *You can do this, Rachel. Think yoga. Think of all the planks and yoga you've done before.*

I slowly bend my elbows. Ignoring the shake in my biceps, I push up from the ground, biting back a hiss of exertion. "One," Seth calls out.

Just five more. Five more, you can do this.

I bend my elbows again, gasping when I felt my muscles beginning to give out. *Fight it. Push through.* I push with as much strength as I can muster, my whole body quivering while I bring it back up into a plank. "Two," all three boys say together.

Four more!

But I don't know if my body can possibly do four more. My arms are shaking violently. I take a deep breath, hovering there in a plank and willing my arms to bend once again. "We are waiting," Seth sings above me and I scowl up at him, hoping he burns in hell for this torture he is putting me through.

Come on. Just four more.

"I don't think she can do it," says Lucas.

"Honestly I'm surprised she was able to do two," says Hunter.

I bend down again, my chest nearly touching the floor. I will my arms to push up, but I remain down. A whimper escapes me and I wince, using every last strength I have left within me to push up from that sticky, disgusting floor that I refuse to clean. But my body is against me. I can't do it.

I can't.

My body falls, landing on the disgusting floor and I gasp, biting back tears at my failure.

"Ah," Seth ruffles my hair. "You lose. Too bad."

"Guess you better get started," says Lucas while looking around at the hell hole that is my life. "There sure is a lot to clean up."

"Yeah, who knows how long this is going to take you," Hunter adds with a chuckle.

I wipe my eyes, not wanting them to see my tears while I pick myself up off the floor. Seth hands me a mop as soon as I'm standing. "Good luck." He pats me on the shoulder and gives me a bitter smile.

"I want it to sparkle." Hunter expands his hands, looking around at the apartment. "I want it to be so shiny I can see my face in the floor."

Lucas passes me and opens the refrigerator. "Maybe we should eat something before we go out," he says, pulling out some milk and chugging it, spilling some on the floor. "Oh, oops. Sorry, roomy. I guess that just makes your job harder."

"Oh, no," says Seth, staring down at the spilt milk. He rubs his chin, and I know he's just thinking of more terrible ways to torture me with. "That's not so nice, Lukie."

"Yeah," adds Hunter, taking one of the glasses filled with yellow liquid and spilling it on the floor. "That's just going to make her work longer."

"Oh, Hunter, look what you just did." Seth points at Hunter's upturned glass.

"Oh my fucking God." Hunter covers his mouth in mock surprise. "I'm terrible."

"No, I'm terrible," says Seth while grabbing the rest of the glasses and running around the apartment, spilling the contents all over the floor and then wiping his dirty shoes in it. "Absolutely, terrible."

"Stop it!" I shout, dropping the mop and following Seth around the apartment. I slip in the spilt water, my legs sliding into an almost split. I grab the couch and pull myself up, ignoring the laughter behind me. "Stop it right now!"

Seth drops the glass onto the floor and I gasp as it shatters into tiny little pieces. "Alright, boys, let's leave her to it," says Seth, motioning toward the door and walking onto the glass, making them break into tinier fragments.

"Bye, roomie," each one says while I watch them walk out the front door, slamming it shut.

I stare at the empty room, covered in spilled water smelling like rotten eggs. I sniff and pick up the mop. I lean it against the wall and sniff again, wiping my eyes. *Don't you dare cry.*

I don't even know where to start. The floor? The sink? The bathroom? *Cinderella probably had it easier.* I wonder what would happen if I just refuse to clean. How long can I stay in a locked room without food and water? Or, really, how long can I avoid them?

Probably a day max.

I sigh and resolve myself to my fate. Just do it and they'll leave you alone. Then you can finally have a proper, decent apartment. And as soon as this is done and over with, you can just hideout in your room.

And they'll leave you alone.

Chapter 6

HUNTER

"Ah, man, that was hilarious," I say while smacking the top of the armrest.

I bite back a groan, pain shooting up my shoulder at the sudden movement. It's aggravating me more and more these days, which pisses me off since it's the start of the football season. And this injury is from months prior. It should be better already. Actually, I thought it was getting better. It didn't even bother me until the summer months. Not until practice started up again and honestly, yeah, I probably shouldn't be playing. Maybe I should be taking a break, but I'm already at the top. After this year and next I could be drafted into the NFL and taking a break now... well it would likely hurt my chances of playing pro football.

I probably shouldn't have pushed it with those pushups. A hundred would have been enough. Hell, ten would have been enough, yet I just had to show off. I narrow my eyes at Lucas. He did over two hundred. Fucking showoff. If my shoulder wasn't like this I could do three hundred. Fuck, I could do five hundred.

I should really see a doctor about this. My hand slides to my shoulder when the pain doesn't alleviate and I try to ignore Lucas and Seth's gaze on it while I rub the tightness out of the muscles. Maybe I should talk to coach about upping my painkillers at the next game. On impulse, my body shudders at the thought of the needle sinking into the sore muscle.

"I can't believe she actually went for it," says Lucas. He guzzles down the rest of his beer in his red cup before tossing it over his shoulder and grabbing another on the tilted coffee table in front of him.

Seth scoffs. "She's a fucking idiot." He chugs the rest of his drink and snaps his fingers at the pledge dressed as a tooth fairy. He prances over and hands Seth another drink. "Of course she'd go for it."

"I wonder what else she'll do," says Lucas, taking a sip from his cup with a mischievous look. He smirks over the room of his cup, his expression turning dark. *Sick bastard. Sometimes I really wonder what goes on in that head of his.*

"Oooooh!" Seth shouts, bounding up from the chair and shoving his legs under him and dirtying the cushion with his muddy shoes. He's obviously drunk, because sober Seth would die from mortification from dirtying anything. *Responsible fucker.* "I bet she'll do anything we tell her to!" he shouts, pointing at Lucas, beer dribbling down from his mouth. "You smart bastard."

Lucas chuckles and shrugs, taking another sip from his cup. "What can I say? I see an opportunity and I take it."

"We could make her clean our rooms." Seth chugs the rest of his drink and snaps his finger for another.

That definitely catches my attention. My room hasn't been cleaned since I moved in. Honestly, I don't even think it was clean then. I just remember unloading the boxes and digging through them occasionally when I can't find something I need. Everything is in a pile on the floor. I don't even use my dresser. It's probably empty. Or filled with Playboys.

I frown thinking about the dresser. My mom helped me get that dresser. I tug out my phone, looking to see if there are any missed calls. One from Betsy—I roll my eyes, I'll put that off until I'm desperate, I don't need any two stars in my life—but none from my mother. I should probably call her tomorrow and see how the chemotherapy is going. I should have asked her about it today.

Why am I such a terrible son? Maybe I should drive over to her place and make sure she has everything.

"Earth to Hunter," says Seth in a low, obnoxious voice, waving his hand in front of my face. "Come in Hunter."

I shake my head. I can worry about Mom tomorrow. "What?" I chuckle, trying to push away my stupid worries.

"What do you think?"

"You know I don't think, Seth."

Seth rolls his eyes. "About psycho roommate." He waggles his eyebrows. "You have a list of chores we could make her do?"

"Breakfast would be wonderful."

Seth faces Lucas and grimaces. "Ah, yeah, your breakfasts are nasty." Seth nearly gags.

Lucas shrugs. "They're not so bad."

I nod in agreement. "Nah, bro. They smell fucking nasty."

Lucas looks down at his phone and smiles. "Looks like I'm up, boys." He sets down his cup and straightens his shirt. "Millie messaged me. Guess it's my turn to be with the sexy, flexible gymnast."

"Oh, man," Seth groans and bows down. "Enjoy. She's a treat."

I smile, and lean back against the couch, ignoring another jolt of pain going up my shoulder. "Have fun."

My thoughts drift to Millie and her huge breasts, her tight ass. Just yesterday I was fucking her and the bitch put her leg over her head. I mean, directly over her head as if it was nothing. I feel my lips curl into a smile at the thought. Definitely need to keep her around for at least the next semester.

Psycho roommate also isn't so bad on the eyes. Sure, she never smiles. Her face seems permanently set in a scowl, but she has a pretty nice figure for not being a sporty girl. Nice ass. Pretty face even when she's angry. Bad temperament. Although, that might be good in bed.

"Hey Seth," I tap my cup, thinking of psycho roommate naked. *How would that look?* "Do you think psycho girl would be good in bed?"

Seth grimaces, his cup to his lips, yet he's not drinking. His expression darkens and I wonder if he'll chuck his drink at the wall. "No," he grumbles. "I think she would be worse than Betsy."

He drinks, not bothering to say anything more on the topic. He's surprisingly quiet, given there's a room full of chicks behind us dropping it like it's hot as Martin shouts about a keg stand.

Although, I'm not sure Seth's assessment on our new roommate is accurate. I mean, how could it be if none of us have really tried fucking her? I side eye him for a moment, taking in his scowl. Seth was never one to get so irritated with a girl before. Other than bumping into me and demanding we clean, she hasn't really done anything crazy. It might actually be fun having her sneak into my room and ride me to the moon and back.

I stare down at my beer, scowling down at its contents. Or maybe I've had too much to drink. This is Seth after all. If he doesn't like her, it's probably for a good reason.

"Hey," Seth hits my arm, smiling over the rim of his cup. I swear the guy always blames me and Lucas for getting him trashed, but it's not my fault he always seems to have a cup in his hands. "You want a nice breakfast tomorrow?" He smiles wickedly.

"Sure, Seth. I'm always up for good food."

Seth rubs his hands together and laughs. "I have an idea."

***

Seth kicks open the door. I stumble inside, nearly falling into Seth, who has completely stopped in front of the doorway.

He looks around. "Whoa," he breathes.

"What gives, man?" I rub my forehead, my head pounding with the fresh beginnings of a new hangover.

I squint in the general direction Seth is looking, trying to focus the two images weaving in and it. I clutch the wall to keep the room from spinning. *Classes and practice are going to be a complete shit show today.* I grimace when the images merge into one and quickly realize we are in the fucking wrong apartment.

The sink isn't caked in grime and mildew. The crowd of glasses, which usually stink up the air with a rotten egg-like stench, aren't cluttering the counter. *These folks are clean motherfuckers*, I think while moving my leg up and down, noting how my shoes don't stick to the floor. *Hell, I can even see my reflection in the floor if I squint hard enough.*

"We're in the wrong apartment again," I groan, starting for the door. "Let's go before they call the cops."

"Stop, you idiot," Seth hisses. "I used my key to get in." He jingles them in front of my face and I squint, taking a moment for everything to click in my drunk little head.

"Oh." I look around again, rubbing my eyes at the organized line of shoes in the hallway. Several of those pairs are mine. The television screen is off to the side with the kayak still leaning against it, with the couch sitting in front. "Wait, this is our place?" *It had to be. Just a sparkly, magical version of the dump we live in.* Even the air

smells of pine and citrus rather than its usual rot. "Wow." I step into
the kitchen, opening the cabinets and seeing shiny clean glasses
staring back at me. "Psycho roommate did all of this?"

"I'm a genius!" Seth shouts, not even bothering to keep his voice
down with arms raised as if he just crossed the finish line. He stalks
over toward psycho roommate's door. "Genius!"

He bangs on her door, laughing maniacally.

"What the hell are you doing?"

"Getting breakfast, numb nuts," he says, continuing to bang on
her door. "Now help me."

I jump at the clicking sound of the door opening behind me, and
it takes me a moment too long to recognize the two figures swerving
in and out are a very disheveled Lucas. He looks around suspiciously
and lifts his legs while staring down at the floor. "Are we in the
wrong apartment?"

I shake my head and the movement makes me instantly nauseas.
Never again. I'm never drinking again. "No, psycho roommate
cleaned."

"Wake up, Rachel!" Seth bangs over and over again on her door.
He scowls over his shoulder at us. "You going to stand there or are
you going to help me?"

Lucas groans and rubs his face. "I've been up all night."

"Really?" Despite my nausea, I waggle my eyebrows. "Millie?"

Lucas grins mischievously, but says nothing.

"In the name of breakfast, get your asses over here." Seth kicks the
door.

"Oh my god." Psycho roommate throws open the door.

Her hair is tied in a frazzled low pony tail. Her pajamas are some
terrible concoction of a long button down shirt patterned with
stripes and hearts with pink fluffy slipper socks. She looks
absolutely... I cock my head to the side, trying to find a word for it.
Definitely not sexy. But not bad either, a small voice says in the back
of my head. *Cute. She looks cute.* I scrunch up my nose at the
thought. Now, that's a word I haven't used to describe a girl in a
long while.

"What the hell do you want now?" She looks at her watch (*who
wears a watch to bed?)* and rubs her eyes for a split second before
raising the watch closer to her face. "It's four in the morning!"

"Breakfast!" shouts Seth, punching the air. "Breakfast!"

I watch Seth continue to punch the air. He's obviously having way too much fun with this. And sure, picking on Rachel, psycho roommate, whatever her face is, was hell of a lot of fun, but Lukie is tired and I'm desperate for a bed. I glance over at my door, wondering if I can easily slip away, but at the same time, I'm quite curious what she'll do with Seth's antics.

I watch as she rolls her eyes and goes to slam the door, but Seth blocks it with an arm and a leg.

"You must be freaking kidding me!" Psycho roommate shouts. She sniffs Seth's neck and I shake my head, wondering if I really am trashed since the bastard's face is turning bright red. "Are you drunk?" I groan, rubbing my temples at the shrill in her voice.

"Not so loud," I moan.

Seth scoffs and grabs her wrist, yanking her into the middle of the room. She shakes his arm off her, but rather than return to her room, she scowls at him. "So what?" he shouts while her hands rest on her hips. "Make us breakfast."

"No." She points her finger at him. "You make me breakfast."

I laugh at that. Seth, make breakfast? I don't think I've even seen him handle the microwave. He does know how to use the phone though and call pizza delivery. At least I know how to unwrap protein powder and swish it around with some milk or water.

I look over and see Lucas grimacing. "I don't think you want that," he says, crossing his arms. "From any of us."

Psycho roommate sighs and her shoulder's slump. She sniffs and looks like she's about to cry. I roll my eyes. For a moment there, she actually looked like she was going to give Seth hell, now she's become this sniveling little girl. That is, until she scowls up at Lucas. "I cleaned this whole place and I didn't even mess it up. The least you could do is let me sleep."

"A race!" Seth shouts while raising his fist in the air. *The bastard has way too much energy for it being 4am.* "We can have a race. Loser makes breakfast."

"No!" Psycho roommate wails, pressing her face into her hands and walking back to her room. "No more." She slams the door shut.

For a moment we all look at each other. Seth's lips twitch into an evil grin which makes me giggle. *God, I really must be drunk.* Lucas shakes his head, but he's smiling and before I know it, my feet are following Seth to her door. All our fists bang on her door over and over again.

"Breakfast Race!" I shout.

"Race!" Lucas and Seth shout together.

"Come on!" shouts Seth. "Just one little race."

"We're not going to stop," I call in a sing song voice, earning a cackle from Seth.

"Not until you face us like a man." Lucas bangs on the door with both fists.

The door opens and my fist nearly connects with her nose. Thankfully, I stop myself and barely have time to get out of her way as she blazes past us.

"Fine," she says, shoving on her shoes and I have to admit, it's quite hot seeing her so riled up, with her hair in a messy bun, now wearing tight yoga pants and a baggy white shirt. I watch her bend over to put on her Chuck Taylor's. She has a very nice ass. However, her choice in running shoes is not the greatest. At least they'll stay on her feet. I glance over and see Lucas and Seth also ogling her ass and grimace. *So they like what they see, too?*

"Well, what are you waiting for, you stupid oafs?" She rises and scowls up at us while placing her hands on her hips. Her scowl is more of a squint and I shake my head, trying to stop whatever thoughts coming to mind.

She is definitely cute.

I'm obviously trashed.

Nothing about this girl is hot and sexy, like Millie.

Ah... Millie... I allow myself a moment to think of big breasted Millie pulling her leg over her head. However, the thought is unfortunately interrupted by Rachel in her cute button-down pajamas.

What the hell is wrong with me?

"Alright!" Seth shouts, leading the way outside the apartment and down the stairs.

Unfortunately, my head is pounding. Thankfully, my vision is no long blurred. But my stomach is definitely lurching at the thought of movement. Fast movement. I'm probably going to throw up in the middle of this race.

"Seth, not too far," I say, but it comes out as more of a moan.

Seth rolls his eyes. "Big baby," I hear him mutter.

He's lucky I'm too hung-over to pummel him for that.

We stop at the sidewalk and I wait for the asshole to give instructions. Seth looks both ways and points at a stop sign about a five-minute walk away. *Oh, thank God.*

"To that sign and back," he says. He towers over Rachel, smirking down at her like some wicked villain from a movie. "Loser has to make breakfast."

"And winner?" asks Lucas.

I size him up. He's a tall man, but he's a rower, not a runner. Maybe his long legs could help him, but he isn't as adept to running like me and Seth. *Well, me on a good day. We'll see how this goes.* I glance at psycho roommate. *Short, can't even do five pushups. Oh, we'll totally destroy her.*

"Winner gets breakfast, Lukie," says Seth. "That's it."

Lucas eyes psycho roommate up and down as if he has other things on his mind. I feel my eyes squinting at him in an absolute failure of a scowl and I move to stand next to psycho girl, silently cursing myself for acting so annoyingly possessive. I glance down at her. Yeah, she is definitely easy on the eyes. Could smile a bit more though.

"On your marks!" shouts Seth, bending down into a starting position. "Get set!"

I roll my shoulders and get into my sprinting position.

"Go!"

I bolt, feeling the wind whipping through my blonde hair. Seth is in front of me, which is no surprise. My stomach lurches and I feel bile in my throat. *Don't you dare vomit.* Seth hits the sign right before me and turns on his heel, making a mad dash back to the apartment. Lucas is right behind me, and psycho girl on his heels. I'm actually surprised she's doing so well. I tap the sign and dash back toward the apartment, nearly running into Seth.

"Let's go, Lukie!" Seth hollers.

"Shut the fuck up!" a neighbor without a shirt on shouts from a window above us.

"No, you shut the fuck up!" shouts Seth while I give the asshole above us the finger.

I turn around, seeing psycho girl about to surpass him. "Go, go, go!" I shout. "Come on!" I don't even know who I'm rooting for. Lukie, or psycho girl?

Lucas's arms pump harder and soon he's leaving psycho girl behind, running across our imaginary finish line. Psycho girl follows after, gasping for breath and leaning over as if she has just run a marathon.

"Breakfast!" Seth shouts, bounding up the stairs. "Breakfast! Breakfast!" He turns around and shouts from the staircase, "You lose, psycho bitch!"

She follows after us, walking slowly as if there are weights attached to each leg. "This isn't fair," she grumbles.

Seth throws himself onto the couch, leaning his head back in the cushions. "I want French toast," he murmurs, already falling asleep.

"An egg white omelet for me," says Lucas, falling onto the couch next to Seth.

I rub my shoulder, trying to get the kinks out of it. I really don't need my shoulder giving out on me today in practice. Our first game is on Saturday, and I really need it up and working.

Psycho roommate whirls around to face me. "And what do you want?"

I scowl back at her. It's not my fault she sucks at sports and I'm in no mood to be treated so rudely. "Coffee," I growl, towering over her.

She shifts nervously in front of me, her mouth opening to say something, but she quickly closes it and turns her attention to the kitchen. *Yeah, that's what I thought.* I whip out my cell phone, turning to my bedroom and closing the door lightly. I am immediately greeted by the smell of sweat permeating off my gym clothes lying in piles around my bed and dresser. I open a window and lean against the wall next to it, inhaling the fresh air deeply to keep my stomach steady. Pressing the dial button, I listen to the rings, hoping she answers. I look at the clock on my dresser, flashing 5am. It's early in the morning, but I know she's an early riser.

"Hello."

I smile at the sound of her voice. "Hey Mom, how are you?"

Chapter 7

RACHEL

I sniff, shoving my hands into my pockets to keep them from punching the air. I try to ignore my roommate's laughter echoing in my head and shake it to keep myself from remembering this morning. *Why did I have to open my door? Would they have kept banging it incessantly?*

Sure.

But eventually they would have stopped and gone to bed. Better a few moments of torture rather than serving them as their slave.

Ugh.

And that race. What the hell? I don't even know why I agreed to something so stupid. Honestly, it was just to stop Seth from going on and on, and for a moment I genuinely thought I was going to win.

Only to realize that stupid asshole, Lucas was just playing with me.

"What the hell is this?" I remember Lucas scowling down at me, holding out his plate as if I served him vomit rather than the egg white omelet he demanded.

I don't know how to make an egg white omelet! Hell, I barely cook!

"Ugh," I remember Hunter groaning, spilling his coffee onto the newly cleaned floor. The floor they made me clean last night! I think my mouth legit dropped to the floor when he did that. "This is disgusting."

"Hey, Rachel," I remember hearing Seth; remember cringing even before turning around and looking at him, knowing he was going to do something completely terrible. I scowl now even thinking about it. *I made him French toast. French freaking toast. He should have been bowing down and thanking me.* Instead, he threw the syrupy slices of bread at my face. I remember standing there, completely shocked while the slices slipped to the floor, leaving a syrupy mess all over my striped blouse. "Aren't women supposed to be good at cooking?"

I don't remember hearing the rest. I think it was something about women being meant to be barefoot in the kitchen. Obviously, it was something misogynistic like that. At the time, I was too focused on my beautiful striped blouse, ruined by maple syrup.

I don't actually remember what happened after. I know I changed and left, which is why I am on my way to the art department now, but I don't actually remember doing those things. I do remember seeing red and nearly punching Seth in his stupid, smug face.

"You'll have to clean this up when you get back, roomie."

Ugh. Even his voice just grates on my nerves.

I groan, walking into the classroom. A part of me perks up at seeing Charlie, Lauren, and Josh all sitting in the back of the room. *Thank freaking God for my new friends. I think they are the only ones keeping me sane.*

"What's wrong?" asks Charlie while I sit in the seat between her and Lauren.

"Yeah, you look terrible," says Lauren. I try not to scowl at her, but I feel it already scrunching up my face. She offers me a soft smile. "Sorry. I mean, you don't look very happy."

"My asshole roommates woke me up this morning, demanding breakfast."

"No," Charlie gasps.

I sniff and wipe my eyes, already feeling the water works about to release. "Yep."

"Please don't tell me you did," says Josh, resting a hand on mine.

I blush while looking down at his hand. *Whatever hell I go through with those idiots, at least I know not all men are like them.* "We had a whole race and of course I lost. So yeah, I did."

"No," everyone says in unison.

I sniff again, grinding my teeth together to keep down a sob. I am not going to cry. I am a strong, independent woman and I am not going to let a bunch of hoodlums break me. "Yeah," I squeak. I sniff several times, trying to calm my racing heart. My face feels like I stuck it into a pyre. Josh squeezes my hand and I hold onto it, trying to put in words the rest of my horrific morning. "And then..." I sniff. *Don't you dare.* "And then they." I swallow and Josh pats my hand.

"They did what?" He leans in close.

I feel my face crumbling and there's no way I can remain strong any longer. "They threw it on the floor," I sob, burying my face in my hands. "The floor I just cleaned after losing the push-up challenge."

"Push-up challenge?" I hear Charlie above me, stroking my head and shushing me like I am a toddler who just scabbed her knees. "What push-up challenge?"

I sniff, lifting my head and wiping my eyes. I pause for a moment, worried I just smeared all my makeup, then scowl, realizing I didn't have time to put on makeup because I was too busy making my five-star breakfast for a bunch of bratty, self-serving pigs. "The place was a mess and I wanted to have a talk about cleaning it together. But they didn't want to so they called for a push-up challenge. Loser has to clean the whole place."

Lauren grimaces. "And you lost."

"Obviously she lost." Charlie motions to me. "Just look at her."

"What is that supposed to mean?" I wipe my eyes.

Charlie shakes her head and pats my hand. "It means you are a bohemian, not an athlete." I scowl at her and she shrugs. "It's not an insult. Just fact."

"Don't worry." Josh winks. "I'm a bohemian, too."

I chuckle before groaning. "What am I going to do? I can't go back there."

"Why can't you just say no?" asks Lauren. "I mean, what are they going to do?"

"Bang on my door until I answer," I say robotically.

"Have an orgy in her room," adds Charlie.

"And then decorate the apartment with used condoms," says Josh, earning a look from all three of us girls. He shrugs. "What? It can happen."

I groan. "So not helping."

"Have you tried taking a look at the rent agreement?" asks Charlie.

I open my bag, digging through my folders until I finally find the yellow one with dachshunds all over it. I take out the rent agreement Seth sent me a few weeks ago, quickly looking through it. I sigh when I finally find what it says. "Just like I thought." I run a hand through my hair, still a mess from having thrown it up into a lopsided bun. "I need to give a two month notice and find someone to take my room."

"So you can leave around Christmas," says Lauren, sounding hopeful.

"I don't know if I can last until Christmas. The boys have me acting like their slave. And besides," I slump, "I don't even know if I can find a replacement. Who would want to live with three loud, messy, horny pigs?"

Silence surrounds me and I whimper. I know I'm being pathetic. I know I should be strong and stand up for myself. Or look at this whole thing with the glass half full like Mom always suggests, but I'm too tired. I went to sleep last night around midnight and was woken at 4am. With that amount of sleep, there is no way I can think logically, or positively about this situation.

"Well, you can always sleep on my couch," says Josh, his hand slipping away from mine. I miss the warmth, but I'm too shy to grab his hand, especially in front of Charlie and Lauren. "And I may have a room for you since my roommate is usually over at his girlfriend's place anyway."

I smile. "Thanks Josh. I may take you up on that."

"Alright class," says a young brunette with short cropped hair and sparkly makeup. I can only assume this is the great Professor Priestly. She kicks the door closed and slams the stack of papers she's carrying down on her desk. She rolls her shoulders back and I grimace when her neck cracks. "Now, shut your mouths, I have a project for you." She turns on the smart board behind her and while it hums on, she flips open the laptop on the desk, quickly typing in what I can only assume is her login information.

"Oh man," Charlie leans over and whispers in my ear. "Professor Priestly has the best projects. This is going to be fun."

"Why do we photograph?" Professor Priestly looks around the room. "Is there anyone brave enough to answer my question?"

Josh raises his hand. "We photograph to remember."

The professor smiles. "True. But if that's the case, then I can just whip out my iPhone and go to town." She looks around the room. "If remembrance is the answer, why do we still have cameras? Why do we still have a dark room? Why are they important?"

I slowly raise my hand and she nods at me. "For the purpose of art."

I cringe when she scoffs. "Art. I guess that's why we are in the art department." Students glance at me while they chuckle and I immediately wish I could just snap my fingers and disappear. *Stupid. Stupid answer.*

"So remembrance and art." The professor continues to pace. Pictures appear behind her, showcasing the campus and various students. One throwing a football with his friends, another displaying girls studying under a tree. All taken with different photography skills and themes. "I guess these two topics blur into one another, however, the answer to my question is a tricky one." She smiles thinly and touches the smart board, changing the picture to historical ones taken of the campus in the early 1900s. "The reason we photograph differs based on the person." She gestures to someone in the front row. "One could take pictures for marketing, but why is it that you market? What is important behind the picture? Others find creating a story through photographs is their reasoning behind the art form. And some," she paces back and forth behind her desk, "like me, want to document history." She taps the smart board, showing several different pictures of people from around the world. "For this next term I want you to choose a topic, whether that be campus life, or lack thereof," her gaze meets the eye of another student, who's ears go pink. "Choose something, and using different photographical themes, I want you to display at the end of this year, why you chose photography. Why this field? Why is it so important?" The pictures continue to change behind her. "You will be graded on your different photographical techniques. Please use ten. I don't want five black and whites and five with selective colors. I want ten different themes. My office is of course open, if you have any questions."

I already feel my hand about to raise. Looking around, hands are rising. Even Charlie's. "But not now," says the professor, turning her back to us and to the pictures on the smart board. "And don't freak out," she chuckles. "We will be learning several different techniques you may use for your project." Professor Priestly claps her hands together. "Now! Today we are going to discuss lighting. It's both our friend, and our foe." She turns around and catches my eye.

I quickly look away and frown. *How the hell am I going to do this project?*

After class ends, I grab my bag and follow Lauren, Charlie, and Josh outside, thinking about what themes I already know and what exactly I can showcase at a campus full of athletes. As we exit the building, my gaze is captured by the peaks in the distance and I wonder if I can try photographing the scenery of Aurora. But it's not the reason why I photograph. *Really, I don't even know why I chose this field. I just want to make art. Does there have to be a reason behind it?*

"You okay there, Rachel?" asks Charlie, throwing her arm over my shoulder. "You're not thinking about your scumbag roommates, are you?

I groan. "No, but I am now." I sigh. "How exactly am I going to do this project?"

"Easy." Josh pulls out an apple from his bag and takes a bite. "Just take it one week at a time," he says between a mouthful of apple. "Start thinking about your topic tonight. That's the hard part."

I sigh and look up at the sky. "I'm going to fail."

Lauren laughs. "You are not going to fail."

"You know what." Charlie steers me into the quad. "You are in desperate need of a girls' night. Why don't we meet tonight at The Cup and we can help you figure out your topic for the project?"

"Oooh." Lauren claps her hands together while jumping up and down. "Girls' night!" She glances over her shoulder at Josh. "No boys."

Josh raises his hands. "I would never impose on girls' night."

"Sounds good to me," I say, pushing back a stray strand on my face. *It will also give me a great opportunity to keep away from my asshole roommates,* I think, but don't say. It definitely puts an extra pep in my step.

Chapter 8

LUCAS

I sigh, rubbing my head and throwing my bag into a corner of the room. I really need to stop staying out late on school nights. I could barely pay attention in my English class. *It's the one class I actually look forward to out of the week and I couldn't even add anything to the discussion. And practice was brutal. Absolutely brutal. But Millie...*

I lick my lips just thinking about her and that perfect body from this morning. Her huge breasts filling my cupped hands, and her long, limber legs... Millie is definitely one for the books. I take out my phone, finding her name. I am tempted to message her, see if she has a few minutes to spare in the middle of the afternoon. I mean, might as well try since the place is empty. I send her a simple question mark. It's not like I need to have an actual conversation. Millie isn't that sort of girl.

I step over the forgotten French toast on the floor while I scroll through my messages. I mean, seriously, I don't know why Rachel can't just clean up her mess from breakfast. *She threw such a hissy fit earlier when none of us enjoyed the lackluster breakfast she prepared. She pretty much burnt Seth's French toast and my egg whites were runny- barely cooked even.* It's not my fault she sucks at doing push-ups and running. *Ha! And she actually thought she was going to beat me in the race!* She should have kept her stupid mouth shut if she didn't want to put in the work.

I walk over to the sink and pour myself a glass of water. It's fucking great I don't have to dig through frog water filled glasses in order to find one semi-clean cup. *I had to give credit to Rachel there. And she wasn't too bad on the eyes, either. A little annoying with the crying...* I stop thinking; my attention completely drawn by a stream of light coming into the hallway through a crack.

I shove my cell in my pocket and walk toward it, finding Rachel's door slightly ajar. *Leave it, Lucas. You don't need more problems on your plate. But it doesn't seem like she's home.*

I take one tentative step forward. My hand rests on the door. *Her door is open, so maybe she is inside.* I rap lightly at it. *If she is home, I will just rope her into making me a sandwich. It's not like she'll say no...* Although, thinking back to the disgusting egg white omelet she made for me, maybe it's better to get her to clean the kitchen. *I could challenge her to do pull-ups if need be. If she can't do push-ups there's no way she can do pull-ups. And having a clean apartment is always nice. I don't have to be embarrassed anymore when I bring chicks back.*

There's no answer. I knock on the door again, just to make sure. *Maybe she's taking a nap?*

I push the door open when there's no answer, slowly so as not to get any unwanted attention, and then fully when I don't see her blonde head sitting or lying on the bed. I stand at the threshold, peering inside at the small and barely furnished room. The chair is barely standing with one missing wheel. *That must suck.* The crappy desk across from the crappy chair is filled to the brim with a variety of items. Books are piled on one side with make-up on the other. *Make-up she doesn't even use. Not that she needs much of it.* A camera sits between both piles.

I step inside, finding several notebooks and photography books strung all over her bed. I raise an eyebrow at the sheets and pillow neatly tidied. *She actually makes it? Huh. Didn't know those sorts of people existed.*

A striped blouse with syrup stains is spread out on the floor with a few vanilla candles sitting next to it. Like she is planning to have a vigil for it. *Talk about a fire hazard if she actually does light them on the floor.*

"Ugh, why do you assholes make me drink so much?" I hear Seth say in the hallway before hearing the door slam. "Practice was terrible! I still did better than half those talentless asses, but still-terrible!"

I roll my eyes. "Wrong question to be asking, you dip shit."

"Lukie, you're home?" I hear him walking down the hallway. I turn around just when he stops in front of Rachel's door. He looks around the room, but doesn't bother to step across the threshold. "What the hell are you doing in here?"

I smirk. "Door was open."

"No way." He takes one tentative step inside and waits a moment. I chuckle watching him. It's like he expects a scythe to come swinging down. He takes another step, followed by another until he's standing next to me in the middle of the room. "Huh. This is it?"

"Right. I was expecting a bit…"

"More," Seth finishes. He strides toward the bed and crouches down low, looking under it as if he's checking for the boogeyman.

I roll my eyes. "What are you doing?"

Seth drags out a suitcase. "I'm looking to see if she has any guns or knives." He unzips the familiar giant suitcase she originally bashed Hunter with and throws open the lid. Inside there are several oil pastels, papers, nice coloring pencils, and a variety of other supplies any typical art junkie would have. Seth rifles through the items. He picks up the oil pastels and reads the contents before tossing them back in.

I shake my head. "She's going to know if you keep doing that." I watch Seth rise. He frowns while looking around the room. "Besides, those aren't allowed on campus."

Seth stalks toward the wardrobe, struggling to open it since it's stuffed full of clothes. "Yeah, but you never know. She is crazy." He pulls out several garments and throws them over his shoulder. One of them hits me in the face and I pull it away.

"Yeah, she's crazy," I say while eyeing a panda hoodie up and down. *Why does she have this weird thing?* "But she doesn't come off THAT crazy." I throw the garment on the bed.

Seth glances over his shoulder, narrowing his eyes at me. "You never know. Maybe she has a stake."

I burst out laughing. "Like a vampire hunter?" I clutch my stomach. My abs pinch in pain as I continue laughing.

"Yeah, maybe she's that kind of crazy. She did try to slice my neck open with her key."

My gaze is drawn to the books on the corner of her desk. I pick one up and flip through the pages. I'm soon fascinated and drawn in by the crisp lines and the intricate detail. It's a city. *New York?* And the use of color is extraordinary. It looks so realistic, as if I'm looking at a photograph and not a work of art. *She may be crazy, by the psycho bitch definitely has talent.*

"What the hell are you doing?"

I jump and Seth spins around. I nearly rip the paper with my death grip. I expect to see psycho roommate there, about to throw knives. Instead, it's Hunter, laughing and pointing while he stands in the doorway. "You should see your faces," he laughs and clutches his stomach. "Oh my god. That was amazing."

"Get in here, you asshole," I drag his ass in and he sits down on the bed, looking under it.

"What the hell are you searching for?" asks Seth.

"Guns," Hunter winces, "or maybe knives. Who knows with this chick?"

Seth nods his approval while I shake my head and turn my attention back to her sketchbook. There are more drawings of squirrels, people sitting on the subway, Central Park; each one with the same amount of detail. I snap the book close and go to her bed, grabbing a book on photography. *Definitely an art student. I wonder what she takes pictures of...*

"What the fuck is this?" I look up, seeing Hunter has moved and is now sitting in front of her wardrobe. He grimaces while holding up a pair of Hello Kitty underwear. "This isn't sexy at all!" He throws it over his shoulder. He pulls out more underwear from her drawer, each one with some cutesy pattern. "I don't see any thongs here."

Seth grabs the camera off her makeshift desk and turns it around before pulling at his waistband and taking a picture of what I can only suppose is his dick. I shake my head, knowing we are in such deep shit when she returns, but at the same time, really enjoying the imagery of her storming in here and screaming.

"Lukie, look!"

"Huh?" I turn to Hunter, who is currently holding up a pink bra over his shirt. The cup size is small and the band is about half Hunter's width.

"Do you think I can wear this?" He waggles his eyebrows.

I roll my eyes and shake my head. "No, you idiot."

I hear Seth chuckling and turn back around, seeing him screw off the lenses from the camera and stuff them in his pockets. I shake my head. Sometimes Seth takes it a bit too far and by the looks of it, that's a pretty expensive camera.

She's definitely going to scream. I can just see it. But she won't do anything, a dark little thought circulates. *She'll probably just cry.*

"Lukie, what the hell are you doing?" asks Seth, motioning to the photography book in my hands. "Here we are, causing chaos and you're learning how to take pictures."

I scoff. "I'm just trying to understand the mental workings of our psychotic roommate."

Hunter rolls his eyes. "Yeah, right. Most likely you have a little crush on Rachel."

I raise an eyebrow. "Rachel, Hunter? So you're calling her Rachel now?"

I take note of the blush flaming Hunter's cheeks and the subtle way he averts his eyes. *Ah, so you like Rachel now?*

"Just do something, Lucas," says Seth. Anxiety fills me as Seth tosses the camera back and forth. *If he breaks that camera, we are all so dead.*

"Hey, it was my idea to come in here." I grind my teeth as he continues tossing it. "Will you please put that down? You are making me nervous."

Seth holds out the camera. "You mean this?"

I nod. "Yes, that. Put it down." I throw the photography book on the pillow and pick up a little pink book. I look at the title, smiling wickedly when I read: **My Diary.** "Look what I have here." I tilt the book back and forth in front of Seth, and nearly sigh in relief when he sets the camera down.

"Ooooh!" Seth jumps onto the bed next to me followed by Hunter, who is currently wearing Rachel's bra on his head. Both breathe down my neck while I open the book to a random page in the middle. "I want to know if she's been writing about us."

"Do you think she'd write about us?" asks Hunter.

Seth shrugs. "Only one way to find out."

I clear my throat and read in a high-pitched voice, "I was accepted into Aurora University today."

Hunter and Seth giggle around me. Hunter smacks his thigh while Seth covers his face.

"Oh god," Seth gasps.

"Lucky you," says Hunter mockingly to the book.

"It's not an Art School or anything," I pause to keep myself from laughing. "But at least it's something to get me started. Looks like a sports school, which I don't know how I feel about." I roll my eyes and hold out my hand. "Someone please give me a pencil. A pen. Anything!"

Seth bounds off the bed and races out of the room. I swear, he runs so fast one would think he is in a race. He returns with a black pen and quickly sits down on the bed, looking over my shoulder while I write inside: **You should feel lucky to be surrounded by such gods.**

Seth and Hunter laugh around me and I flip through the pages, finding another entry and reading, "Dear Diary, tomorrow I leave for Colorado where I will start my new life at Aurora University."

"Oooh, exciting," Hunter says in a girly voice.

"I'm worried I won't make any friends." I pause and take out the pen, writing: **Duh!** I clear my throat and continue, "And I wonder if photography is really the path for me."

Seth rolls his eyes and flops down on the bed. "Oh my god she is so boring."

"But," I raise one finger, "at least it is something for now. Maybe after a year I can get into Juilliard or Colombia after I build up my portfolio."

Hunter and Seth groan.

Hunter grabs the book from me and flips through it. "I want something more interesting. Sex. Drugs. Give me something!" He frowns and continues flipping through the pages violently. "Poetry, poetry, photography." He groans. "Nothing. Absolutely nothing!"

"Well, I just want to build up my portfolio and go to an art school," I say in my high-pitched voice while fluttering my eye lashes and flicking my wrist.

Seth scoffs. "Yeah, right." He grabs the book from Hunter and throws it across the room, where it lands neatly in front of Rachel's feet.

Chapter 9

RACHEL

I stare down at my journal resting at my feet, blinking several times and wondering if I am ever going to awaken from this ongoing nightmare. I glance up at the boys lounging on my bed, before looking down at my book. Again. I glance back and forth for a while, still trying to figure out why they were in my room and what they were doing.

"Do you think she's going to scream?" I hear Hunter whisper to Seth.

My vision goes red. My nails dig into my palms and I grind my teeth keep myself from exploding. "What..." I breathe and it takes everything within me to keep myself calm. To keep myself from lunging and ringing their muscled veiny necks. "...Are you doing..." I take a step forward and Lucas and Hunter shove themselves up from my bed, "In my room?" My eyes land on Seth, who is still lounging on my mattress as if he owns it. As if nothing could possibly be wrong with this situation.

Seth scoffs, rolling his eyes. "If you didn't want us in here, then why didn't you lock your door?"

"Because you assholes were throwing food all over the apartment I just cleaned!" I shout, unable to keep my voice down. I grab my diary and throw it at Seth's head.

He rolls over, barely dodging it and pushes himself up. "For fuck's sake you really are psychotic," I hear the bastard mutter while pushing his goons outside the door.

"Out!" I shriek, slamming the door shut behind them and locking it.

I look around at the underwear and bras thrown all over, finding my camera resting not in the same place. I lurch, grabbing it and having a look. *Where are the lenses?* I wonder, turning it over like an idiot. *Like I would really find lenses on the back of my camera.* I swipe the notebooks from my bed and dig through my rumpled clothes in the drawer, throwing more garments around the room, but finding absolutely nothing.

Oh God! What if they broke it?

I turn my camera on, praying it still works and they didn't destroy the one expensive thing I own.

I release a breath when it beeps on. *Thank God.*

What if they deleted everything? Not like I have much. *They better not have deleted anything.*

I click the display and nearly drop the camera. I snatch it before it hits the ground and click again, seeing another floppy piece of meat surrounded by curly brown hair.

I scream, gripping my camera and nearly ripping it into two as I throw open the door and stomp out into the middle of the living room. Seth is on the ground rolling around on the floor, laughing maniacally as his idiot goons chuckle in the kitchen.

"Who did this?" I shout, showing the dick pic around and earning even more laughter from Seth.

Nothing.

No answer.

It's like I am living in a Hell house.

"And where the hell did you put my lenses?" I walk to Seth, towering over him as he continues rolling around on the floor laughing. A sneaky little thought goes through my brain, telling me to kick him. Hard. But violence is never the answer.

Maybe.

"Well?" I lean over.

Seth covers his mouth, sputtering with laughter.

"Where is it Garcia?" I shout. Really, I should kick him. I should kick him in the dick and then take a picture. See how he likes that little remembrance of art.

I stalk over to Hunter and Lucas. I go up on my tiptoes, but I don't even reach their eye levels. I'm too short and they're too tall. It still doesn't stop me from scowling at the giant Thor look-alike. "Where are my lenses?" I shout.

Hunter shakes his head. "I don't know what those are."

I groan, setting down my camera on the kitchen counter. "Well," I turn to Lucas, who just stares at me. He just stares at me as if I'm growing two heads. *If I don't find those lenses I just might.*

I grab a dirty frying pan from the kitchen sink, still sticky from making Seth his stupid French toast, which still lies on the floor. Seth peaks over the couch, crawling to stand but still struggling through his laughter. "First time seeing a dick, Rachel?" He says between giggles. "You should enjoy it. Knowing you, you'll never see another again."

I must have gone completely batshit crazy. I whip the pan behind my head and release it, hoping it hits Seth in his stupid face. Instead it hits the couch and lands on the floor with a clatter.

Seth stares at it, mouth open. "You psycho freak!" He shouts, bounding up from the couch and stalking toward me.

"Yeah, what the actual fuck?" says Hunter behind me.

"Just give me my lenses." Seth stops in front of me, finger in my face, yet no words escape his lips. "Now," I say, turning around and finding a glass filled with dirty water. "Or else—"

"Ah fuck this," I hear Lucas behind me. I glance over my shoulder, watching him reach into Seth's pant pockets and dig out the lenses for me.

He grabs my hand, placing the lenses in my palms and wrapping my fingers around them. I am too shocked. I don't know if it's because he looks like he's going to murder me or it's because I'm not expecting such kindness from one of Seth's bros.

"Thank you," I breathe, not knowing what else to say.

Lucas rolls his eyes and strides back to the couch. No one says a word and before they can make me do anything else like clean the French toast or wash the dishes, I run back to my room, slam the door and lock it.

***

So, maybe I should have cleaned the bathroom last night. I stare around me, at the mildew and the socks cluttering the sink. Why do they put their socks in the sink? There are even several pairs soaking in some brown water. The soap clings to the top, as if giving up and trying to escape. I spent the whole night before scrubbing the disgusting, sticky floors and salvaging the kitchen that, unfortunately, I decided to leave the bathroom up to chance. At the time, I wasn't thinking about my dire need for a shower.

Even now I wonder if I truly need a shower. Sure, I probably still smell like airplane and there are a couple days' worth of dry shampoo in my hair, but it's girls' night out! I want to wear my finest and drink large mochas while I discuss art. That's the way college life is, right? Staying up late with friends and having meaningless debates about art styles and themes.

I scrunch up my nose. *Alright, Rachel, just keep your flip flops on and close your eyes. It's not like you need to shave or anything. Just wash your face, pits, and hair. It'll be fifteen minutes max.*

I try not to gag as I push back the glass door, immediately welcomed by the hair still stuck in the drain. *I said close your eyes!* I grimace, closing my eyes and stepping inside. *Thank God I brought my flip flops.* I turn on the water, sighing when the hot water hits my skin, wiping away the airplane stink, the stress from the move, and the stress of living with complete assholes.

I turn around and lather my hair with shampoo. I wince, hearing something banging in the background, but I push those thoughts away. It doesn't matter to me what those idiots are doing. Soon I will be out at a cafe with Charlie and Lauren and discussing the big project. *Never mind the noise.*

I turn off the water, hearing the bass banging in the background and realizing one of the assholes is blasting some sort of rap music. I hear some talking and a shout while I wrap myself in a towel and open the door just a hair, peeking through the crack and finding at least six strangers I don't know lingering in the hallway. Possibly more in the living room.

I look around at the bathroom, only now realizing I don't have a change of clothes. *Really?* I sigh and look at the ceiling. *Are they doing this on purpose? They really want to make my life a living hell now, don't they? What did I ever do to them to deserve this kind of treatment?* I roll back my shoulders. *Come now, Rachel. You are not going to let this get to you,* I decide while throwing open the door. *It's a thirty second walk to my room. No big deal.*

"Hey Seth!" A girl stands between me and my room wearing a black mesh top and a bright pink push up bra underneath. She stuffs her hands into the back pockets of her high waisted shorts and smirks at me. "Who's this?"

"Excuse me," I say, reaching for my doorknob, yet she pushes my hand away. I frown, tightening my hold on my towel. My skin prickles in the chilly air. I stare at the girl, quickly realizing it's the gymnast the boys have been passing around and stop myself from rolling my eyes.

"What is it Mitzie?" Seth strides toward the gymnast, throwing an arm over her shoulder and looking me up and down with a stupid smirk.

"It's Millie," the gymnast corrects with a pout.

"Ah, really?" Seth nuzzles her shoulder. "I kinda like Mitzie."

"This," Millie gestures toward me. "Who's this?"

"Excuse me," I say, reaching for my doorknob again. "Just trying to get to my room."

"That's psycho roommate," says Seth, steering Millie away from my door. "Ignore her."

Millie glances over her shoulder. "Why does she look like a wet rat?"

Seth pokes her nose. "Excellent question."

I roll my eyes and turn toward my door, finding another unwanted guest wearing a football jersey standing in front of it. He wreaks of beer and leers down at me, barely balancing on his two feet and nearly stumbling into me. "Psycho roommate huh?" he says, taking a swig from his red cup. "What sport do you play?"

"Excuse me."

"She doesn't play sports, Tom," Lucas calls from his place on the couch, his arm slung around a brunette with breasts nearly bursting from her tight top.

"Then, like," Tom hiccups, "what are you even doing here?"

I scoff and shove past him. I open my door quickly and before he can open his mouth and say something else, I slam it in his face. I lean against my door, sighing and closing my eyes. *Just get ready and leave. Who cares what they think? Not you.*

"Man, what a bitch," I hear Tom behind the door and shake my head, biting back the tears threatening to fall.

I grab a brush and run it through my hair. I apply moisturizer all over my face and body and stare down at the mess of clothes around me, nearly screaming as I recall finding those jerks in my room going through my things. *Tomorrow. Tomorrow we are going to talk about privacy and not going into my room.*

I choose a simple short black dress to wear with my black ankle boots and a leather jacket to top it off with before blow drying my hair and applying makeup. I decide to go simple with my eye makeup, keeping it to an eye liner and mascara duo accompanied by a bold red lip. I top it off by putting on a black wide brim hat. I gaze back at myself in the mirror, happy with my look and ready to seize the world with my new girlfriends.

I grab my bag and my keys and lock the door behind me. I pull on the doorknob, ensuring it is definitely locked this time. I really do not need any guests wandering in there and deciding to steal a few of my possessions. Especially given what happened earlier today.

When I turn around I see Seth, Lucas, and Hunter staring at me. Their guests are still drinking, not even paying attention to me, but how am I going to slip past the boys if they won't stop staring at me? I touch my hair, wondering if it's a knotted mess, but that doesn't make any sense. I pull out a mirror from my bag, wondering if my lipstick is smeared or on my teeth.

Nope. Totally fine.

I look up, still seeing their gazes on me.

"What?" I say, shrugging on my backpack and inching toward the door.

Lucas shakes his head and looks into his beer. "Nothing," he mutters.

Seth says and does nothing, even though Millie is currently sucking on his neck. He just continues to stare at me with this dopey wide-eyed expression.

I pass by him slowly, imagining him as a lion and me an antelope, walking as slow as possible and hoping he doesn't notice. Or maybe he's a T-Rex and I'm Doctor Alan Grant. I reach for the door, feeling deja vu all over again. I pull it open and step toward my freedom.

Almost there. Nearly there.

Hunter slams the door shut with one hand. "Are-aren't you forgetting something," he says, his voice sounding unusually high pitched.

I look up to the ceiling. *Why?* I whine in my head. *Why can't I have just this night?*

"What am I forgetting, Hunter?" I deadpan, waiting for some stupid excuse as I stare at his stupid large hand resting on my only exit.

He looks around. "Um." He chuckles while I shake my head at him.

Seth pushes Millie off his lap and pats Hunter on the shoulder, earning a hiss and a grimace. "What Hunter is trying to say," Seth starts, quickly removing his hand from Hunter's shoulder, "is you have left the kitchen in a complete mess." Seth gestures to the kitchen. The sink is currently filled with dishes from this morning as well as glasses and an assortment of beer bottles. The French toast I painstakingly made this morning is being kicked back and forth between Tom and another jersey wearing jock.

I look at Hunter, who is nodding his head vehemently.

"You must be joking," I say, trying to keep my voice down.

"And don't forget about our rooms," Hunter adds. "You need to clean those, too."

"You can go fuck yourselves for all I care." I reach for the door, but before I grab the handle, several party goers swarm around me. Tom picks me up and hauls me back into the kitchen. "Stop it!" I shout, smacking his shoulder. "Put me down now!"

Millie and her clique point at me and laugh. "Look at the little rat!" says one, giggling over her cup.

"Put me down!"

"Alright," says Tom, dropping me onto the kitchen floor. I feel French toast squish under my butt and groan, picking myself up and wiping my bottom. *I really hope that doesn't stain.*

"Alright, Rachel, get going!" says Seth while shooing at me. "It's not going to clean itself."

"Yeah, Rachel." Millie saunters over me. "Get going." She pours her drink on the front of my dress. I barely register what is happening. Only that my front is cold and I smell like beer. I stare down at my dress. Silence surrounds me.

"What the hell, Mitzie?" I hear Seth. "Why did you do that?"

"I don't know. I just felt like it."

"Well, you shouldn't have. Just..." He groans. "Just leave her alone. God!"

In front of me is a cloth. I look up and see Lucas handing it to me. A sob escapes me and I clamp my eyes close, biting back another.

"Oh, is she going to cry?" I hear a girl behind me say mockingly.

I grab the cloth and stalk back to my room, slamming my door and locking it behind me for what seems to be the tenth time today.

I wipe my black dress, trying to get the beer out of it, but there's no way I can salvage it for tonight. I sniff. *I really liked this dress. It was cute and casual in a not trying kind of way. Perfect for dates, cafes, and long autumn walks.* I sniff again. *It's not the end of the world.*

I shrug out of my dress and lay it neatly on my makeshift desk, careful with it despite the fabric already soaked with beer. I grab a short floral-patterned dress. It's still cute and goes with my accessories, but still. I really, really wanted to wear the black dress. I run my hands over it, scowling when I hear laughter behind me.

"I bet she's crying," I hear Tom slur soon followed by Millie's giggles.

"The dress is like a cheap knock off," one of the girls cackles. "It wasn't even that cute. You did her a favor, Millie."

I throw open the door. It knocks into the wall and I stalk outside ready to... ready to... I grab the mop still leaning against the wall and go for the television.

"Wait!" I hear Lucas, but I don't care.

An eye for an eye... or whatever the saying is.

I stand beside the television, holding the mop by its dusty head while aiming the pole at the screen. I swing it back over my head.

"No!" I hear the boys shout together.

Out of the corner of my eye I see Lucas's gaze filled with horror. I turn my head slowly, slightly reminded of a scene from the Exorcist. I feel my lips split into a grin while I stare back at boys, huddled together behind the couch.

"Please don't," says Lucas, putting his hands together.

"Not the TV," says Seth, coming around the couch.

"Stop," I say, taking a practice swing at the television, stopping right before I hit the screen.

"No!" Everyone shouts together.

"Why are you such a psycho bitch?" asks Millie.

"What do you want?" asks Hunter. "We'll do anything. Just leave the TV out of this."

I drop the mop and tap my chin thoughtfully. My eyes go to Seth sitting on his knees on the floor. "Everyone, go home." I look around at the crowd of strangers.

They look at each other curiously, yet they don't bother to move.

"Go. Home." I annunciate each word with a tap of my mop on the ground.

Millie rolls her eyes and I fight the need to whack her in the face with my mop. "You're not going to listen to her, are you, Seth?"

Seth hangs his head.

Millie leans over and taps his shoulder. "Seth?"

"You heard the lady!" shouts Hunter, running for the door and swinging it open. "Party over. Everyone out."

Millie scoffs, but still doesn't move her ass from the couch. "Seth?"

Seth sighs and slowly stands. "Out," he says to Millie.

If I was a better person I would have felt sorry for her. But, instead, she smacks the couch and stalks toward the door, casting me a dark scowl. "Whatever," she mutters.

Hunter shuts the door when everyone is out and all eyes are on me. I still don't bother to drop the mop, or move from their beloved TV.

"Alright," starts Seth. "You got your way. Everyone's out."

Hunter groans. "I didn't even get laid." He throws himself on the couch and stares up at the ceiling. "My good luck lay for the game tomorrow."

"You'll live," I say.

"Alright, give me the mop," says Lucas, reaching for my weapon.

I lurch away from him and aim it at the screen.

Lucas's hands go up, but it still doesn't stop the scowl from returning to his face. "What the hell? We did what you want."

I tap my chin again, feeling on top of the world for once in a very long while. "Hmmm, I don't know. The kitchen is a mess again, the bathroom is completely destroyed, and someone said something about messy rooms."

Seth narrows his eyes on me. "So?"

I twirl the mop in front of me before taking another practice swing at the screen. The boys gasp in unison. Lucas even falls to his knees. "No!" shouts Hunter.

I laugh manically. "Well, get to it, boys."

Chapter 10

HUNTER

This fucking sucks.
       This really fucking sucks.
   Sure, going through her room while she was out, definitely an ass thing to do. Keeping her from going out... also an ass thing to do. Millie dumping beer on her dress... not my fault. Not Lukie's or Seth's fault, either. Threatening to destroy the TV...? Like, what the fuck?! What a fucking batshit crazy bitch! It's like she's completely lost it. Who threatens the number one most important thing in the household?
   Psycho bitch. That's who.
   I glance over at her, now sitting on the couch while watching some girlie Netflix show. Gilmore Sisters? Gilmore Family? Something stupid. The mop is resting next to her while she types away at her phone. It's completely unguarded. Seth catches my gaze from across the room. He's been put on trash duty while Lucas cleans the bathroom. Ah Lukie. Poor bastard lost at rock paper scissors. I definitely don't want to be him right now.
   Seth nods toward the mop and I nod back at him. I set my wash rag on the counter and slowly step toward Rachel. I grimace when my footsteps cause the floor to squeak. Seth scowls at me, yet Rachel remains glued to her phone. *Hell, why have the TV on at all if you're just going to stare at your phone? It's a complete waste of energy.*
   I'm standing right behind her and the mop is only a foot away. I watch Rachel as I reach for it. Slowly, so I don't draw attention. Nearly there. And I know as soon as I grab that mop there is going to be hell to pay. Just need to get it.

The phone rings and Rachel grabs the mop, quickly bounding up from the couch. I stumble backward and quickly grab my wash rag and return to scrubbing beer off the counters. *Fuck! I nearly had it!*

"Sorry!" Rachel says into the phone while pacing back and forth with the mop over her shoulder.

She sort of reminds me of a military sergeant. A sexy, bratty military sergeant. I hate to admit it, but there is a part of me that is completely turned on by this whole fiasco. She can be quite bossy. And it makes me wonder what she would make me do to her in bed.

"Ugh! You would not believe my night." She tosses her head back and stares at the ceiling, something I notice she does pretty frequently. "Well, seeing how I don't trust the boys to clean up their shit, I'm kinda stuck here. And who knows if they'll break into my room." She sends both me and Seth a dark scowl. I ignore the shivers going down my spine. "You know what, why don't you guys come over here? I would really like to have both your opinions and I really, desperately need this study night."

I drop my wash rag at the same time Seth drops the trash bag in his hands. The bottles rattle inside as they hit the floor and one even rolls out. We send each other a look across the room.

Like hell she's having people over, Seth's eyes read.

I know, right? I try to say with my eyes. I turn back to psycho bitch still pacing back and forth. I'm about to yell that it isn't fair, but I immediately clamp my big mouth closed. She is way too close to the TV.

"Okay, perfect." Rachel beams and twirls around. Her gaze meets mine and once again I tell myself that the fluttering in my heart is nothing. "I'll see you soon. Bye!" With a click she shoves her phone into her leather jacket and throws herself back on the couch.

Seth steps in front of her, his hands on his hips. "What the hell was that?"

"What the hell was what, Garcia?" Rachel deadpans.

"You get to have a party after you just kicked out all our guests?"

"Yeah!" I shout. Rachel turns around and I feel my face heat. "It's not fair," I say more quietly, grimacing at how idiotic I sound.

Rachel rolls her eyes. "It's not a party. It's a study group, which I was happy to have outside this apartment, but you assholes decided to keep me here." She motions around the room. "And so here I stay."

"Alright you fuck faces!" shouts Lukie while stalking out of the room. I stifle a gag when I see the hairy and grimy rag in his hands, which he chucks into the trash bag. "Switching time. There is no way I am spending my whole night cleaning that bathroom." He points down the hallway at said bathroom. He looks around the room, his gaze pausing on Seth standing in front of Rachel with his hands on his hips. "What's going on?"

Seth motions to Rachel. "Why don't you ask our tyrant?"

Rachel scoffs, but says nothing, stuck in a stare down with Seth.

I guess I will have to be the one to inform Lukie. I lean in close to him, not wanting to distract Seth from whatever stare competition he is in with Rachel. I mutter, "Rachel is having friends over."

"What?" Lucas nearly shrieks. He stalks over to stand next to Seth. "After you threw out our guests? What the actual fuck?!"

Rachel bounds up from the couch and twirls the mop in her hand before aiming the handle at Seth, who quickly jumps back. It's like that thing is a sword or something, the way she handles it. "Like I said before, it's not a party, it is a study group, which I had planned for somewhere else originally until you assholes got in the way. Now!" She levels the mop at Lucas, who stumbles backward, nearly falling into the TV. I yell, lunging over to grab him, but thankfully the asshole balances himself. "You don't want to clean the bathroom. You know the rules. Rock paper scissors. Loser cleans bathroom."

The three of us shuffle into a circle. The thing about Lucas is we know he always chooses rock. Even when he tells himself not to choose rock, his hand just moves naturally into that position. Maybe it's because he's a rower? I'm not quite sure, but Seth and I both know he's the one responsible for the nasty condition of that bathroom and neither of us are cleaning up that shit. I glance at Seth, and he meets my gaze.

Paper? I question him, hoping he understands.

He gives me a curt nod. *Paper.*

"Alright, are you ready?" asks Rachel.

All three of us groan in response.

"Rock, paper, scissors, shoot," we say in unison.

Seth and I shoot paper, while good old reliable Lukie, shoots rock.

"God fucking dammit!" He throws his hands up in the air. "I demand a rematch."

Rachel clucks her tongue and shakes her head. She pouts mockingly and points down the hallway. "You know the rules, Lukie."

Lucas runs his hands through his perfectly coiffed hair, frazzling it a bit before turning on his heel and stomping down the hallway. "This fucking sucks!" he shouts before slamming the door closed.

Rachel giggles and sits back into the couch, placing her hands behind her head and watching Gilmore Sisters with a terrifying smirk. Once again, I ignore the seductive whispers in the back of my head, wondering what it would feel like having her above me, taunting me.

***

There's a knock at the door and I watch Rachel open it, revealing two sexy little things. One in a short skirt and knee-high socks, and the other in a short dress and stiletto boots. *Wow. If this is a study group, then Rachel needs to invite me.* The brunette looks around while the blonde sniffs the air. They look at each other before shrugging and entering inside, dragging along their black satchels. They even have cameras slung over their shoulders.

Just what kind of study group is this?

"Hi!" Waves the blonde in my direction.

"'Sup?" I nod.

"I'm Charlie and this is Lauren," she motions to her brunette friend in the knee highs, who's still looking around at the place.

"Rachel, you didn't tell me you had such hot friends," says Seth while throwing the bag filled with trash over his shoulder. I swear he has been working on that thing for the past thirty minutes, taking his sweet time loading it up when it would take anyone ten minutes max. Maybe less.

Rachel rolls her eyes and motions her friends toward her room. "Ignore them."

"Who's there?" Lucas calls from the bathroom.

"Rachel's hot friends," Seth calls back.

Lucas's head peaks out from the room and he blows his bangs out of his eyes. "They're hot?"

"Very," I nod in agreement.

He rips the yellow gloves sticking to his arms off and tosses them in the sink and smiles down at the two girls, who are currently trying to contain their giggles behind their hands. Rachel shakes her head while crossing her arms.

"Why hello," says Lucas, holding out a hand. "I'm Lucas."

"Charlie," says blondie while taking his hand.

"Lauren," says the other.

"Rachel, you should have told us they were hot," says Seth while elbowing Rachel in the ribs. "Hot girls are always invited."

I nod. "Always."

There's another knock on the door and all our heads turn and watch while Rachel strides toward it. I expect there to be another, hoping for a redhead, but instead a wormy, skinny, weasel looking guy stands in the entrance. He smiles at Rachel and I instantly don't like him. I don't like the way he pushes up his black rimmed glasses, or the way he slinks into the apartment. He sticks close to Rachel, his hand brushing against hers and I fight the temptation to grab him and throw him up against the wall.

I turn to Seth, who is also eyeing this dude up and down, narrowing his gaze and cocking his head to the side. I notice Lucas crossing his arms and his expression darkening.

"Hi, I'm Josh," he says with a slight wave, looking between us hesitantly before turning his gaze back to Rachel. "Sorry to intrude like this. I'm also having some problems coming up with a proper theme to the project."

I hate the blush on her cheeks, the shuffle in her feet, and the way she seems to fluff out like a Pomeranian about to receive a treat. She flicks her hair behind her shoulder and smiles shyly up at him. "No problem. We should stick together, right?"

Oh hell no, you should not!

Josh looks around the room, dropping his bag from his shoulder down to his hand. "Where should I put my stuff?"

"We'll just go to my room," she motions toward her door.

That guy. In her room? No fucking way.

"Why don't you study out here?" asks Seth, and I'm so glad he beat me to the punch. He nods to Lucas and they both grab an end of the couch, moving it back to make more space in the living room, revealing—embarrassingly—dust, crumbs, protein bar wrappers, and used condoms.

Rachel groans and smacks her forehead while I grab the mini broom and dustpan to sweep up the mess. Blondie and her brunette friend giggle behind a hand while four-eyes grimaces at the mess. "I guess you weren't wrong about those orgies," blondie whispers to four-eyes as I walk pass her to dump the contents into the trash bag.

"Thanks, but I think we'd be better off in my room."

"No, no, no," says Seth, grabbing a cushion from the couch and throwing it down on the newly clean floor. "You've got your Gilmore-whatever here, easy access to some drinks."

"But—"

"We're pretty much finished," I add, motioning around the room. I have to say, we did a fantastic job. The place nearly sparkles with all our efforts. Although, I'm quite interested to see what Lucas did with the bathroom. "We won't be in your way."

Rachel glances over to Lucas. "Please tell me the bathroom isn't disgusting anymore?"

Lucas makes a face. "It's... better." He shrugs to the girls. "You can put your ass on the seat without worrying about it biting your cheeks off."

Rachel looks up at the ceiling while the girls burst into laughter. "Duly noted," says the brunette, still laughing while she grabs a cushion and sits down on the floor.

I scowl when I see four-eyes sitting next to Rachel, his leg accidentally bumping into hers. She chuckles nervously, but the bastard makes no effort in moving his leg. I lean against the counter, scowling down at them while I watch him lean in close over her shoulder. Seth and Lucas sidle up next to me.

"Who is that punk?" asks Lucas, nodding to whom I can only assume is four-eyes.

"I can't remember his name," says Seth, shaking his head.

"I hate him," I mutter.

"He's a grimy little weasel, now ain't he?" says Seth.

"You know, we might be able to get some more ideas by looking at some art," I hear four-eyes say while blondie goes to the bathroom and the brunette goes to grab something from Rachel's room.

Of course. Now that she's alone he's going to sink his claws into her.

"Oh?" Rachel's innocence is really grating on my nerves. At times she can be a bossy, demanding little bitch and other times she reminds me of a lost puppy dog with not a single brain cell going on in that pretty little head of hers.

Mr. Four Eyes is definitely a creep, yet the way she looks at him, it's like she doesn't even see it.

"Yeah, we could check out the art museum this Saturday. Get a few ideas. Maybe go for coffee afterwards."

Hells to the fuck no. She's not going to any of that shit. Just when she opens her mouth, I blurt out, "Rachel's going to the football game on Saturday."

Four-eyes pops up his head, meeting my stare and I feel Seth and Lucas's gazes on me, but I refuse to break eye contact with the asshole.

"What?" asks Rachel, her voice completely confused. "No, I'm not."

Think Hunter. Think. Although, thinking has never been my strong suit.

"Well, we need you there," Lucas adds, his voice quivering and he looks over to me trying to find something else to say to steer her away from four eyes.

"For the tailgate," says Seth. "We need you there for the tailgate. All of us roommates go at the start of the year. To support Hunter here," Seth smacks my shoulder and I grit my teeth to keep from crying out. A groan escapes and I scowl at Seth who immediately moves his hand. One of these days I am going to have a serious talk with him about not smacking injured shoulders.

"Yeah, it's for good luck," says Lucas. "You wouldn't want Hunter to lose the first game of the year."

Rachel scoffs. "That sounds completely—"

"Oooh, a tailgate, that sounds like fun," says blondie, entering the living room like an angel sent down from the heavens. "I want to go."

"Yeah," says the brunette. "We're studying tonight. Let's enjoy the weekend."

Rachel looks between her friends. "You'd actually go?"

Blondie nods. "Yeah, I don't see why not."

"We can go together," adds the brunette. "Make sure these boys treat you right." She winks at me.

Rachel sighs and shakes her head. "Fine." I hold back my smirk when I see Josh's shoulders slump. *Take that, asshole.* "But we need to actually make progress tonight." Rachel scowls up at us. "Don't you boys have rooms to clean?"

I raise my hands up. "We're leaving."

I nod to Lucas and Seth, who nod their approval. *One point, bros. Zero points, weasel guy.* I walk back to my room, closing the door behind me. I take one look and groan. Fuck. I really hate cleaning. Where do I even begin with this fucking mess? *Just fuck it and jack off,* I think while throwing myself down on the bed, kicking off my shoes while unbuckling my jeans. My thoughts drift to Rachel and her dark scowls and her cute little freckles.

Chapter 11

RACHEL

I look around at the crowds of students, alumni, and parents chugging back beers and grilling hot dogs under tents. For a tailgate, there are hardly any cars. Just a line of tents with crowds of people weaving in and out. I stand under one, set up by Seth's track and field freshmen, holding a cup of beer I've barely touched. Looking around, I wonder when I can sneak away. Going to the art museum with Josh would've been way better than this. *We could've looked at art and discussed it over coffee. It would've been like a dream come true. Now, I'm just standing around awkwardly and wondering what to do with myself.*

I grimace when I see Millie, remembering just the other night how she dumped beer down my dress and called me a wet rat. My eyes narrow on her as she strokes the arm of some guy. An arm not belonging to Lucas or Seth. Hunter is at practice so obviously she can't be with him. *Now, now, don't slut shame the girl, Rachel. Women are allowed to have sex with whomever they want whenever they want. Like men.*

However, she was a complete and utter bitch to me the other night and I assume it was only to look good for the bros. The least she can do is be a little loyal. Millie's gaze lands on me and she flicks her hair behind her shoulders before flipping me the bird and sucking on the finger provocatively.

I scrunch up my face despite my need to act unbothered and turn back to Charlie and Lauren who are chatting up one of Seth's track friends. "Why am I here again?" I mutter in Charlie's ear.

She smiles politely at the guy as he goes on and on about his intense training schedule and leans over to me. "Because it's fun," she mutters behind gritted teeth and nods again at the guy. "Well, isn't that fascinating. Will you just excuse us for a moment," she says, wrapping an arm around me and turning us around.

I spot Josh leaning back in a chair in the middle of the tent, looking absolutely bored. "Alright, I'm calling it," I announce, setting my beer down on the plastic white table. "I'm getting out of here."

"Oh come on," says Lauren. "It's not that bad. Drink your beer and cheer up."

"Yeah," says Lauren before gulping down another swig. "We only just got here."

"Yeah, but Josh is miserable," I motion toward him, "I'm miserable and there is a completely viable art museum we could be enjoying ourselves in."

Lauren and Charlie share a look. "You mean discussing what eyes your baby will have and what your first born should be named?"

My face heats up so much I worry it's going to melt off my body. "N-no! What are you talking about?" I take a swig of beer and grimace at the bitter taste.

"Oooooh Rachel and Josh sitting in a tree," sings Charlie.

"K-I-S-S-I-N-G," Lauren continues singing.

"Who's kissing?"

I turn around and jump when I see Seth standing right behind me.

"No one's kissing anyone," I say quickly, and cast dark looks at Charlie and Lauren not to say anything.

They giggle behind their hands and I'm tempted to swat the both of them.

"Rachel was just about to make her getaway," says Charlie.

I scowl. That's just about the next worst thing to say.

"No," says Luke, taking my cup and scowling at the contents. "You've barely done any damage. Party foul!"

I scoff. "Party foul?"

"What does party foul mean?" asks Lauren, taking another swig from her cup.

"It means you've broken a party rule," says Seth as he looks into my cup. "In this case, not finishing a beer within the hour."

I roll my eyes. "It tastes gross."

Lucas smirks and casts a glance to Seth. "You know what that means?"

Seth nods and grabs my arm, pulling me through the crowd and toward several long plastic tables pushed together. I glance over my shoulder and reach out my hand. "Save me!" I shout to Charlie and Lauren, who simple shake their heads.

"Have fun!" Charlie hollers.

"But not too much!" Shouts Lauren.

I barely catch Josh's curious look before I am swarmed by people and being coalesced into a herd of people all standing around the table. I stand on my tiptoes and see two people on either end of the table, wearing blue Aurora jerseys. One even has black smudges on his cheek while the girl standing next to him has her jersey tied into a knot, exposing her very toned abdomen and her huge cleavage.

"We're next," says Seth.

My face heats when I realize he is still holding my hand. I don't tug it away, telling myself that if I let go I will most likely get lost and I don't know the way back to our tent. *Yeah, keep telling yourself that. It doesn't have anything to do with the fact he's super hot.*

"Next for what?" I make myself ask, not wanting to think in depth the inner workings of my messed up mind.

"Beer pong!"

I shrug. "I don't know how to play."

Seth rolls his eyes. "Just listen and do what I say."

"You'll have to chug if the ball goes into your cup," says Lucas from behind. I turn and nearly bash into his muscled chest. He doesn't bother looking at me. His focus is on the beer pong game. I try to look away, but he really has a handsome face. Chiseled jaw. Nice eyes. Definitely nice lips.

I quickly turn away. *Oh God, what is wrong with me?*

I grimace when I see the ball go into a cup after being cleaned on someone's jeans. "Isn't that unsanitary?"

"Very," says Lucas.

The big breasted lady and the guy with the war paint cheer and high-five each other and then Seth is pushing us through the crowd toward the table. Red cups in front of us are being refilled with beer and I'm standing in a huge crowd of strangers covered in blue. I shift awkwardly on my feet, really wanting to sprout wings and fly away from this. I know about beer pong. Anyone who has seen a cheesy rom-com knows about beer pong, flip cup, and keg stands. It doesn't mean I know every rule in the book. Nor that I want to.

"Just shoot it in the cup," Seth whispers in my ear while handing me the ping pong ball. "And don't fucking miss."

"Great last words," I mutter.

I aim the ball at a cup, but I'm quickly stopped by Lucas, whose arms wrap around me and pull me slightly backward. "Don't let your elbow go pass the edge of the table," he whispers in my ear and a tingle of shivers roll down my spine. I swear, my head is about to blow from the heat.

I gulp and nod awkwardly and then aim once more. I throw the ball and watch it sail, going straight into the middle cup without bouncing off any others. "Oh my god!" I shout, jumping up and down and clapping my hands. "I did it!"

Seth rolls his eyes and bats me to the side. "Yeah, yeah, yeah. You didn't fuck it up. Great job." He aims the ping pong, shoots, but it bounces off the rim and is quickly caught by the guy on the opposing team.

I pout at Seth mockingly. "Ah, you missed."

He shakes his head at me. "Be careful, Rachel. Your competitive side is showing."

"Ha! Yeah right."

The guy hands his lady counterpart the ping pong, who shoots and lands a direct hit. Seth hands the cup to me and I take a sip. "Wrong!" Says Seth, shaking his finger at me. "You gotta chug it."

I groan.

"Chug!" shouts Lucas.

"Chug! Chug! Chug!" Shouts the crowd around us and I grimace, gulping down every last drop of beer in the cup until it settles heavily in my stomach. I gasp when all the liquid is gone and grimace around the crowd. They cheer and the guy prepares his shot, aiming it for the cup in the front. He shoots and it goes in.

Seth takes it and smiles at me. "Cheers," he says, saluting me for a moment before gulping down the beer.

The ping pongs go back to the opposing team, since, Seth explained, they were able to get two shots in a row. We continue aiming and throwing, chugging and laughing, until finally, we lose the game and are forced to down the rest of the beer. Lucas leads us back to the girls, who are once again talking to a group of boys. I'm surprised to see Josh hasn't left his spot in the chair.

"Oh, well, look who it is," says Charlie, throwing her arm around my shoulder. "A bit pinker and a bit drunker. Do you want to go home now?"

I shake my head and she throws back her head and bursts into laugher.

"Your friend sucks at beer pong," says Seth, scowling at me. For a second, it seems like he's doing it playfully. I don't know what to make of that.

"Hey, I take insult to that," says Lauren, touching her chest.

"Why? It's the truth."

I shake my head and cross my arms. "What are you talking about? You were just as terrible if not worse."

"That's a lie and you know it." Seth leans in, smirking down at me with those full delicate lips.

"Oh, really?" I wonder briefly how his lips would taste. They're only an inch or two away. It wouldn't be so hard to just lean in. "Lucas, what did you think?"

Lucas shrugs. "Both of you suck."

"What?" shouts Seth, whipping his head over to stare up at his friend.

I smile smugly. "See. We both suck. But I've never played so at least I have an excuse." I glance back at Charlie and Lauren, who are smiling and sharing a knowing look. I frown. *What's going on? What do they know that I don't?*

"Everyone knows out of the group, I'm the best at beer pong," I hear Lucas say from behind.

"What?" Seth shouts. "Prove it. Me against you."

I glance over my shoulder and see Lucas smirking. "Loser finishes the bathroom."

Seth scoffs. "Loser finishes the bathroom and cooks the other breakfast for a month."

"Two months."

I shake my head, *Ugh. These boys. Although, I'm glad to know they weren't just placing these ridiculous games to torture me.*

"Rachel will be my partner," says Lucas, wrapping his arm around my shoulders and dragging me roughly toward him.

As a response I choke back a burp. The thought of chugging more beer really making me feel quite heavy in the belly area. "I think I need a bit of a break," I say, trying to make my getaway, but Lucas is strong and doesn't let me go.

"No, it wouldn't be fair if you don't play, Rachel," says Seth, smirking at me.

Why does this asshole need to rope me into this? I scowl back at Seth. "It's not fair to have me play if I've already been drinking."

Seth raises a finger. "Fairer than if he plays with one of your friends." He points back and forth between Charlie and Lauren.

I groan. "Why me?" I glance over my shoulder and ask Charlie, already feeling Lucas tug me away.

"Are you okay?" asks Charlie, pulling Lucas's hand away from mine.

"Yeah, we're here if you want to stay," says Lauren. "You don't have to go."

"Oh, come on!" shouts Seth, throwing his hands up in the air. He's about to say something else, but Charlie and Lauren's scowls instantly shut him up.

I really need to learn that trick.

I look back at the boys. Well, a part of me really wants to go play another game with them. Maybe one more... just to see Seth's face when Lucas wins. It'll be wonderful watching Seth be forced to clean the bathroom. And make breakfast for two months.

"I'm fine," I say while taking a step toward Lucas and Seth. "I'll play one more game and be right back."

"We'll be here!" shouts Lauren, waving goodbye as once again, Lucas grabs my hand and drags me away.

We come upon the table, now with two different teams operating it. I groan, feeling the weight of the beer in my stomach and look around frantically.

"Is there a bathroom nearby?"

Lucas stares down at me darkly. "You can't be serious," he says, rolling his eyes. "We just got here. You could've gone at any point."

"No, I really need to pee." I shift back and forth quickly. "Like right now."

Lucas shakes his head. "Hold it."

I grab his collar and pull him down, meeting his wide eye dark gaze. "It wouldn't be fair to you if I fuck up the whole game, because I gotta pee. Now tell me where the toilet is, or I'm leaving."

Lucas sighs and runs a hand through his hair. "Fine." He pats Seth's shoulder. "The bitch needs the toilet."

I roll my eyes. *Just when I thought we were getting to a first name basis.*

Seth glances over his shoulder and shakes his head. "Bitches," he mutters. *I regret ever wanting to kiss him.* "Well, hurry the fuck up. Game is almost over and you're up next."

I turn on my heel and push through the crowd. Then stop when I realize I have no clue where I'm going. I turn back just when Lucas grabs my hand and pulls me off to the side, toward the trees at the edge of the tents.

"The bathrooms will be packed right now so your best bet is the great outdoors." He smiles back at me. "Think you can squat?"

I don't even warrant that a response. Sure, I'm from New York. I'm not so acquainted with the great outdoors. But when a girl's gotta go, a girl's gotta go. I'm not so uppity to refuse a chance at peeing in the boys' restroom or in a dank alley if I really must. I look around at all the men peeing on the side of trees. A couple are making out against a tree. The girl's leg is wrapped around the guy's hip while his fingers are pretty much down her pants. I blush and quickly look away, wondering where is the perfect pee spot.

"Well," says Lucas, turning around. "Go."

I look down at where we're standing. There's no coverage. We're in the freaking middle of the woods and he just expects me to squat down in front of everyone else? There's no way I can pee here. Not where everyone will be able to see my bare ass. I look around and find a large tree about a two-minute walk away.

"Lucas," I say quietly.

"Don't tell me you've gotta shit."

I wince. "No, but do you think you can stand guard while I pee behind that tree over there."

Lucas turns around and sees where I'm pointing before looking down at me disdainfully. "Fine, but hurry up."

I run up the slight hill toward the tree. It's more difficult than normal. I think all the beer has finally hit, because I'm giggling. I hear Lucas muttering on behind me about bathroom duty and how it's all my fault he's stuck with the shitty end of the deal. Literally. I don't bother telling him that he and his bros started it, especially since I need him to play guard. I run behind the tree and relieve myself, happy to know no one is going to come and bother me.

I quickly zip my jeans and run out. "Finished, let's go," I say, wobbling down the slight hill. "Can't be late, right!" I yell at him, laughing as I look back behind my shoulder.

Lucas, with his long legs, easily catches up to me and grabs my hand. "Careful," he mutters.

I feel so giggly, like I have been breathing in laughing gas all day. The sun above me is shining so brightly and the music booming in the background puts an extra pep in my step. I stumble into Lucas, my ankle gives out from underneath and I see the ground coming closer toward my face. I close my eyes, waiting to eat dirt, or to at least feel some sort of pain.

Instead, when I open my eyes, I see Lucas with his arms around me. He's pressed up against another tree. "For fuck's sake, woman," he groans while rubbing his head. "Be careful."

He opens his eyes, his gaze trapped in my own. My breath hitches when they dip down to my lips and I feel that itch in the back of my head once again, telling me to be naughty. Telling me just to go up on my tiptoes and claim his mouth for mine.

You need to get back. Charlie and Lauren will be waiting for you. Seth will wonder where you are.

But my body betrays me. Just when my feet lean up into my toes, Lucas slams his lips down on mine. His arms tighten around me, forcing me toward him. One hand slides up the front of my shirt, playing with the base of my bra. I gasp and feel his tongue entering me, stroking and entwining around mine. I press myself against him, overcome by warmth and the need to have more. My leg lifts and he catches it, holding it near his hip while he grinds himself against me. A moan escapes from my lips and my eyes instantly open.

What the hell are you doing?

I rip my mouth from his and take a step back. Our breathing is frantic. I feel his hands stroking my waistband, trying to pull me back. A part of me wants to return to that warmth. To feel him press up against me.

We're outside. OUTSIDE!

"We shouldn't be doing this," I breathe, quickly turning around.

My eyes widen when I see Seth standing just a few feet in the distance.

Watching us.

Chapter 12

SETH

Where the hell are those assholes? The table is just about to be free and they're nowhere in sight. *Leave it to Ra-psycho bitch to fuck everything up.* I don't even bother looking around the porta-potties knowing those are going to be incredibly crowded. I follow a group of hippies walking barefoot through the mud and grass, passing a joint between them toward the group of trees on the hill just on the outskirts of the tailgate tents.

When I get to the edge I see Lucas pressed up against a tree, making out with some blonde bitch with a nice ass. I smirk. *Good work, Lukie. I wonder how this one will taste in bed.* But there's something oddly familiar about her clothes. Black ankle boots, skinny jeans, a blue and white polka-dotted sweater.

My eyes widen

No, it can't be.

She turns around and I feel the world around me tilt and shatter like glass.

It is.

Rachel's eyes land on me and widen for a split second before she tilts her chin up and stalks pass me, nearly tripping over her own feet. Against normal protocol I reach for her just when she nearly smashes head face first into a pile of leaves and twigs. I gently help her up, but she pushes me away.

"I'm fine," she slurs.

I stop myself from rolling my eyes. *Bitch, you are the opposite of fine.* Lucas stops next to me and we both watch as she weaves back and forth. It's like watching a deer learning how to walk. "I guess those beers finally kicked in," he says, shaking his head. "We should probably catch up with her before she wreaks havoc on some poor passerby."

I watch him go. Not knowing what to do with myself or with this terrible feeling overcoming me. *Why was she kissing him?* I don't even want to think of the implications of my anger. I'm not the jealous type, especially with a girl any of my bros hook up with. Any girl who comes into contact with my bros will eventually get passed on to me.

But this is psycho bitch we're talking about.

I force myself to follow them, telling myself it doesn't matter if they were kissing. She can kiss whomever she wants. Even if it's not me. Not like I want her to kiss me or do anything else with me for that matter. Hell, she's not even that attractive. I look around, finding a group of girls passing around Jell-O shots. They look like they're from some sorority dressed up in some sort of cowgirl get-up with blue and white tie-dyed shirts. Another group of girls on my other side are older, possibly seniors, and doing body shots. I smile. There are plenty of girls for me to hook up with here. I don't need piss poor rating Rachel.

I stop dead in my tracks when I come to the tent, seeing Rachel smiling down at four- eyes. *I don't know why that bastard had to show. It wasn't like we invited him. Just Rachel and her hot friends.* I can't take my eyes off Rachel, no matter how hard I try not to care about the sway in her step or the slur in her voice. Her cheeks are so pink I'm wondering if she'll pass out at some point. "Fucking idiot," I mutter when I see she's holding another drink.

"Don't worry, it's water," says one of Rachel's friends. The blonde one. Christine, was it? She pats me on the shoulder and nods at Rachel when I give her a confused look. "She's drinking water. Poor girl came back and told me the world won't stop swirling."

I scowl when I see the worming asshole stand and motions to the now vacant seat as if he is a freaking butler. Rachel smiles and drops into it, tossing her head back and leaning in. I wonder if she will actually pass out.

I scowl when four-eyes doesn't leave and continues saying whatever it is he has to say. *Fucking bastard giving her a seat and not leaving her alone.*

"Whatever," I say to the blonde bitch before turning around and smacking on my most charming smile at Lucas.

I saunter over him and waggle my eyebrows, stopping whatever boiling I feel under my skin as I remember his lips locked on Rachel's. "So," I start, grabbing a cup and quickly chugging it. *Need to drown whatever this is.* "I saw you sucking face with psycho bitch," I say, trying to sound funny, but I grimace at the high pitch in my voice.

Lucas chuckles and looks away. "Yeah, it just sort of happened."

I fist bump him before quickly pouring myself another beer from the keg. He raises his eyebrow. "Easy there. We still have all day."

I bat my hand at him. "I'm totally fine."

Lucas rolls his eyes. "Uh huh. That's what you said last time."

"So, Rachel," I say, taking a smaller swig of the beer. "Is she a good kisser? Gonna fuck her tonight?"

Lucas shrugs. "I can't really say anything. I barely tasted her. Besides, look at her," I follow the motion of his hand and scowl once again when I see her talking to four eyes. "She's totally wasted. I can't fuck her if she's not going to remember anything. She probably won't even remember the kiss."

I'm so angry and I don't even know why. She's over there, talking to that wormy little bastard after kissing Lucas. Why is she being such a slut? Now that she's kissed one of the bros she thinks she's a guy magnet. Is that what she thinks?

I should calm down. I shouldn't even care. Yet, I find myself being drawn to her, walking step after stupid step toward her until I'm standing next to four eyes, cup in hand, staring awkwardly down at her.

She stares up at me, her mouth slightly parted. I imagine them on me, her tongue flicking against mine. Her soft moans when I deepen the kiss. My hands on her ass drawing her closer and pressing her against my hard cock. Those sweet lips on my dick.

What the fuck am I thinking? I'm obviously trashed.

My face heats as I realize I've been staring at her mouth for longer than appropriate and both four-eyes and psycho bitch are staring at me as if I've suddenly sprouted polka dots all over my body. I take a moment to set down my cup, anywhere far away from me. I've obviously had way too much if I want psycho roommate. After collecting myself I turn around and in my most asshole voice I say, "Get lost, Four-Eyes."

I hear Rachel gasp as I stare down the wormy bastard, whose gaze narrows on me. He opens his mouth to say something and I swear I will punch him in his fucking ugly face if he so much utters a word. Instead, he turns to Rachel. "I'll be with Charlie and Lauren if you need anything."

"I'm so sorry, Josh," I hear Rachel say, but I continue watching four-eyes slither away, back to blondie and her brunette friend.

"Why are you such an asshole?" Rachel asks while throwing herself back in the chair and spilling a little water on her sweater,

I take the cup from her so she doesn't make herself even wetter in the chill air. *Don't need her getting sick. And then getting me sick*, I quickly add.

"That guy's an asshole," I say, pointing at whatever-his-name-is. "Me," I point to myself, "I'm an asshole, but not as bad as him."

She narrows her eyes up at me. "Really? How is he an asshole then?"

I wince, trying to come up with something, anything, but I'm completely dry. *I'm sure there's something. My asshole radar wouldn't be going off if there wasn't.*

She shakes her head and clucks her tongue at me, instantly reminding me of said tongue being down Lucas's throat and not mine. "See?" She leans her head back, giving me an ample view of her long slender neck.

"Fine!" I throw up my hands. "First, Lucas, now four-eyes? I see you're a busy girl."

She scoffs. "What?" I cringe at the shrill in her voice.

"You heard me." I rest my hands on my hips. "I didn't peg you for the type of girl to open your legs to just anyone, Rachel," I say, hating how I sound right now.

Why am I making a big deal out of this? It's nothing! Nothing!

"You," she stands up and digs her finger into my chest. Startled, I step back, bumping into the table "A guy who shares your women and fucks his way around campus, are slut shaming me?"

I gulp, my mouth suddenly feeling very dry. She looks so cute, scowling up at me, her nail digging into my chest under the fabric of my shirt, and I think if I don't say anything now I just might kiss her.

No more drinking ever again. NOT EVER.

"It's different," I breathe, completely captured by the freckles peeking through her minimal makeup and her slightly parted glossed lips.

"How is it different, Garcia?"

If I don't get away from her now I really will kiss her. I push her away and turn on my heel, grabbing her cup and downing the rest of the water. *Water for the rest of the day. For the whole week. No. THE MONTH.*

"It just is," I yell, quickly stalking back to Lucas.

I hear her laugh bitterly behind me.

I pass by blondie and the brunette, feeling their stares, but deciding to ignore them. It's nothing. Absolutely nothing. I'm just drunk and need to sober up. Then everything will go back to normal. And I'll be fine.

"What was that all about?" Lucas asks me, but I don't stop. I can't stop. I'm going to that football game and I am going to focus my attentions where they're needed. Finding me a cheerleader to fuck.

"Seth?" I hear Lucas call when I don't respond.

I shake my head. "Let's just get to the game."

***

I have no clue if we're winning or losing and I'm not even trashed. In fact, I've stopped drinking completely. I can't stop staring at Rachel on the other end of the bleachers. I don't know why she has to stand as far away from me as possible.

Well, maybe I do just a bit.

But why does she have to stand next to four-eyes? Four-eyes who continues touching her shoulder and stroking her hair behind her ear; who continues whispering into her ear as if they were sweet lovers. She's so drunk she doesn't even know what's going on. I watch her jump up and down and cheer, clapping her hands and laughing at something four-eyes said.

At least someone is paying attention to the game.

I grind my teeth when I see the wormy asshole take her hand in his. I hate the way she blushes, or the way she smiles. The way she looks at him as if she likes him. My heart stops. *What if he takes her somewhere? She's so drunk she might just follow him.*

"Excuse me," I say to Lucas, pushing him to the side.

Lucas, the big oaf that he is, stumbles backward. "What the fuck, man?"

I ignore him and continue shoving my way through the bleachers until I'm worming myself in the middle between jerk-off and Rachel.

She sighs. "What the hell are you doing?" she asks, her words aren't so slurred as before, but her eyes are still a bit bloodshot. Thankfully, her cup is filled with water.

"There's a better view here," I say, looking down at the game. Oh, so we are winning, great. "Go, Hunter!" I shout, clapping my hands. I look down at Rachel, whose arms are crossed with a scowl. "Why, did I worm in on the little date you were having?" I touch my chest, looking pained. "Poor Lucas will be so heartbroken."

Rachel shakes her head and looks away from me. "You are such a jerk."

I shrug. "If the shoe fits."

"Why can't you just leave me alone?"

"Because it's funny to see you act so pathetic."

She scoffs. Her nose scrunches up as she scowls at me and I'm tempted to poke it. *What is going on with me?* "I am not pathetic."

I scoff. "Oh, you are so pathetic. Everything about you screams 'save me' or 'why are you so meeeeeaaaaan to me?'" I laugh bitterly. "I can't help it. It's like you're asking to be tortured."

"What will it take to end the roommate contract?"

I roll my eyes. "You have eyes. Read the fucking contract, sweetheart."

"I have, but it means I will have to leave at the end of the semester. What would it take for me to end the contract immediately?"

I glance down at her. *Fuck. I don't need to go roommate searching again. And those assholes won't help. I just know it.*

"I want to enjoy my college life," she continues. "I don't want to be constantly fight with you and your bro-hoes on cleaning and partying."

I sigh. *I really don't need this right now.* But then again she's looking up at me so sweetly. I wonder if she'll do anything to end it. If she'll even succumb to tasting my cock.

"If you fuck all three of us, then I'll allow you to break the contract," I say, barely hearing the words come out of my mouth.

I love the way her eyes widen with my words and watching all the different emotions come across her face. Anger, relief, embarrassment, and maybe a hint of intrigue.

She opens her mouth.

"Hunter is down!" shouts the announcer.

I whip my head back to the game, seeing players and the referees surrounding someone in the field.

"Wow was that a hit! I sure hope Hunter is okay. That did not look good."

Chapter 13

RACHEL

I cannot believe I actually kissed Lucas. Lucas! Asshole Lucas who made me make him an egg white omelet. Asshole Lucas who dropped milk on the floor after I lost the push-up battle. Lucas with the dark looks and the sexy lips. I still feel his tongue slipping briefly against mine. His teeth grazing my lips, his hands on my waist.

I'm obviously drunk and I'm sticking with water for the rest of day. Ugh. And good old Seth ruining what would otherwise be a pretty good day out with the roommates with his slut shaming.

Just what is his problem, anyway?

It's not like he and Lucas don't share their girls.

Oh, God. Is that what he's expecting now? Are they going to toss me back and forth?

I'd rather die.

"If you fuck all three of us, then I'll allow you to break the contract," I hear him say through the crowd's cheers.

Great. It is that. He thinks exactly the way he's not supposed to. *Ugh. Why me? Why do I get myself in these situations?* But if I just do it, then I can immediately move out. Possibly sleep on Josh's couch for a week or so before. I'm sure I can find something available. There is the whole issue of working with Seth, but I can always change my shifts around so I never see him. That shouldn't be too hard.

But they're all such jerks. I don't know if I can respect myself if I allow myself to sleep with all three assholes. I'm about to tell Seth, fat chance, but then I hear, "Hunter is down! Wow was that a hit! I sure hope Hunter is okay. That did not look good."

I whip my head around, watching as players surround him. The referees are speaking and I see a man carrying a stretcher running out to him. Hunter is lying on the ground, holding his shoulder. *What happened?*

Lucas comes up behind Seth and grabs his shoulder. "Let's go check it out."

"I'm coming too," I say, following them onto the stairs and down the bleachers.

Seth and Lucas look at each other before shrugging in unison and continuing down the stairs. They move quickly, easily through the crowds whereas I have to push through in order to keep up. Seth waits for me at the bottom of the staircase and grabs my hand, pulling me behind him. "Geez, you are annoying," I hear him mutter. I follow him around the field until I come upon Hunter on the stretcher, holding his shoulder and moaning.

"Fuck, Hunter, what did you do?" Seth asks.

"Got hit in my bad shoulder," Hunter growls. His eyes are clamped shut, his hair wet and sticking to his sweaty face. "I think my hand is broken. Can one of you call my mom? She said she would be watching the game. I don't want her to worry."

"On it," says Lucas, already taking out his cellphone.

Why does Lucas have Hunter's mother's phone number?

"What hospital are you taking him to?" asks Seth.

"University of Colorado," says the medical technician. "Don't worry. At the worst it's just a fracture."

"Fuck!" shouts Hunter as they push him into the ambulance.

I watch the ambulance drive away. "I want to go," I hear Seth say.

Lucas shakes his head. "You've been underage drinking. Not the best place to be. I'll go and call you if anything's up." He nods toward me. "You better take her home."

Seth and I watch Lucas walk away with the cellphone pressed to his ear.

"Hello, Ms. Smith?" I hear Lucas say as he walks away. "Yes. Yes. Don't worry. He'll be fine. I'm on my way there now."

***

The walk home is quiet. I kick an empty red cup ahead of me, walk two steps, and then kick it again. I hope Charlie and Lauren aren't too upset with me for bailing. I messaged them earlier, but I still haven't received a response. Maybe they are at some after party.

What a day.

I still feel the effects of the booze, yet I'm walking in a straight line and my head doesn't seem so discombobulated. Nothing is quite as fun as it once was. I really hope Hunter is okay, which is weird since the guy has been an asshole to me since I first moved in.

Still, I don't like seeing someone get hurt. I shiver, remembering the way he looked on that stretcher. *As if he was trying to keep everything in, but deep down all he wanted to do was shatter.*

I watch Seth unlock the door, throwing it open. It bangs on the wall and I shuffle inside, depositing myself on the couch like a sack of potatoes. I lean my head back and sigh. Home sweet home. Seth sits down next to me and doesn't say anything. He turns on the TV and flips through the channels, running through all fifty of them before repeating again. I grab the remote from him and change it to some reruns of Buffy.

Once again, he doesn't say anything.

I sigh and try to focus on Buffy run after vampires and stake them in the chest rather than Hunter lying on a hospital bed. I'm surprised to glance over and see Seth watching. *I thought he would've left by now.* His head turns and he meets my gaze. His hair is sticking up all over the place and I'm tempted to push it back down. It's weird he can be sexy when he looks so unkempt.

I narrow my eyes when I see a smirk overcoming him, knowing what he's about to say is going to annoy the crap out of me. "So, how was it?"

"How was what, Garcia?"

"Your first kiss."

I roll my eyes. "What is this? A girl's sleepover? Are we having a bonding moment here?"

Seth scoffs. "Your first kiss with Lucas."

I shake my head and set my gaze on the TV screen. "Wouldn't you like to know," I mutter.

"Yeah, I would."

"Why?"

Seth chuckles while he sits up higher on the couch. He leans in close and I watch him flutter his eyelashes. "Because I have such a crush on him," he says in a girly voice.

"Oh, whatever," I say, taking the cushion behind me and hitting Seth in the face with it.

He laughs and throws the cushion on the floor in front of the TV. "Oh, come on now. Tell me."

"You want to know?"

"Yes, I think I should have the right to know what my best bro—"

Before he finishes I lean into him, pressing my lips against his. I smile when I see his eyes widen. My tongue slides against his bottom lip and before he can do anything, I pull away. I smirk back at him, his expression completely taken aback. "I guess I can shut you up."

I go to leave but Seth grabs me and pulls me back to him, his lips slamming down on mine. My mouth opens for him and his hungry tongue slips inside to dance with mine. My hands slide up his chest. Up into his hair while his wrap around me. We fall onto the couch, my back going into the cushions. My legs part for him and he presses his hard cock against me through his jeans, making me moan. He answers my moan with one of his own and I swear to God this feels absolutely wonderful.

Which frightens me.

I should push him away. I should tell him to fuck off. That I'm too drunk to be doing this or that I'm too drunk to know what I'm doing. When in reality, I haven't had a drink in the last two hours and I know exactly what I'm doing. My fingers play with his waistband. My hand pulls his shirt up. My palms press against his spine. He shudders when I nip his bottom lip.

Stop, Rachel. He's an asshole. You've got to stop this.

But his kisses feel amazing. It feels like they are pulling me further and further into an abyss I have no chance of escaping. And all I want to do is dive deeper inside.

There's ringing and we stop. His eyes staring down at me, widening as if just realizing who he's been doing this with the whole time. He quickly sits up. His warmth leaving me immediately. I run my hands through my hair while he answers the phone. My feet are already taking me to my room.

"Yeah?" I hear him say, while I close the door, barely catching a glimpse of his eyes on me.

I lean against the door, biting my lip. What the hell is wrong with me? I touch my lips, still feeling his touch.

"Broken?" I hear Seth say.

It's probably Lucas calling about Hunter. I bang my head against the door. I kissed two boys in one day. I am a slut. A total slut. And they are two of my roommates. Unbelievable.

"Okay, well, keep me in the loop. I'll see you and Hunter at home."

I hear some shuffling and then footsteps before a knock. I sigh, already knowing what Seth would want. I need to remain strong. I can't give in.

I take a deep breath and open the door, seeing Seth standing there. He smiles down at me. It's soft. Something I'm not used to at all from him. "Hunter's going to be okay," he says, taking a step toward me. I tell myself to step back, but my body remains rooted. *Traitorous body.* "He has a concussion and a broken hand. His shoulder is still messed up. Probably more so now than before. But he will be okay."

I nod. "Good. I'm glad to hear it."

He steps forward again, an arm reaching around my waist and pulling me toward him. "Now," he breathes seductively, "where were we?"

Be strong, Rachel.

I pull away from him and I'm glad when my body actually listens to me and creates space between us. "Nowhere, Seth," I say, rolling my shoulders back. "We were nowhere."

Seth scoffs and shoves his hands into his pockets. "Really?"

I nod. "Really, really."

He licks his lips and I remember that tongue toying with mine. The memory lights a fire in the pit of my stomach and I feel that itch in the back of my head, urging me to capture his lips with mine. *No, remain strong.*

"And may I ask why?"

I shake my head at him. He really needs to ask why this is a bad idea? There are so many reasons why I shouldn't sleep with him. I don't even know where to begin. "Because you're an asshole, Seth." I scowl at him and cross my arms. "You've been an asshole to me since I moved in. And I wouldn't have any respect for myself whatsoever if I continued whatever it is we were doing."

I wait for Seth's response and I'm shocked to see the hurt flash in his eyes. It's only for a split second and then the usual, dark, cruel Seth appears. "Fine," he says, turning on his heel. "Your loss, bitch."

I watch him stalk through the hallway and the kitchen before slamming the apartment door closed.

Chapter 14

SETH

I fumble with my keys, groaning when they fall to the ground and I'm forced to lean over and swallow back the vomit threatening to spew from my mouth. *I drank way too much last night. Even after that whole thing with Rachel.* I scowl while picking up my keys, immediately reminded why I left in the first place. *Stupid bitch blueballed me. She fucking kissed me and then she left me wanting. Such a fucking cock tease.*

I unlock the door and kick it open, peaking around and finding it dark and quiet inside. I slam it close, waiting for Rachel to come out and yell at me to keep it down. I watch her door for the longest minute in the world, but there's no answer and once again I feel irritation set on my shoulders while I stalk toward my room. *Fucking bitch doesn't even want to face me.* I know I'm being ridiculous, possibly even childish, but who cares? She's the one who started this whole mess with first kissing Lucas and then me. I slam my bedroom door closed behind me, this time getting a groan from Hunter to, "Keep it the fuck down man!"

I cringe. *That's right. Hunter's home from the hospital. Dude must be doped up on pain meds.* I lean against my door, banging my head against it several times while I try to drown out the images of Rachel dragging me into that kiss on the couch. *Her lips had been so soft.* I look down at myself, feeling my cock growing hard just recalling her moans when I pushed her down; the way her legs opened and wrapped around my waist.

Sure. That kiss I shared with Rachel was fucking hot. Doesn't mean anything, though. I smile as my thoughts drift to Millie from the night before. Good ol' reliable Millie. Flexible. Big breasts. The cool girl next door who doesn't give a fuck which of us bros she gets to sleep with. I force the memories of Rachel away and think of Millie at John's house party climbing on top of me, riding me while pressing my face in between her breasts. *Who cares if I couldn't stop thinking about Rachel and that kiss the whole night... or that I kept imagining Millie as Rachel...?* I grimace, remembering Millie's sloppy kissing. Or lack thereof. *Well, the sex was good... sort of...*

I groan and run a hand through my hair, which is probably sticking up and matted in all sorts of places. I feel greasy and slimy as if my skin wants to peal itself away from my body and run away. *Last night should have been hot. I had been so fucking horny, anyone would really do. But it still wasn't the same... who cares if Millie isn't the greatest at kissing... or at least not as great as Rachel?*

Nope, not this guy. Don't care one bit. Not at all. Rachel isn't even hot. Not like Millie hot. She's just some pitiful excuse of a female and at the time I was just feeling desperate. And right now, I'm just irritated that she didn't get my rocks off like she seemed to be advertising.

I strip myself of my clothes and stride over to my bed, falling into it. The bed shakes and squeaks with my weight. Work starts in just a few hours and I need some sleep if I'm going to be able to survive any of it. I close my eyes and try to will away any thoughts of Rachel and those seductive lips away.

Unfortunately, I fail miserably as I find an image of Rachel appearing before me behind closed eyes. I imagine her naked and reaching for me while moaning my name. My hand slips down my body to my hard length, twitching and pressing into the bed. I grab it and give it several earnest strokes.

"Rachel," I moan into the bed.

***

Work sucks, which is why I am hiding out in the stock room while Miss Blue Balls is handling the front of the store. We've just gotten a huge wave of customers, and really, I should be out there helping, but then again, I don't want to. And why should I? She thinks I'm an asshole, so why change any of that? Let her think I'm an asshole.

The stock room is pretty quiet and does wonders for my pounding head. I hear the bell ring with the entrance of more customers and some mumbling from several people in the front. *You should probably go help her,* a small voice in the back of my head whispers. *That's the tenth time that bell has rung.* I grind my teeth and force myself to remain in my chair. *Fuck that,* I tell the stupid small voice. *I'm an asshole. Asshole! She can handle it on her own. Bitch is probably going to quit soon anyway.*

I eye a pair of Hokas and immediately grab them, unpacking the box and looking down at the blue and white shoes. *I can't help her now. I'm too busy looking at these sexy beasts.* They're the Rocket X. Lightweight. Thick insole with a comfortable fit. I've tried them on at least a hundred times but they are two hundred dollars over my budget. My budget being free. And sadly, even a track star isn't enough to get the returned Hokas given to me by the store owner.

"One of these days," I whisper to them while petting the side of one. "One of these days you will be on my feet."

"Garcia, are you going to work today or what?" I hear Rachel's shrill voice ask from behind.

"I am working," I say, putting the shoes back inside their box.

"Oh really?"

"Yeah, really," I say, glancing over my shoulder and watching her cross her arms.

I ignore the memory of her falling back against the couch, or the way she tossed her head back and moaned. Or at least, I try to ignore the memory, yet it leaves me wanting much more than I know she's willing to give. I purse my lips while turning around. *Millie,* I tell myself. *Think of motor boating Millie's giant breasts. Not of stupid psycho bitch.* But rather than Millie coming to mind, I wonder what Rachel would do if I motor boated her, instantly imagining her hands clawing at my shoulders.

"What the fuck is wrong with me?" I mutter while shoving the shoes back onto the shelf.

"The problem with you," says Rachel coming around to face me, her hands on her hips now while she glares down at me, "is that there's a huge line at the counter with your stupid name on it," she says while pointing at me.

I roll my eyes. "So? You seem to be handling yourself fine."

"Handling?" She throws her hands up into the air. I swear if her eyes get any bigger they'll pop out of her skull. The imagery definitely kills any boner I have. "I'm not handling it, you asshole." I roll my eyes again. *Here we go...* "There are customers looking at shoes, customers asking about runner's belts, customers wanting to test out their running gait," she counts on her fingers, "and you're in the back just twiddling your fingers."

I shrug. "What can I say? I'm busy." I look her up and down, taking in her black leggings, converse shoes and pink work shirt. She's wearing a high ponytail today, which I have to say is quite hot. I kinda want to pull it and see if her eyes will bug out. "I guess you would know nothing about that." I smirk and give myself a mental high five. *Nice burn.*

She scoffs and before I realize what she's going to do, she's stepping around me and grabbing the chair. "Whoa!" I shout, trying to hold onto the armrests, but it's too late and she's surprisingly strong when she's pissed. She swings the chair sharply, dumping my sorry ass onto the floor.

"There!" she shouts when my knees smack against the hard ground. I groan while picking myself up. I catch her storming out of the stock room, her ponytail swishing to the side from her jerky movements. "Busy my fucking ass," she mutters.

"Fuck, you gotta be kidding me," I yell, stalking out of the room and stopping immediately when I see at least ten or fifteen people in the store room turning their eyes on me. Several make a face, most probably from my language and I chuckle awkwardly while I shift back and forth from foot to foot.

"Excuse me," someone waves from the counter, sounding annoyed while holding a runner's belt and several packets of GU. She shakes them and scowls at me. "I've been waiting forever and would really like to buy this."

I search for Rachel, finding her at the treadmill watching a customer's gait and sigh, not even finding myself capable to scowl at her. She wouldn't notice anyway.

I smack on my best smile and stride toward the cash register. "Let me help you with that." I take the belt and packets and ring them up quickly. "Did you find everything alright?" I ask while glancing at Rachel, who casts me a devious smile.

One point, Rachel, I think while my fake smile softens into a real one.

***

I grab my bag in the stock room and watch Rachel shrug into her denim jacket. She seems to be avoiding my gaze. I'm quite shocked she was able to pull off today at all. Maybe she won't be leaving the store any time soon. I watch her clock out and quickly leave. *She's not even going to wait for me?* I stuff my time card into the archaic looking device and run after her. *Why isn't she waiting for me?*

Better yet, why am I running after her?

"Hey!" I shout, running faster when she doesn't pause. "Wait up!"

"What do you want?" she asks, not bothering to look at me. She stuffs her hands into her jean jacket and keeps her head down against the wind.

I slow when I catch up to her. "What? We're heading in the same place," I say while gesturing in front of us.

Rachel laughs bitterly. "Doesn't mean we have to talk to each other."

I shrug. "There's a party going on tonight. The guys and I are going. You could come along... too." I cringe at how awkward I sound. *What the hell is wrong with me?*

Rachel is already shaking her head. "I can't. I have that big project I'm working on for photography. I still have no clue what theme to pick or what to do for it exactly."

"I could... help you," I say and immediately regret it. What the hell am I even saying? I'm an asshole. She thinks I'm an asshole. Why am I being so nice? I feel like a puppy begging for attention from its master. And all for a kiss. *A stupid little kiss that means absolutely nothing,* I remind myself.

She looks at me then and I feel my face heat when my eyes go to her lips. I remember them feeling soft, her tongue like velvet as it brushed against mine. She raises an eyebrow at me. "You can help me?" She chuckles. "And how exactly can you help me, Garcia? Art isn't even your thing."

I try to think of something to reply with, but my mind is already carrying me far away, imagining her moans as I suck on her tongue, nip at her bottom lip. I imagine my hands playing with her nipples, her head thrown back in bliss.

I clear my throat when she continues staring at me and quickly say, "I know Aurora. Aurora is beautiful." I wave a hand around us at the houses we walk pass. "And I love Colorado. I'm sure there's something there you can take a picture of."

Rachel shakes her head. "I doubt you could help me." She looks at the sky and sighs. "Most likely you're just going to take me somewhere, and leave me out in the woods to defend myself against rabid wolves and drunk homeless men." I grimace at the imagery. "And then I'll fail my photography class."

"Why would I do that?" I ask. "I'm an asshole, but I'm not pure evil."

Rachel shrugs. "You haven't been the nicest as of yet."

"Scouts honor," I say, holding up two fingers.

Rachel laughs, covering her mouth with one dainty hand. "I doubt you've even been a boy scout."

I shrug. "You'd be correct."

"Then no deal."

We're coming up to the apartment. At least a ten-minute walk away when I get a dirty little idea. "First one home then," I say with a wink.

She throws her hands up in the air. "No, not another challenge."

"First one home wins. And if I win you have to join me on a tour of the town."

Rachel shakes her head. "No."

"Yes," I say, laughing and bolting ahead.

I feel the wind under my feet. I don't even bother looking back, already knowing I'm flying so far ahead of her while she's stuck in the back. I reach the staircase easily and when I turn around I see her in the distance, gasping to keep up with that heavy backpack on her shoulders. Her cheeks and nose are pinked from the chill air. Her nose is scrunched up in irritation. *Probably because she lost. Again.*

She stops in front of me, slumping over with her bag sliding off her shoulders and onto the sidewalk. "Damnit," she says between gasps.

"I win!" I shout while raising my arms into the air in victory.

She inhales deeply while straightening herself. "You promise not to leave me out in the middle of the woods?"

"I promise to make sure you are returned home safely," I say, holding out a hand which she takes and shakes firmly.

"Next Saturday," she says without breaking eye contact.

I nod curtly. "Next Saturday."

We walk up the stairs together and there's a bounce in my step. I'm going to spend a whole day with Rachel. Rachel with the soft lips and the cute freckles. Rachel, the art girl with small breasts and a nice ass. And I'm completely excited.

I must be dying.

Something must be seriously wrong with me.

I unlock the door and find Hunter in the kitchen, trying to make a protein shake with one hand while Lucas sits on the couch playing Mario Kart on the TV.

"Hey," says Lucas, waving one hand at us. He smiles softly and I glance at Rachel, seeing her return the smile.

My heart falls and all excitement leaves me.

Before I can say anything to Lucas, or Rachel, I catch Hunter's scowl out of the corner of my eye, aimed in my direction. "You," he says, pointing at me with his bandaged broken hand. "You were the one making all that fucking noise this morning."

I roll my eyes and throw my jacket onto the couch before sidling up next to him to pour myself a glass of water. "So?" I ask with a shrug.

"Why can't you keep it down?" He groans. "Just for once."

I give him a dark scowl. "Why are you whining like a pussy?"

"I'm in pain, you asshole," says Hunter, shoving past me and downing his shake with one long chug.

"Are you sure you should be going out tonight?" asks Rachel from the couch. She's sitting next to Lucas. Too close. Like thigh-brushing-thigh close.

"What the fuck is that supposed to mean?" asks Hunter, slamming his glass down on the counter.

"Hunter," I say in a warning voice. The way he's speaking to Rachel is completely uncalled for. Sure, he's in pain, but he doesn't have to take it out on all of us. Especially Rachel, since she's just showing her concern.

"You just," she waves at him while trying to find words, "don't look like you feel too well. It's okay to take a break every now and then."

"Oh, shut the fuck up," mutters Hunter as he walks toward his door. "Who asked that bitch anyway," he adds before slamming his door closed.

I sigh and run a hand through my hair. *Maybe he should talk to someone.* My gaze lingers on the door as a dark thought enters me. *Maybe he's going through withdrawal.* I stare at Hunter's door, wondering if he's going to be alright. A broken hand isn't good, but it'll heal pretty quickly. But his shoulder has been messed up for over a year now and Hunter still isn't treating it with the attention it needs. He's going to tear it if he's not careful. If it isn't torn already.

"Ignore him," says Lucas. "He's had it pretty rough today." He hands Rachel a controller and smiles at her. "Play with me?"

I step forward, instantly needing to wedge myself between them. I tell myself I'm just irritated that the bastard didn't ask me to play, but really that doesn't make any sense. Rachel is sitting too close to him. Lucas is actually smiling at her. And she's not even undressing. She's fully dressed, sitting next to him, playing video games. Very poorly I might add. But still, he's still smiling at her. Practically cuddling with her. In front of me.

It's nothing. Stop being so weird, I tell myself while striding toward my room. *Still. They look like the perfect couple.*

Chapter 15

RACHEL

It's Saturday and I still can't believe I'm going out with Seth. Or that he even offered. Which is weird in itself. The whole week has gone by like a complete blur with Hunter mopey around the flat and Lucas casting me little smiles here and there. I still can't get the idea of kissing Lucas and Seth out of my head. *I kissed both of them. On the same day.* Part of me feels completely mortified by the idea of kissing two boys within a span of a few hours. I have never done that before. Sure, I've kissed boys here and there and gone out on a few dates. I'm no virgin Mary. But I'm also not the type to go from sleeping with one guy one day and another guy the next day.

Not like that's a bad thing or anything.

I just have never done it.

And I don't know how to feel about it, yet, because the other part of me really wants to kiss again. Both of them. Even Seth, who, despite his asshole personality, is actually a really good kisser. Who would have thought?

I glance over at him, walking next to me down the sidewalk toward campus. He looks freshly bathed. His hair moves easily with the breeze. *It was soft when I ran my hands through it,* I remember faintly. My face heats when I remember the way he moaned, how he pressed against me. I remember feeling his hard dick through the jeans and the need for more. *No,* I tell myself. *You do not need any more Seth.* Honestly, I don't think I would be feeling so torn if I kissed someone else after Lucas. Even Hunter would have been a better choice than Seth, even though he is also a bit of a jackass. Even more now after his injury.

And then there's Josh.

Sweet Josh. I should be kissing him and not Seth. Josh with his beautiful eyes and his gentle ways. *He even asked me if I wanted to go to the art museum today.* I frown, remembering how sad he looked when I turned him down. *Other plans I told him. Other plans with a guy who wants to make my life a living hell.* I should have said yes to Josh and played sick for Seth.

But I am a bit curious as to where he plans on taking me today. *Not to mention, he woke me up at five this morning.* Someone who wakes up at five on a Saturday definitely has big plans. There's no way I could play sick with this much curiosity going through me.

I gaze into the distance as the sun begins to climb over the mountain tops, casting golds and crimsons and lighting the small quaint town in its glittering rays. It's beautiful. Aurora is absolutely beautiful, and even in its autumn beauty I wonder what it will look like once snow begins to fall.

"There," Seth says while pointing where I've been looking. "That would make a beautiful picture."

I level my camera and look through the lens. It is a beautiful picture, but I can't get the lighting right and there are telephone poles and wires in the way. *The picture is just going to fall flat compared to the beauty in front of me,* I tell myself while lowering my camera.

"Did you get it?" Seth asks. He smiles and looks over my shoulder to look into the display.

I shake my head. "No." I sigh and try to ignore his pestering gaze. I don't even know how to explain myself. I just can't take pictures. I'm not the greatest photographer in the world and I guess at this rate I never will be. "I can't get it right," I say instead, not wanting to unload all my pent-up baggage. He already thinks I'm crazy for some reason. No reason to add fuel to the fire now.

"You can't get it right?" He looks at me, his brows furrowing while he purses his lips. "What's that supposed to mean?" He waves at the mountains. "Just take it. Take hundreds. Then you can look at it after and decide which is the best."

I roll my eyes. "That's not my method."

"Then you're going to have a whole lot of nothing if you don't take at least something." He watches me with crossed arms and nods toward the mountains. "Just one picture. Not that hard. You just push the little button at the top. I can take it for you if you want."

I scowl at him, immediately recalling the last time he touched my camera. "No, that's quite alright," I say while putting my camera up to my face. "I don't need any more dick pics."

He chuckles and, in that instant, even if it is a crappy shot, I push the button and hold it, taking at least ten shots of the mountains in the distance. I go to open my display, but Seth is already sprinting ahead of me. "Look at it later," he calls, waving at me to join him. "We won't have time for everything at this rate."

This really is going to be interesting, I think while slinging my camera over my shoulder and running after him.

The entire day I follow Seth around Aurora while taking pictures of coffee shops, the lighting in the surrounding woods, people playing music in the small college town square and every time I question whether or not it's the right shot, Seth pressures me to push the button no matter what.

And I have to hand it to Seth, he's really good at getting me to do what I don't want to. *I never realized before how much I questioned myself,* I think while flipping through the display screen on my camera, chuckling at one shot I took of Seth making a face at some dog poo he stepped in. *I probably shouldn't use this for my project,* I tell myself while quickly pressing the button and staring at a beautiful picture of the woods just on the outskirts of town. I find myself scrutinizing the picture, yet finding absolutely nothing wrong with it. The light slips in through the trees perfectly, showing the difference in shadows and depth.

I wouldn't have taken this without Seth, I realize, glancing up and watching him placing our orders at the cash register. After spending the entire day around campus, Seth and I wind up at The Cup. It's a cute little cafe situated in the heart of town and we were able to swindle a table next to the window from an elderly couple a few minutes prior. I gaze out the window overlooking the town when I see Seth heading back toward me.

I don't need him knowing I was looking at him.

"Coffee will be ready in a few minutes," he says and sits down in the chair across from me. "Wow," I hear him say and look over, catching him taking my camera and looking at the picture with the woods. "You're actually pretty good."

I smile. "Thanks to you." I shake my head when my gaze catches on the initial first shot of the day with the sun rising over the mountains. "I wouldn't have been able to capture anything if it wasn't for you."

Seth shrugs. "You just gotta let go. It's like running."

I raise an eyebrow. "How is photography anything like running?"

Seth nods to the waiter when he sets down the coffee mugs in front of us. My hands instantly reach for the warmth, inhaling the intoxicating scent of mocha before diving in and licking cream from my lips. When I look up I see Seth watching me, and I flush.

"Well, running has always helped me let go," he says, reaching forward to wipe cream from my upper lip.

I watch him lick the white residue from his fingers. I shift uncomfortably in my chair as I remember his kisses on the couch. I cross my legs tightly, accidentally touching his leg with my foot. His nostrils flare and I ignore the tightness I feel in the pit of my stomach. "How so?" I breathe. I run my hands through my hair to give me something to do other than stare at his lips.

Seth shrugs. He looks at the window for a moment as if seeing something that isn't there. "Dad walks out, go for a run. Mom can't pay the bills, go for a run. Guys are assholes at school, go for a run." He shrugs again before taking a sip from his filtered coffee. "It's just how I've always been able to let go of the stress."

"Really?" I ask, imagining young Seth going through all that. It's hard. He's definitely a dick, but now hearing it I realize that there is a reason for the tough exterior.

"What do you mean 'really'?" Seth says between sips of coffee.

"You went through all…" I wave my hand, not wanting to repeat everything. It's probably hard enough saying it. Especially in this society when men shouldn't show their feelings.

He shrugs and casts his gaze back to his coffee. "It doesn't really matter. Running has always helped me through the shit."

I nod, pressing my lips together into a thin smile. "I guess I should try it some time."

His gaze pops up to me and he smirks while leaning back in his chair. "You? Try running?" He looks me up and down. "I thought you hated us jocks?"

I roll my eyes. "Well, you don't make it easy to like you."

Seth scoffs. "What do you mean? You had an attitude before I even met you."

"I did not," I say a bit too loudly. I slump down when I feel several students casting annoyed looks in my direction.

Seth leans in close, his nose nearly brushing mine. "Did too," he says while his gaze dips down to my lips.

I lean in close. Our lips are only a breath away. My nose nuzzles gently against his. Briefly. "You were a complete asshole to me the first day," I whisper. "You called me stupid."

Seth chuckles softly. He doesn't move away, which sends a thrill through me like none other. *Is he enjoying this as much as I am?* I wonder. *Does he want to kiss me again?*

"Because you couldn't find the fucking door. Anyone with eyes can find the fucking door. Doesn't mean all us athletes are jerks."

"Well, athletes can't have a normal conversation," I say while I lean back and look around the cafe. *We're in a café,* I remind myself. I notice Seth copies my movement, his body mirroring mine.

"I can have a normal conversation," says Seth. His gaze lingers on my lips.

I scoff. "It's always sports this and sports that," I say while flicking my right and left hand as if balancing the words in the palms of my hand.

"I can talk about other things."

"Like what?"

I watch him search his small little brain for anything. "Sex," he says.

I roll my eyes. "Please."

"And food."

"Really?" I cross my arms. "You can talk about your culinary prowess? Or which wine brings out the best flavors of meat?"

Seth makes a face and shakes his head. "Who discusses that bullshit?"

I roll my eyes. "People who talk food, dummy."

"Fine," says Seth, leaning in close. I stop myself from copying his movement, knowing no good will come from playing around with Seth. None at all. "And what exactly do you and your art buddies discuss?"

"Art history, of course," I say. "And we debate modern art aesthetics. In my English class we are discussing symbolism and the correlation between Heart of Darkness and Apocalypse Now."

Seth nods appreciatively. "I like reading. Sometimes I read the little articles in Playboy."

I smack my head and stifle a groan. "This is exactly what I'm talking about." *And exactly the reason why I need to forget that kiss.*

Seth chuckles. "Well, we're talking now," he says. "Isn't that something?"

I smile at him and push a lock of hair behind my ear. "I guess."

"We can say I like debating proper discussion etiquette." He shrugs. "That sounds fancy enough."

I giggle over my mocha. "Very fancy."

"Hey, Rachel." I jump and glance to my left, seeing Josh hovering above us with his hands stuffed into his jean jacket. He shifts awkwardly from foot to foot and glances between me and Seth. My eyes widen as I realize what he's already suspecting.

It's not a date, I want to shout, but before I can say anything Seth says, "What the fuck do you want?"

My mouth is still open when I look at Seth, my eyes already narrowing into a scowl.

"Oh, um, nothing," says Josh, looking at the floor. "I just wanted to say hello is all."

"Well, you've said it," says Seth, rolling his shoulders back while scowling up at Josh. It's like he's trying to make himself taller like a grizzly bear about to attack. "Now go away."

I shake my head. "I'm so sorry, Josh."

"How's your project coming along?" asks Josh, smiling shyly back at me and thankfully ignoring everything coming out of Seth's stupid mouth.

"It's going great," says Seth. "Now beat it."

"Seth, shut it," I say. "Its fine, Josh. I'll talk about it with you at study session next week."

Josh beams and nods. "Sounds great. I'll see you there." He waves at me before grabbing his to-go cup from the counter and striding out of the cafe. I watch him go, wishing I can run along with him right about now rather than stay with this jerk who seems to think he's better than everyone around him.

A jerk, who's a very good kisser, a dark voice reminds me.

I ignore that idiotic thought and scowl at Seth. "Why are you such an asshole?"

"I don't like the guy,' says Seth while watching something through the window. *Probably some hot girl not wearing a bra,* I think while rolling my eyes. "There's something off about him."

I shake my head. "You know what. Forget about me and the jock crowd. You also have an attitude toward us artistic folk."

Seth makes a face. "I do not."

I nod. "You sure do. You probably think all of us are prissy."

"Well, you are," he says while gesturing toward me. "Your very attitude wreaks of snobbery."

I point at him. "See this is the problem. You should be nicer to us artists. Not all of us are uppity."

Seth rolls his eyes. "And why would I do that?"

I shrug before taking another sip from my mocha. "I'll give running a try if you give art a try."

"Where would I even begin with that? There's absolutely nothing about art I would enjoy."

"Photography," I say while shaking the camera at him. "You love Aurora so much you could try photographing it. You do know all the best places. And wouldn't it be great to capture your college life while you still can?"

Seth shakes his head. "I don't even have a camera."

"I can loan you one," I say, my whole body brimming with excitement. "I have so many different cameras. Just promise me," I say, lifting one finger, "no dick pics."

Seth smirks. "If you give running a chance, I'll give photography a chance," he says while holding his hand out to me.

"Deal," I say, smiling and grabbing his hand, giving it a firm shake.

***

Why am I doing this? I wonder when I wake up the next morning at an ungodly hour. It's Sunday. S-U-N-D-A-Y. No one should be up at this time. Especially after waking up at five the morning before. I groan, blinking my eyes to try to keep them open. The sun hasn't even risen and here I am shrugging into my leggings and stuffing my feet into tennis shoes. I don't even have a sports bra. I guess a normal bra will just have to do for now. I throw on a grey sweater over it all and hope it's enough to keep me warm from the outdoors.

I open my door, seeing Seth standing in front of it, his hand in a fist like he was going to knock on it. He slowly lowers it and looks me up and down. A shiver goes down my spine. It feels like he's undressing me with his eyes. I am instantly reminded of the last time he stood here at my door, and a part of me wants to tug him inside and go back to bed.

And not for sleeping.

"What?" I ask while gesturing to myself. "Is something wrong with what I'm wearing?" I turn around as if there could be a hole he spotted in the back of my leggings, but there's nothing.

"No," he breathes, shaking his head. "It'll do."

It'll do, he says, I think, feeling annoyance weigh down my shoulders. *Meaning I'm already doomed.* He is of course dressed in tight running pants and some sort of track cleats and a long-sleeved shirt that definitely highlighted his toned body. *I don't think I am ready for this,* I keep telling myself while I follow him out the door. *Sure, after giving him a cheap camera last night after our day out and making plans to run this morning, I of course didn't think about the moving part. The only thing I thought of was we had such a nice time and I wanted to hang out with him again.*

Like a freaking idiot.

I walk slowly down the stairs, while he bounds down them, all ready to shoot off into the rising sun. I'm instantly reminded of some of those girls who pick up a hobby to impress a boy they like. *But I don't like him,* I tell myself.

You just want to do him. I groan and rub my temples. *Two days of waking up impossibly early. Ugh. What has my life come to? And now I can't even think straight.*

He's running in place while he waits for me. He will probably be doing that a lot on this run.

"Alright, so the key to running is all in the breathing," he says to me while running in place as if it's the most natural thing for him. "You keep a good breathing rhythm, you'll have a good run."

I make a face. *What is that supposed to mean?*

"Since you're a beginner you don't need to worry about speed," he says. "Keep your hands at your hips while you run and keep them easy. Don't fist them like you're going to punch someone in the face."

I might just punch him in the face for making me get up this early. But a deal is a deal. I try running and he tries photography. I just don't know what's going to happen if I hate this. Which I suspect I will.

"Alright, let's go!" he says, sprinting down the sidewalk and toward the stop sign.

I groan and move my legs into probably the slowest jog anyone has ever done. I keep my hand at my hips and try not to fist them, but it's probably only been like thirty seconds and I feel like giving up. *Don't most people do like a couch to a 5K challenge for this? Shouldn't I run one minute and walk five minutes?*

Watch me hurt something.

Seth is already waiting at the stop sign while I run toward him. He's still running in place like the freaking marathon man and hasn't even broken a sweat.

"I don't know if I can do this," I say between gasps while running in place. My legs move sluggishly underneath me and I wonder if I ever moved them this quickly outside gym class.

"Let's just do ten minutes," he says while running. He's not even gasping. He could probably make pancakes while doing this.

"How long has it been?" I whimper, sounding like a pathetic child about to throw a tantrum.

He looks at his watch. "Two."

I groan and he laughs. "You can do it. Look we're almost at three," he says while showing me his watch. I watch it click away, reading 44, 45, and 46 before he runs across the street and sprints to the next stop sign.

Oh my God he really is going to be the death of me.

Several stop signs later I am walking behind him, having reached my ten-minute mark while he dashes back to the apartment. There is no way I can keep up with him, but having run ten minutes in one go has me feeling like a freaking queen. Like I can accomplish anything. I can actually run ten minutes. I died the whole way, but, still, ten minutes is definitely a win.

I stomp up the stairs, not able to control any part of my body as I swing open the door. It's still early. No one is up and Seth is probably already back in his room, planning our next running date. I really hope he isn't planning on me doing this tomorrow morning with him. Or lengthening it anytime soon.

I drag myself into my room and grab my towel and a sweater set before continuing to drag myself through the hall and toward the bathroom. I throw the door open and stifle a scream as I see Seth standing there completely naked. He stares back at me with wide eyes while yanking for his towel hanging over the shower door to cover himself with.

"For fuck's sake," I hear him mutter.

I should go, yet my legs won't move. His body is made up of lean muscle without an ounce of fat. I am completely captivated. And his dick... definitely a good enough size for me. "I am... I am so..." I stutter as I try to turn around.

Once again my body completely betrays me.

"Well, are you staying or going?" he asks.

I glance back at him. I should go, but I'm stepping toward him. My hand is pushing on the door, clicking it closed and locking it behind me. But I'm not on the right side. I'm standing in front of him and I know there's no way I'm letting this opportunity escape me.

I want to kiss him again. I want to feel him again.

"Staying."

Chapter 16

SETH

I stand in the middle of the bathroom and stare unblinkingly back at Rachel. I don't really know what to do with myself since I got here first. But she's still not closing the door. She's just standing there, wide eyed, with a hand covering her mouth.

"Well," I start, feeling myself growing hard. "Are you staying or going?"

I expect her to go running and screaming back to her room, but instead the door closes behind her and she strides toward me. "Staying," she whispers. I'm so completely shocked she's still in the room with me I have no clue what to do.

I lean toward the shower, not breaking eye contact as I turn on the hot water. I have to hand it to Lucas, he really outdid himself with the whole shower cleaning bit. Too bad I can barely have a look since Rachel is staring up at me with an all too cute expression on her face.

I really should be yelling at her for just barging in on me like this.

Instead, I am completely intrigued by what's she going to do.

She doesn't say anything as she pulls off her grey sweater and tugs down her leggings until she's standing before me in a pink bra and underwear matching set with a cute little bow in the middle. I nibble on my bottom lip, seriously wondering if this is happening or if I've suddenly found myself stuck in some naughty sex dream. *No complaints if I am, although I really hope I don't cream the bed.*

"So, are you getting in?" I breathe.

I should be better than this. I've slept with loads of girls. At least thirty. And yet, I'm completely turned on by Rachel standing in her underwear in front of me. My cock is twitching underneath the towel and I feel so fucking timid right now. Like I'm a virgin all over again.

Although I've never been shy in my entire fucking life.

She juts out her chin and unhooks her bra, letting it drop next to her before dipping down to pull her underwear down. My mouth feels dry while I watch her move. Her shoulders are freckled just like her nose. Her breasts, while smaller than Millie's definitely are sizeable enough to play with in the palm of my hands. Her stomach isn't toned, but it doesn't matter. She looks amazing. Absolutely amazing and I can't take my eyes off her when she slips inside the shower. Dropping the towel on the floor, I follow her inside and slide the door closed.

The water hits us and I don't know what I should do here. Does she want me to touch her, or is she just taunting me? Flaunting her sexy body around as punishment for my cruelty? She throws her head back, allowing the water to hit her face. It drips down her body, soaking her from head to toe. She moans while turning around and allowing the hot water to hit her shoulders, while I'm just standing in the chilled, steaming air growing a massive boner.

I grab a bar of soap and rub it against her back, which gives me something to do. The water drips against my prickled skin. She shifts her body so more of it hits me, wetting my hair. Her ass wiggles against my cock and I bite back a moan. Rubbing the bar against her shoulders, it slips from my hands and slides down her back. I watch it clatter onto the ground, but I find myself completely incapable of bending over to grab it as Rachel continues to rub her ass against my dick. I shiver, feeling the beginnings of precum slipping from my slit. My hands circle around her as I nuzzle her neck with my forehead, pressing kisses into her shoulder blade.

I can't believe this is happening. The thought slips through me just when Rachel is turning me around. I step back, wondering if she's going to toss me out of the shower. If she's going to seek her revenge this way. I mean, I have been an asshole. I can't really blame her for leaving me in this predicament.

Instead, she takes my hand and pulls me close to her. So close, my cock is between us, jabbing into her stomach while my lips are hovering just a hair's breadth above hers. She tilts her head up and I see the water captured in her lashes. Her curly hair damp and resting on her shoulders. A moan escapes my lips as I contemplate pressing them against hers. Her hand slips between us and gently strokes the head of my cock, eliciting another moan.

Fuck, I'm really going to lose it if I don't know where this is going. "Do you..." I start, my voice too high pitched. I grimace and clear my throat. *Let's try this again.* "Do you maybe want to—"

She moves onto her tiptoes and presses her lips against mine while her finger continues stroking the sensitive flesh at my tip. I moan and pull her to me, wrapping my arms around her waist while her arms slide over my shoulders. My hand slips between us and cups her breast, massaging it before tugging delicately on her nipple. She moans, opening her mouth for my tongue to slip inside and slide against hers. I'm hungry for more. I want to hear her moan more. I grab her leg and lift it up on my hip, pushing her back against the wall and thrusting my cock against her stomach.

I'm so horny I want to just thrust it inside her, but I don't have any condoms, and I can only assume she hadn't thought to bring any either. I moan in frustration as I thrust against her again. I'm so wet with need. I will probably cry if she leaves me now. I will probably beg if she does.

My hand slips down her front, stroking lightly at her clit. Her thigh tightens around me, holding me steady and I can't help but wonder if she is really going to get me off here, in the shower. I've always thought of fucking in here, yet Lucas always kept it so nasty I didn't think I could convince any girl to join me.

We are keeping this bathroom fucking clean no matter what after this.

I continue stroking her clit with my thumb while my index finger brushes against her entrance already wet with slick. "Yes," she whispers in my ear before nipping my earlobe. "I want it. So bad."

I moan, feeling myself getting close as she continues pumping her hand in a steady rhythm. My finger pushes inside her and she moans between kisses on my neck, sucking at the sensitive flesh and making me thrust rapidly in her hand.

God, I just want to come. I want to fuck her and I want to come. I move faster while rubbing her clit. My finger thrusts into her and is soon joined by another. She moans and tosses her head back. I bite my lip to keep from moaning, but with one last thrust and a guttural groan I release myself in her hand. My cum spilling out all over her stomach and fingers.

She washes it in the water while I find myself slipping to my knees and parting her pussy lips. I slide my tongue against her clit, tasting her sweetness. God, she tastes so fucking good. Unbelievably good. My fingers continue going in and out of her while I stroke and lap at her clit. Her hand covers her mouth, keeping her whimpers at bay until finally she stills around me. I look up, watching her bite her hand while whimpering her release.

She moans between her gasps while I stand, pressing sweet kisses into her neck, her throat. My hands stroke the length of her arms. I can't stop touching her. And I try not to think about how much I really don't want to share her.

***

The memories of that morning keep replaying in my head like a rerun marathon I usually find on the TV. And in no way can I possibly think of anything else. All of yesterday, after our little rendezvous in the shower, I spent locked up in my room to keep myself from questioning Rachel like a little bitch. Even now, the questions are going through my head.

Do you want to do it again?

What does this mean?

Do you hate me or do you like me?

But at the same time, all of yesterday I found myself asking similar questions of myself.

Why did I do that?

Do I want to do it again?

Do I hate her or do I like her?

"Psst," someone whispers to me, swatting my shoulder. I scowl in his direction, but he only scowls back. "Can you please stop that?" he asks while pointing at my pencil, which I've been tapping furiously against my desk. "I'm trying to pay attention."

I sigh and instantly drop it, watching it roll toward me. It drops into my bag. I rub my chin and try to read whatever the professor is writing on the board, but my mind returns to Rachel's moans and the water glistening on her skin.

Does she want to do it again?

I bounce my leg up and down and press a hand over my mouth. *She could've left and she didn't. Why? Why did she stay? Had she been thinking about the kiss? I mean, she must have been thinking about the kiss.*

Or was she trying to get out of the contract?

I scowl as I remember my drunken encounter with Rachel at the game. *Well, she did want to leave so sleeping with me would be a good start.* "Fuck," I mutter when I bang my knee against my desk. All eyes turn to me and I meet each of them with a dark look. *So, what if she wants to leave,* I tell myself. *She knows the rules so one down. Two more to go.*

But do I really want her to go? Especially when I want to do it again.

"Alright, class is dismissed," says the professor and I bound from my seat and nearly sprint toward the door, throwing it open and striding down the halls toward the exit.

Should I tell the boys? I wonder while digging into my pockets and looking through my phone. There's a message from Millie, which can wait. None from Rachel, but then again I don't think she has my phone number. Why would she need it anyway?

But should I tell them?

I bite my bottom lip. I can't deny that a part of me really doesn't want them playing around with her. And we haven't even laid out the terms of what sex really entails. *There wasn't penetrative sex. There was just some playing around. She got off. I got off.*

I imagine Rachel and Lucas together. Rachel's mouth pressing against Lucas's lips while he's shoved up into a tree. The way his hands wrapped around her. I shove my phone into my pocket. They don't need to know anything.

I step out into the sunlight and walk down the small paths toward the college town. I smile while memories of Rachel seep back into me and I remember how she smiled at the various places I took her in town.

I take the small camera she loaned me out of my bag and snap a picture. I look at the display. It's not so bad. Not as good as Rachel's photography. I think of showing it to her later, wondering if she will be happy I'm giving the whole art thing a try. Maybe she will even smile at me, lean over my shoulder and nuzzle her cheek against mine while giving me a few key points of advice.

I scowl. *Stop thinking about her,* I tell myself. *Just stop it.*

Chapter 17

HUNTER

I stalk home, holding my bag in my hands rather than over my shoulder. It still fucking hurts. My hand is getting better, but practice fucking sucked. I wasn't able to do anything other than run a few laps and watch the fucking scrimmage. This is really going to set me back. Forget my hand, my shoulder is completely fucked. I can't even put my bag on it let alone throw.

What am I going to do?

I'm supposed to be a football star. The NFL is already looking for the best players. It's my junior year. I shouldn't be sitting on the bench. I should be out playing. What's Mom going to do if I don't get onto a team after I graduate? I stop in front of my door and rummage for my keys in my pockets. I hiss when I move my shoulder just the slightest bit and groan when a packet of my painkillers slide out, landing on the cement. I groan, slowly reaching for them with my good shoulder. I pick up the packet and stare at them, my body urging me to take just a few. Just one. I need just one. I shake my head. No. I don't need that on top of everything else. I need to get better, not just numb my pain. If I don't get better...

How am I going to be able to pay for Mom's chemo?

I push the key into the door and kick it open. My gaze lands on Rachel standing in the kitchen washing dishes and I scowl. I'm really not in the mood to deal with her. Are those my dishes?

She opens her mouth while her hand scrubs at leftover egg.

"I'm cleaning fucking nothing," I say between clenched teeth while kicking the door close behind me.

"Oh," she breathes, still watching me with wide green eyes. She's dressed in black leggings and thick knee-high grey socks with an oversized, high necked blue-green sweater. The sleeves are baggy and she continues pushing them over her elbows. "Is everything—"

"Just leave me the fuck alone," I mutter, shaking my head and biting down another surge of pain going up my shoulder and through my neck.

I stomp through the flat, ignoring her eyes on me and make it to my room, slamming the door shut. I drop my bag and lean my head against the door. I'm just feeling sorry for myself. Coach decided to bench me after it was apparent I could do nothing and now I'm taking it out on anyone who gets in my way.

I close my eyes and release a groan. This wouldn't be happening if I got a physical therapist last year when I was initially injured. Sure, the hand is definitely broken. There's nothing that will fix that for now except for time, but my shoulder. That could've been dealt with last year and I wouldn't be in this downward spiral of asking coach for drugs every game.

Just the look he gave me today when I asked him again.

"That's for game day, son," I remembered him saying to me, giving me that disdainful look. Like I was some drug addict looking for my next fix.

I shiver, remembering the shot they gave me on game day, how it instantly took all the pain away. I cringe. What the hell have I come to? I'm not a junkie. I'm a football star.

This isn't how I planned for everything to go.

I stride over to my bed and fall into it. I gaze up at the ceiling. I should probably go to class, but what's the point? I'm so far behind on everything. I'll probably fail this semester, like all the others. Which never mattered, because I was playing. I have my plan and all.

But what if I fail?

What if I can no longer play?

What am I going to do then?

I can't think about this shit anymore, I decide while pulling out my cellphone and search through my contact list. I stop when I find Millie's name and send an eggplant emoji with a question mark. She'll help me take my mind off this. A good fuck is all I need. I stare at the three dots, waiting for some sort of estimate of time.

I scowl when I read: Too busy. At practice.

I scoff. "Well, good for you." I toss my phone across the bed and stare up at the ceiling. I don't know what I'm expecting. She's a fuck buddy. Not a friend. Not a girlfriend. I shouldn't expect her to drop everything just to be with me, or take care of me. Hell, she wasn't there when I broke my hand so why should she be there for me now?

Three knocks pull me from my thoughts and I lift my head just when the door creaks open and Rachel pops her head inside. "Hi," she says while entering a little further, pushing my bag to the side. She looks around briefly, sniffing at the mess and probably the sweaty odor. "I was able to scrounge up some cucumber sandwiches." She shows me a plate with several mini sandwiches cut into triangles. "I was wondering if you would like some."

I grimace at the small sandwiches. Cucumber what? "I'm not hungry," I say, while rolling around onto my good shoulder and facing the window.

"That's fine." I hear her set the plate onto my desk. "Are you okay? Do you want to talk about it?"

I roll my eyes. "All I want to do right now is fuck, psycho bitch."

"Are you sure?" Her voice is so fucking aggravating. It's all hesitant and filled with pity. "You seem like you could—"

"Just go the fuck away," I say while punching the bed. "I don't want your pity. I want to be left the fuck alone."

I wait for her to say something stupid, or to insist, but instead the door closes. I sigh. I'm not surprised. It's for the best anyway. I don't want anyone's pity. The way the coach stares at me, my teammates, hell, even my friends are driving me so fucking crazy. Yeah, I got hurt. Yeah, all my dreams and plans are going up in flames. Doesn't give any of them the right to treat me as if I'm going to shatter at any point.

Even though I just might.

The door opens and slams into the wall and I jump, cringing as another jolt of pain goes up my shoulder when I whip my head around too fast. Rachel stands in the door frame with a pair of my tennis shoes scowling at me.

"Just what the—" I hold up my arms as she throws the shoes at me, completely missing me.

"Put those on!" she shouts while crossing her arms. "And get on your coat. We're going for burgers."

"But—"

"Move!" She turns on her heal.

I blink while I slowly bend down to pick up my shoes, completely stunned. Just what the hell got into her? And is she planning on feeding me poisoned burgers? I shove my feet into the shoes, not even bothering to untie them or lace them properly. I'm too afraid what she's going to do to me if I take my sweet time.

"Hurry up!" she shouts from the living room.

"I'm coming," I call back, biting down the urge to smile.

***

I watch Rachel throw back her head and moan, totally spellbound as she continues to chew her hamburger while we sit outside the burger joint. There's a red and white plaid umbrella above us while we sit in at a wooden picnic table on the sidewalk. The other picnic tables don't have their umbrella's up, but then again most normal customers would rather sit inside. It's probably a little too cold to be doing this, but the joint was completely full inside and sitting in stuffy air with people shouting over each other while eating this crap is never my thing. Thankfully, the owner was kind enough to give us blankets. Rachel looks all comfy wrapped from head to toe in the big red and white plaid blanket. She's wearing a huge black wool scarf and matching hat to complete the comfy getup.

Cute, I think while watching her chew. *Bossy, but definitely cute.*

"Well, aren't you going to eat?" She motions toward my cheese drenched fries and my giant two patty burger, which I haven't even touched. I've been too engrossed watching this weird art girl eat as if she never had a burger in her life.

"I'm working on it," I say while grabbing a French fry and shoving it into my mouth.

"This is the best," moans Rachel in between bites of her food.

I chuckle. "Don't they have burgers where you're from?"

She shrugs. "Yeah, but this is my first one in Colorado. And it tastes even better after getting paid."

"You sound like Seth."

I notice her cheeks go a bit red at the mention of the track and field star. The way she looks away from me makes me wonder if the idiot did something to her. Again. Well, I can't deny my joy at getting her to clean the flat and drive her crazy, but sometimes Seth really did take things too far. And, I don't even know why. She's cute. Definitely not a big breasted Playboy Bunny hottie, but she's very cute. I'm beginning to wonder if that's my niche. So many guys I know go for big breasts, nice ass, long legs, brunettes or blondes, and sure, I like girls. I like lots of girls. But I'm beginning to think that cute and bossy are definitely my type.

I wonder what Seth's type is? He seems to go for lots of girls, but I've never seen him act so cruel to any of them like how he acts around this girl. I try to imagine Seth making a move on Rachel, but it's hard. Most likely he would just make fun of her, pull her hair and she would respond with some shouting and scowling. *Doubtful that would ever get anywhere,* I tell myself. *But still, she seems completely enamored with her burger. She still refuses to look at me.*

"So, do you want to talk about it now?" she asks, her gaze now pointing daggers at my shoulder.

I sigh and shake my head. "Not really."

"But won't it make you feel better getting it off your chest?"

I raise an eyebrow. "I'm not a little girl."

"And I'm not a psycho bitch," she responds while leaning in close to me.

I really can't stop smiling. "Fair enough." I take a bite of my burger, and it really is good. Usually I eat whatever junk is closest without paying any mind to taste, just so long as it fills me up and keeps my engine running. But this. It really is fantastic.

"See," says Rachel with a dopey smile. "I told you."

I nod. "You sure did." I take another bite and think of my mother, so skinny and small compared to the robust woman she used to be before the cancer hit. I remember her making stuff like this in the kitchen before the disease hit. I remember her singing while she cooked, which would drive me crazy since she was so tone deaf.

I really miss those days.

"Are you okay?" asks Rachel, putting her hand on mine.

I shrug. "I was just thinking about my mom."

"Your Mom?"

I nod. "She's at home now. In remission." I stare down at the ketchup and mustard mess in front of me. "She has breast cancer. Lost both. She's not really... the same."

"But she's okay now?"

"For now," I take another bite. I don't really want to talk about this. The bros know all about my mom, but we never talk about her. We never talk about anything emotional. Just party hard like there's no tomorrow. But everyone has their problems and this thing with my mom has always been like a dark cloud over the group. It just hovers above us, always there yet never mentioned. Just like my shoulder.

"I'm so sorry I didn't know." Rachel's hand slides away and I watch her set down her food and lean back against the bench. She looks off into the distance, her gaze staring at the snowy peaks around us.

"Well, I didn't tell you."

"It must be hard watching your mom go through that."

I hang my head, shaking it slowly. "It's even harder now, not being with her. Knowing she's suffering and I can't do anything for her."

"But she lives in town?"

I nod. "I can't be far from her. Not now. I want to be there for her if anything happens. Dad..." I imagine my father walking into the kitchen while my mom sang, sliding his hands around her waist and pressing a kiss against her cheek. He hasn't done that in such a long time. I sigh, wondering if he's even helping her at home now. "Well, he keeps busy with work. I think it's too difficult for him to be around like he used to. I always hoped I could support her with football."

Rachel makes a face and I laugh. "Football?" she asks.

"Yeah. I want to join the NFL, but with this banged up shoulder, I don't know if it'll be possible."

Rachel looks at my weakened shoulder. "Why would that stop you?"

I chuckle. "You wouldn't understand."

She crosses her arms, her chin jutting out while giving me that defiant look that turns me on so much. "Try me, Hunter."

"Okay," I say hesitantly, trying to put in words what has been on my mind since last year. More like since high school, which is when I planned this whole thing after discovering Mom's illness. "If I want to make it to the NFL I need to be seen. I need to play my hardest, my best. I need to be the fastest, the strongest."

"Like a lean mean fighting machine?"

"Exactly," I say while pointing a fry at her. "And in order for scouts to see that, I need to play. Not be on the bench." I cringe, remembering practice and how I barely played. *I barely did anything today and I probably wouldn't be able to play in the next few games.* "I'm so young and already I have this injured shoulder, making me a liability." I slam my hand down on the table, suddenly agitated by everything screwing up my life. "I'm twenty-one and I'm injured already."

"But getting injured is part of the game. Doesn't every athlete get injured at some point in their career?"

"The thing is," I say quickly. "This injury could shorten my career. Who would want me on their team, knowing my shoulder is probably already wrecked?" I don't wait long for her answer as I say, rather loudly, "No one. No one would want me."

"But can't you fix it?" she asks while motioning toward my shoulder. "There are physical therapists that can help you. And haven't you been playing with it, despite the injury?"

I don't want to tell her about the drugs. I don't want her to know. For some reason, I want her to see me at my best, not as some drugged up football player who needs an injection at the start of every game in order to be able to play.

"Physical therapists cost money," I say instead. "And the only reason why I made it this far is because of my football scholarship. Which I could also lose."

"But shouldn't they have physical therapists on this campus for athletes?" Rachel motions around herself as if they are everywhere.

And since this is a sports college, they probably are everywhere.

I don't say anything, knowing deep down she's probably right.

"I'm sure you can find someone easily," she continues. "They can give you exercises to help with your shoulder."

She stares at me for a moment and I swear her eyes twinkle in the lamplight. I feel like I'm in some harlequin novel. One of the naughty ones Mom used to read. I can't stop looking at the fire in her eyes, the way her hair frames her face or how full and kissable her lips look.

"You shouldn't let this injury break you. You're too young. I'm sure with some work, you can fix your shoulder and get off that bench."

I swear her positivity is infectious, because even now I feel like fighting. I can find a physical therapist tomorrow. I can do exercises. I don't need to give up on my dreams. I look away from her, feeling a smile threatening to spread. "Thank you," I say while standing, offering my arm. I try to ignore my joy when she accepts it. "You've really taken my mind out of the gutter."

She beams up at me, still holding onto my arm with her dainty little hand. "No problem," she says. "I couldn't let a roomie suffer. Even though you are a complete jackass."

I throw back my head and burst into laughter. "I guess I've earned that title. But if you weren't such a psycho—"

"Rachel," she interrupts, levelling a smirk at me. "My name is Rachel." She juts out her chin and purses her lips. I swear if I don't look away now I will kiss her. "You call me Rachel, then I won't call you Jackass Number Three."

"You promise?" I ask while holding out my pinky. "You pinky swear?"

She shrugs while taking my pinky with hers. "Not aloud anyway."

We walk back to the apartment arm-in-arm and I feel like we are leaving a date. *Can I call this a date?* We're laughing. We're talking. It's more of a date than I've ever been on with a woman. Usually, it's drinks and then a quickie in the bathroom, or at someone's place. But, for once I don't really want this to end with a quick fuck and a promise to call later. Actually, I don't want it to end at all. It's nice to know she lives in the same apartment as me since it won't end. I'll see her tomorrow. And the next day. And the next day after that.

So what does all this mean?

Why am I feeling like this?

We stop in front of the door and I watch Rachel take out the keys from her pocket. Her cheeks are still tinted pink. Her hair falls over her shoulder and I find myself pushing it back so I can see her face. She looks up at me, her eyes stunned but not moving away. My hand strokes the side of her face and she leans into my palm.

Does she want this? I wonder while I lean down. She's going up onto her tiptoes, her lips press lightly against mine. They feel soft, just like I expected them to be. I slide an arm around her and pull her to me. I hear the keys jingle as they drop to the ground, but I don't care. She opens her mouth and my tongue hungrily enters. Her hands slide up my front, wrapping around my neck and pulling me toward her as she moans. I gasp as she nibbles on my bottom lip, my cock twitching as she presses her thigh against it.

The kiss is over as quickly as it began and I'm left gasping for breath and wanting for more as she quickly enters the apartment and escapes into her room. I lean against the door, gazing at her room while I rub my lips. I should probably enter, but I'm completely stunned.

Now that was a kiss, I think. Before I return to my room, I secretly wonder how I can get more.

Chapter 18

RACHEL

W hat the hell is wrong with me?
Seriously, what the hell is wrong with me?

First I kiss Lucas, then Seth. Then Seth and I pretty much get down and dirty in the bathroom, and now Hunter. I lean against the door, banging my head against it as I try to wrap my pathetic little brain around this whole week.

Just how did all this happen? Am I really so horny that I will go after the closest thing with a dick, which so happens to be my terrible, asshole roommates? I whip out my phone and send a quick text: MEET ME AT THE CUP IN TWENTY!!!

I wait for a response, the first being Charlie: OOOOH. EXCITED.

Then next being Lauren: OH NO! WHAT HAPPENED?

I shove my cellphone back into my backpack and grab my bag. I open my door, looking both ways to make sure the coast is clear before I tiptoe across the living room. Hoping no one will notice me, I open the door slowly, cringing as it squeaks. I look around myself, wondering if any of the bros heard. No one opens their door. They must be busy sleeping or... sexting or something. Not bothering to risk any more squeaking, I slide myself through the small crack in the door and shut it behind me as quietly as possible.

Next thing I know, I am sitting at The Cup, tapping my fingernails on the table furiously while I wait for the girls to arrive. Unfortunately, my brain takes that time to go over all the crazy events. Over and over again. As if I don't have enough problems on my plate. Between my photography project, work, classes, and surviving my first semester, I did not need 'hooking up with roommates' on my growing list.

The bell on the door rings and I look up, as if I'm some sort of prairie dog, but it's only a couple on a date and not Charlie and Lauren. I grimace. *Oh, God, I really hope they don't bring Josh. I really don't need him thinking I'm a slut. A horny, dirty slut.* I blush as I recall Seth on his knees in the bathroom, or Lucas pressed up against the tree. *God, I am so dirty.*

But it was hot.

Very hot.

"Alright, girl, I need the deets," says Charlie as she comes floating in with several shopping bags on her arms. Lauren is hot on her trails.

"Please tell me you didn't invite Josh," I say before either of them can go up and order a cup of coffee.

Charlie gives me a look. "I didn't see him in the chat. What's up?"

"Yeah," says Lauren while sitting down in the chair next to me. "Did he do something?"

I shake my head, groaning while rubbing my temples. "Maybe it was a bad idea to meet here."

"What's going on?" asks Charlie, sitting down across from me.

I lean in close and the girls copy my movement, eying me with bated curiosity. "I did something stupid," I whisper. "And I need you to promise to keep this to yourselves."

Charlie squeals. "Oh, I am dying to know."

Lauren leans in closer. "What is it?"

"I may have kissed my roommates."

Lauren's eyes widen. "Really?" she whispers. "Which one?"

I shake my head. I really don't want to say it again, but Lauren is just blinking back at me. *She totally doesn't grasp the seriousness of this situation.* "I kissed my roommates," I say again, putting emphasis on the plural part of 'roommates'.

"All of them?" asks Charlie, her voice a bit too loud for my liking.

"Sssh!" I press a finger to my lips. "Keep it down."

"Oh, sorry," she whispers. "So... all of them?"

I nod. "All of them."

"Oh man, girl," says Lauren, her head slightly tilted up while gazing at the ceiling. "What a treat."

I scowl. "What do you mean 'what a treat'?"

Charlie clears her throat. I swear it's in an attempt to keep from laughing as she tries to hide her face from me with one hand pressed against her mouth. "I think Lauren means," she begins, coughing once again, "is that you are one lucky woman."

"What?" I nearly hiss to keep myself from shouting. "How in the world am I lucky?"

Charlie waggles her eyebrows. "Oh, they are hot."

Lauren nods her approval. "Very hot."

"Are they any good at kissing?" Charlie makes a kissing face at me which only makes me blush harder.

Honestly, I was not expecting the conversation to take such a wild turn. I was expecting some slut shaming, maybe a few 'ewws', and some 'what were you thinkings'. Not a high five for a job well done.

"Yes," I say while pushing back my hair, twirling the strands around my finger. "They are all very good kissers."

Charlie nods. "You lucky girl."

"Is that it?" asks Lauren. "Is that the only thing that you're upset about? Kissing isn't a crime, Rachel."

I feel my face heat even more and wonder if it's just going to erupt in volcanic lava at this point. I try to ignore Lauren and Charlie's shared look. "Oh, there's more?" asks Charlie while both of them lean in.

I groan and smack my head. "Yes," I whimper.

"Tell us," says Lauren, her hands tapping on the table in excitement. "I gotta know. My love life has been boring lately."

Charlie cringes. "Yeah, mine too. Let us live through you!"

"Sssh!" I shush them again while looking around. I grimace, noticing several people are looking our way before leaning in. "Seth and I may have shared the shower the other day."

Both girls gasp. "No!" they say in unison.

I nod. "And we didn't really... wash up."

Lauren smacks the table several times while Charlie covers her mouth. They look at each other and squeal.

"Sssh!" I shush again. Everyone in the cafe is looking at us as if we've all sprouted several heads.

"Wait, so who do you like more?" asks Lauren.

I shrug. "I don't know. I don't think I can answer that."

"Well, you must like one of them the most," says Lauren.

Charlie waggles her eyebrows at me. "Unless you like all three equally."

I grimace. "How is that even possible?"

Charlie shrugs. "It can happen. It's not like you have to choose these days."

Lauren chuckles. "Oh, Charlie. Knowing you, you would keep all of them for yourself now, wouldn't you?"

Charlie glances over at me. "Which is why, Rachel, I'm going to give you the same advice I would give myself." She flips her hair over her shoulder. "Go for all of them. Who cares?"

I open my mouth to say something but Charlie holds up her hand.

"It's the twenty first century," she continues. "Relationships can be whatever you want them to be." She shrugs. "Why not just enjoy your time with them and see where it goes. And if you still can't choose, there's nothing wrong with having a little harem for yourself, now is there?" She waggles her eyebrows at me.

I scoff. "I don't know if I can do that."

Although, I find it very difficult not thinking about them in my bed. All three of them with their big arms and their toned abs, treating me like a goddess. I imagine Hunter nuzzling my neck, stroking his hands up and down my leg while Lucas lies between my legs, sucking and licking my womanhood. In my dream Seth is on my other side, cupping my breasts while hungrily kissing my mouth.

I smile wickedly while Charlie and Lauren go on about how annoyed they are with the men in their lives. It's hard to pay attention with such wanton thoughts running through my head and I really wonder if having such a harem is a possibility.

***

I return home from an annoyingly long day at school. And I am absolutely exhausted. I push the door open with my shoulder while I shuffle through. I've been up since six in the morning going over my pictures, attending English and math classes, discussing my theme with art students out of my friend group, studying at the library, checking my work schedule, and now all I want to do is throw myself into bed and stay there for the rest of the night.

When I look inside I see Hunter drying the now clean dishes, Lucas setting up boxes of pizza on the table with a single flower sitting in a small glass of water. The entire place is clean. Still. It's actually a miracle it hasn't gone back to the disaster it was before. The bros turn toward me, smiling in unison while halting whatever it is they are doing.

Just what am I looking at right now?

It's like the bros have turned themselves into the Stepford wives. And I can't decide yet if it's creepy or not.

"Hey, welcome home," says Lucas, striding over to me and handing me a pristine plate. "Want some pizza?"

"Yes," I say tentatively, taking the plate and walking very carefully toward the table. Just what are they planning? Are they going to dump the pizza all over me? Did they do something terrible to my room? And where is Seth? A part of me wants to go to my room and see if he is waiting there with destroyed film everywhere, but then again that doesn't make any sense. Especially when Seth slams open his door and comes running into the living room with the camera I loaned him earlier.

"Hey, Rachel!" He waves the camera with a smile. "I was wondering if you would like a look at some photos I took earlier."

I look around the room as if somehow I have stepped into another realm where people are nice and do nice things. Did I wake up this morning in a dream? Although, that wouldn't explain the exhausting day I had. I take a bite of pizza and nod. "Sure," I say through mouthfuls and motion toward the couch. "I'd be happy to look."

Seth and Lucas sit down on either side of me while Hunter grabs a cushion and sits on the floor. It's like we are one big happy family and I'm not so sure what to think about it, especially since it was only a week ago that we were at each other's throats. Hunter eats his pizza while Lucas throws an arm casually around my shoulder, peeking over it to get a look at the camera. Seth glances back and forth between Lucas's arm and the camera as if he might rip it off and swat both men away from me with it.

"So, I only took a few," begins Seth.

I gasp and swipe the grease on my jeans, taking the camera into both of my hands. "Wow," I breathe while flicking through the display. "You really have captured the light wonderfully." He's taken a few simple pictures of track and field athletes and students going to and from school. Most likely without their permission, which I will have to talk to Seth about probably in the coming days. It's not so polite to just take pictures of people without asking them. However, he really captured the beauty of Aurora in the morning. Most likely he took it during his run.

"Wow, Seth," says Lucas, taking the camera from me. "I didn't think you had it in you."

Seth scoffs. "I can be artsy when I want to."

Hunter glances at the picture and nods his head. "Artsy," he murmurs. "I'd like to see some of your pictures sometime." Hunter glances up to me and my gaze dips to his lips, recalling our kiss from the previous day outside the apartment.

I clear my throat and nod. "Sure," I say, taking a bite of pizza to ensure I don't say anything stupid.

There's a buzz and Lucas takes out his phone from his jean pocket, looking down at the screen while Seth takes the camera back from Hunter. "How has your project been going anyway?" asks Seth while turning off the camera.

"Definitely better. You really helped."

Seth graces me with a smile and I instantly recall the look he gave me when he asked whether or not I was going to shower with him. His moans echo in my head and I shift uncomfortably on the couch.

Is it just me or is it getting hot in here?

"Millie messaged me," says Lucas. His thumb hovers above his phone while he stares down at it like it's an SAT test and he's stuck on a math question.

"Oh, Millie," says Hunter while nodding his approval.

"You're still sleeping with her?" asks Seth.

Lucas casts a dark glare in Seth's direction. "Aren't we all?"

Seth shrugs. "I guess."

I really have nothing to add to this conversation so I stand from the couch and place my plate on the counter. *It's none of my business who they sleep with,* I tell myself, but despite knowing all that is true I'm still getting pissed Lucas is getting text messages from Millie after our kiss. Or that Seth pretty much admitted to sleeping with her even though he hooked up with me.

But why am I getting upset? None of us are in a relationship. They can sleep with whomever they want. Even if the girl happens to be a stupid, mean, cruel bitch. Doesn't matter to me whatsoever.

"So, should I go?" I hear Lucas ask.

I'm actually surprised they don't all hoot and holler and go on about her big tits. Seth shrugs and Hunter nods, but no one really says anything. Lucas looks around the room before his gaze catches on me.

"Well?" he asks, without saying who exactly he is talking to.

I shrug. "Up to you, man," I say, cringing out my attempt to sound like a bro.

Lucas smiles. Hunter chuckles, shaking his head. He slowly stands and looks around the room. "Alright, who's coming with me to Tom's house party?"

I shake my head. "I have my project."

"I need to... study," says Seth without looking at anyone in particular.

Lucas raises an eyebrow. "Study?" he asks. "You actually study?"

"Now I do," says Seth, quickly leaving the couch and striding back into his room. "Now, if you don't mind me, you fuckers," says Seth, opening the door to his room and standing in the threshold, "I have some studying to do." He slams the door shut behind him.

Lucas and Hunter give each other a look before getting up and shoving on their shoes.

"Are you sure you don't want to come with us?" asks Hunter.

"It might be fun," adds Lucas.

I shake my head, smiling and waving at them. "You go on ahead. Maybe next weekend."

I hear the door click while I finish cleaning the kitchen. I put the pizza box in the refrigerator and stride toward my room. Before I enter, I see Seth standing in his doorway out of the corner of my eye. He watches me, looking me up and down for a moment and my face heats noticing the want in his gaze.

"Do you want to study together?" he asks, a book in his hand while he pads toward me.

I shrug, entering my room, but keeping the door open. He follows me inside, kicking the door closed behind him and stands in the middle of my room, looking around, possibly wondering where to sit. I pat a spot next to me on the bed and he quickly walks over, sitting himself closer than expected.

"So did you really want to study, or did you just want to talk?" I ask while digging through my bag, finding my camera. We haven't talked much since our time in the shower and, though I've been keeping up with my running schedule, I notice he hasn't invited me to go with him since the first time.

Seth opens his book. "Why did you stay?" he asks while not looking up.

I shrug. "Why did you offer?"

Seth chuckles. "I thought you would run away."

I smile. "I didn't."

Seth snaps his book closed and leans toward me. I remain rooted in my spot, staring into his eyes. He's so close. His breath is on me. His lips just centimeters away. And I want him to kiss me. I want to do more with him, and it scares me acknowledging I would ever want anything to do with this asshole.

"No," he breathes. "You didn't."

I stare at him, waiting for him to say more, to do something. But he just stares at me. As if he's trying to memorize my face. His hand strokes my cheek with the backs of his knuckles. I release a breath I didn't know I was holding and he licks his lips. His hand slides to the back of my head. He leans into me as I allow him to pull me toward him.

His lips brush mine lightly, hesitantly, as if he's too shy to ask for more. I press my lips against his, my tongue stroking and urging him to open for me. He moans softly as his mouth slackens and I move myself closer, deepening the kiss and stroking the fires inside him. His hands stroke my hair away from my face. They cup my cheeks and pull me closer. I move my legs so I'm straddling his waist.

He quickly pulls away. "This is so weird," he whispers. His face is tinted pink.

"Yeah, it is," I say. His hands stroke up and down my thighs several times before he reaches around and cups my ass, pulling me so I'm on my knees straddling him. My mouth lingers just above his. "Are you going to be an asshole to me after this?"

He chuckles. "Probably."

I decide I don't care as I push him down on my bed. In my lust, I find myself growing more forward. He gazes up at me in shock and wanton desire. His fingers slide underneath my shirt, playing with the lining of my bra.

"Is this what you want?" I whisper while pulling at his shirt.

He pulls his shirt all the way off, throwing it into a heap at the foot of my bed while I unbuckle his jeans. "Yes," he says, his voice hoarse. "This is exactly what I've been wanting."

I claim his mouth with mine and his hands tug at my shirt, pulling it off my body before going to my bra clasps and unhooking it. My breasts spill out and he cups them, enveloping and sucking lightly on one nipple. I gasp, digging my hands into his hair as I toss my head back in bliss. His hand slides down the length of my back to cup my ass, tugging my pants down. I undo them and he continues tugging while the other slips inside my panties, dipping into my wet entrance while his thumb strums my clit.

I arch against him, whimpering and moaning my need while he continues to suck and toy with me. His hand pulls my panties down, cupping my bare ass and pulling me toward him. My fingers slip under his waistband to stroke his leaking tip, twitching and begging for attention.

He moans, halting his movements as my hand circles around him. I give him a gentle jerk. A whimper escapes his lips and he thrusts himself into my hand. "I brought condoms." His voice trembles as he says the words in my ear and I push away from him, looking down at his pink tinted cheeks, his pleasure soaked gaze, drunk on want and need. His hair is going in all directions. His lips swollen with desire.

I smile down at him, pushing back his hair. He takes my hand and kisses the palm, his cock twitches in my other. I jerk him again and he shudders. With one more he moans. I feel so powerful having him like putty in my hands. "Well, what are you waiting for?" I whisper into his ear. "Put it on."

Seth moves quickly, pulling down his pants and underwear. Digging into his pockets, he finds a condom and rips the package open with his teeth. I stare down at his cock. He's so big and hard. It makes me even more wet knowing he'll be pounding it inside me. As soon as the condom is on, he leans back on my pillows, waiting for me as I crawl on top of him. I lean forward, as if I'm going to kiss him. He opens his mouth, waiting for me, but I lean back before he can capture my lips. He growls and grabs my hair, pulling me back toward him and slamming his mouth against mine, stroking my tongue with his while his hand slides down to play with my clit. I angle his cock at my entrance. He bites his bottom lip as I slowly sink down on top of him, a hoarse gasp escaping him as I take him all in. I run my hands through my hair, putting on a good show as I rock my body and ride him.

"This is," he shudders again, "so good."

I capture his mouth, kissing him hungrily. He flips us over and grabs my leg, lifting it over his shoulder and angling his dick deeper, pounding it into me harder than before. I gasp. My fingernails dig into his thighs as I meet each thrust. His gaze remains on mine. My gasps turn to moans and then shrieks as he continues pounding inside me. His mouth slackens, a hoarse moan escaping his lips.

"More!" I shout while lifting my other leg over his shoulder. My heels dig into him as he thrusts deep inside.

He grabs my hands and pushes them down into the bed, gripping them painfully as he continues to thrust into me. "Do you like that?" he says between gasps.

"Yes," I whimper, turning my head away.

He mouths my neck, his teeth grazing against the sensitive skin. I arch my back, pressing myself against him. I feel as if I'm flying. Higher and higher up. My legs tighten around him and I don't know how much more I can take. He stills above me. Lifting his head, he moans, "I'm going to come soon." He thrusts into me again and I groan. "Please, tell me you're close."

I nod. "Don't stop," I whimper, meeting each of his thrusts.

He slides his hand between us, a finger stroking my clit as he continues thrusting inside me, going faster and faster. My moans grow into shrieks and then suddenly I'm gripping him, screaming his name over and over again as he shouts his release.

Seth falls on top of me, his head nuzzling my shoulder while he mouths my collar bone. I gasp, stroking circles on his back.

"That was amazing," he says between mouthfuls of air.

I nod. "Yeah," I breathe, but worry digs into my dreamlike state and I wonder what life will be like with the roommates now that I've actually slept with one of them. Am I the next Millie? Will they shuffle me around for a bit until they finally tire of me?

Seth nuzzles my shoulder, breathing me in as he continues kissing me. He lifts his gaze up, pressing his lips against mine. Already I feel him hardening against my leg. "I have another condom," he whispers while looking away. "Do you want to do it again?"

My hands slide up his arms and I angle myself so he's sliding his wet dick against my clit. "Yeah," I whisper into his ear, smiling when I feel his dick twitching against me.

Who cares about all that, I tell myself, kissing him hungrily while wrapping my legs around his waist. *I'll worry about it tomorrow.*

Chapter 19

LUCAS

I sigh as I walk home. The party was completely boring and I just wasn't in the mood for Millie. I groan and rub my head wondering what is wrong with me. She was so available for the taking in her short skirt and low-cut tank. And those boots, I look up at the sky. Thigh high and so sexy. I imagine doing her, completely naked with just the boots on. It would have been so easy. Yet, I couldn't stop thinking about Rachel and that kiss we shared at the tailgate. I had wanted more, but things had become so busy with rowing.

Not to mention, her door is always shut these days.

I wonder what Rachel would look like in thigh-high boots, I think while unlocking the door and entering. I pause in the doorway as I hear moaning sounds coming from down the hall. I smirk. *Studying huh?* I think while I glance at Seth's door. I stride toward it, trying to listen in and figure out who it is, but I frown when I realize it's not coming from Seth's room. And it can't be Hunter since he's still at the party, drowning his pain in pills and booze like usual.

I glance down the hall, my eyes widening as I realize the girl screaming her pleasure isn't one of Seth's girls, but is in fact Rachel. *Who the hell is fucking her?* I scowl, thinking of the four-eyes she brought to the tailgate.

Oh please, anyone but that.

I knock on Seth's door, wondering if he saw or heard anyone enter the apartment while I was away. I mean, its fine and all for Rachel to invite over whomever she wants. It's her home, too. But I can't help but worry she's hooking up with someone who's just going to hurt her.

I shake my head. What the fuck am I thinking? I'm not Rachel's guardian angel. I'm barely her roommate. I knock again when no one answers and wait. Something isn't right about this situation. I open Seth's door slightly, the door squeaking on its hinges. I expect to see Seth passed out on his bed. Probably with some chick. But no one is there. And his phone is on his desk. He'd never leave home without that thing superglued to his hand. I look down the hall again. The moans are getting louder. My eyes widen. *No, it can't be.* The guy is moaning now and I grimace. *Could it? Is Seth really in there with Rachel.* I scowl as the guy continues to groan, his tone growing more frantic and I realize that it sounds a lot like Seth.

But why? He hates Rachel.

I waltz over toward Rachel's door and stare at it. She's screaming her release while the guy I suspect to be Seth shouts his. I don't know why I am just staring there, listening to this when I should just go back to my room. I have half the notion to knock on the door. Another part of me wants to storm in there and drag Seth off of her.

Although, I should be glad it's him and not four-eyes.

I sigh and shake my head, striding to my room. With one last glance at Rachel's door, I enter and shut the door behind me with a soft click. I go to my bed, dumping myself in it and leaning back on the pillows.

But there's no way I can sleep.

Really, I should be happy Seth is with Rachel. I've been wanting to hook up with her since we kissed. Every time I recalled that strange day I couldn't help but feel aroused. Her lips had been so soft. She had felt so good in my arms. And I wondered what it would feel like to go all the way with her. If it would feel even better than Millie.

I'm sure Seth will give us all the dirty little details. I'll probably get a message from him soon and Hunter and I can have our turn.

I scowl as I think of Hunter having his way with her. She's a free woman. Neither of us have any claim to her. However, I don't know how I feel about *sharing* her with Hunter and Seth. In fact, I really, really don't want to share her. The thought worries me, since we built these bro rules on the idea that bitches wouldn't come in the way of our friendship.

But possibly Rachel just might.

I hear the door open and realize it's probably Seth leaving Rachel's room.

"So, goodnight," I hear Seth, which only makes my mood darken.

"Goodnight," I hear Rachel whisper.

I imagine her wearing his track shirt as she says the words, which only makes me angrier. The door closes and I hear Seth pad back to his room. And then I wait. I pull out my phone, wondering just what he will say. If she's the best thing he's had all year or a boring fuck. I continue staring at my phone, flipping through social media as I wait, but the bastard hasn't texted anything. Nothing at all.

I restart my phone, wondering vaguely if he sent it and my phone is just acting funny. Really, that wouldn't make any sense, but I don't want to think of the implications of Seth not sending us that text. My phone turns on and I type in the passcode. And then I wait.

I wait.

And I wait.

I open my eyes, not realizing I had closed them. Already the morning rays shine in through my window. But I could care less about morning and the fact that I barely slept at all last night. I search for my phone, finding it face down on my floor. I grimace. The screen is cracked from having fallen. Just wonderful. I wonder about trading it in at the nearest shop while I quickly type in the passcode. I smile when I see I've missed a message and quickly press on the app.

I frown.

It's from Millie.

I MISSED YOU LAST NIGHT.

I roll my eyes and search for Seth's name. Nothing. He sent nothing. The last message was from yesterday, demanding I get pizza. I stand and groan. My head pounds and the world sways, which won't help me at all for today. And I have rowing practice later, which makes me feel even more miserable. I stumble into the kitchen and pour myself a glass of water, guzzling it down while Seth slams the door shut, strutting in and sweating from his morning run.

I smirk at him, waiting for the inevitable. *Maybe he will just tell me in person,* I think, trying to be reasonable. *Maybe Rachel exhausted him so much last night that he just passed out.* The thought leaves me with a very dirty image of Rachel riding Seth so hard her bed breaks, which annoys me more than it should. "Morning," I say casually, despite the prickle of annoyance brimming.

Seth nods at me, gasping while he grabs for a cup and downs several gulps of water. "Morning," he says between mouthfuls. "How was the party? Did you hook up with Millie?"

I shrug. "Party was pretty boring." I don't want to admit to him I turned Millie down. I don't want him knowing whatever is going through my pathetic little head. Especially since I don't even understand what is happening in there. "What did you get up to last night?"

Seth downs another glass of water. I notice he doesn't even bother looking at me as he answers, "Nothing. Just studied and went to bed early."

Fucking liar, I want to yell at him. I clench the cup in my hand, tempted to throw it at him and demand to know the truth. The least he could do is tell me he fucked Rachel. "That's it?" I ask while he strides back to his room.

He shoots me a weird look. "Yeah." I notice he glances at Rachel's door before entering his room. I scowl. *Fucking asshole,* I think as I throw my glass into the sink. Thankfully it's plastic and doesn't shatter into a million pieces. I'm probably being such a drama king right now but it doesn't matter. It doesn't matter whatsoever. Maybe Seth will just message us about it later.

I spend the entire day looking at my phone, waiting for Seth to fess up and tell us he slept with Rachel. And every time I look down at my screen I see absolutely no text messages from him. I see one from Hunter about how he's so hung over from Tom's party. And another from Millie wanting to meet up later. I ignore both. I'm tempted to throw my phone across the room when I see by the end of my English class in mid-afternoon he still hasn't texted us about Rachel. I even go to my rowing practice and fuck everything up, not able to think about anything, but my stupid phone. By the end of practice, not only has my coach asked me if anything is wrong, but I still haven't seen a single text message from that fucking bastard.

I return home, pissed, throwing my bag down on the floor and scowling at the top of Seth's stupid head. I kick the door closed harder than I really need to. It slams shut, rattling the glasses on the counter a bit.

"Fuck, man," says Seth as he turns around in the couch. "What's wrong with you?"

What's wrong with me, you ask? Oh, that you are a fucking little good for nothing liar. "Oh, go fuck yourself," I nearly shout at him. I want to confront him. I want to yell at him and let him know I heard him and Rachel going at it last night. Instead I bite my tongue as Rachel opens her door and strides into the living room.

She looks between Seth and me with wide, concerned eyes. "What's going on here?" she asks.

Seth shakes his head. "Nothing. Lucas was just being an ass," he mutters while flipping through the channels on my TV.

"Oh," Rachel breathes. She smiles at me and I feel like everything around me becomes soft and fuzzy as if I'm in one of my mother's favorite soap operas. "Actually, Lucas, I was meaning to talk to you about something."

"You were?" Seth and I say in unison.

I give him a dark glare while Seth glances back at Rachel, worry all over his stupid face. I smirk. *Oh, so you're worried about Rachel needing something from me. How interesting.*

"Yeah, we got this new product in the store. It's some sort of electrolyte thingy."

I chuckle. "Electrolyte thingy?"

"Yeah, it's called Nuun or something like that," she says while flicking her hair behind her shoulders.

I laugh. "That's not new. And why do you need me?"

Rachel's shoulders slump and I know she feels offended by whatever is that I said. I try to take pity on her and wrap my arm around her shoulder. "I can help, whatever it is."

Rachel smiles up at me. "Well, I was wanting to get some photos for the website and I was hoping to get some pictures of you using it. Maybe I can also get an article out of you about how it helps with your rowing."

Seth scoffs. "You don't need him for that. I can help you."

I give him another dark glare. He glares back at me.

"I want to get more people in the store," says Rachel. I break my staring contest with Seth and smile down at Rachel. *Yeah, Seth. She wants a rower. A rower who doesn't make up rules he's just going to break.* "Not just runners. I think the stuff we sell can be beneficial to everyone in sports."

I nod. "Sounds like a great idea. I'm your man."

I glance over my shoulder at Seth, noticing his frown as he leans against the couch cushions. *He's obviously hating every bit of this.* I smirk. *Well, that's what you get for being a fucking liar.*

"When would be good for you?"

"Never," I hear Seth mutter.

"At the row meet on Saturday," I say.

Rachel nods. "Thank you so much, Lucas."

"It's a date," I add, knowing it will piss Seth off even more. Seth watches me as I stride over to my room. I smirk at him over my shoulder. If he doesn't have to text me about his comings and goings with Rachel, then neither do I.

Chapter 20

RACHEL

I stand at the edge of the river, watching Lucas and his team race each other in the water. If I know absolutely nothing about running, then I know even less about rowing. But Lucas looks absolutely amazing. His thick, muscled arms pull the paddles (or whatever they're called in rowing) back and forth in the water. I'm able to get several amazing shots of him at work.

It's also nice to be away from Seth.

Ever since our night together, things have been strange. It's like he keeps avoiding me and I have no clue what to think about that. That night was amazing. He was amazing. But now he's just treating me as if I'm some sort of leper. Honestly, I really can't be surprised. Seth has never proven himself to be anything more than an asshole.

Although, he did help me with my photography project.

But everything seems to wbe on edge now. Lucas and him seem to be in this ongoing war, yet there's no yelling. No hitting. Nothing to actually show that they are mad at each other. But the energy has changed. They don't talk to each other and both of them cast each other dark looks when they think I'm not looking.

It also doesn't help that Hunter is still going out drinking. He comes in so late in the morning, completely trashed and spends his days sleeping rather than going to classes. At least he's nicer to me. And picks up after himself these days. But I'm really worried about him. I had hoped my little talk with him would help, but it seems like all he got out of it was a kiss. I really don't know what else I can do to help him.

Lucas's boat docks and he jumps out, helping his crew drag it out of the water and back onto land. I watch him speak with his coach.

His strong hands shake his opponents'. It's a typical autumn day, yet he's only wearing shorts and a long-sleeved shirt, which hugs his muscled, perfect body. He's very hot. So totally hot. Hunter and Seth are hot, as well, but Lucas looks like a freaking European model. Meanwhile, here I am, standing in jeans and a leather jacket, wondering if I should have brought my big fluffy scarf.

He strides over to me, slicking his wet hair back with a smile that should be criminal. I try to think of something, anything to say to him. Unfortunately, I have no clue what just happened in his rowing meet thingy. So I smile and say, "That was great."

"Did you get anything useful?" he asks while pointing at my camera.

I nod dumbly and pick it up as if I just noticed I was carrying it. "Yeah, I got several great shots. Did you, um, win?"

He chuckles and wipes the water from his face with his shirt. "Yeah, you could say that. Do you need any other photos?"

I flip through the display on my camera seeing pictures of him holding the Nuun bottle, putting the powder into his water bottle, drinking it, as well as several photos of him rowing. "I'll just need a close-up photo of you and some questions answered for the blog," I say while smiling at him, hoping I don't look like a complete idiot.

He nods. "Sounds good. We could go rowing. Might make for a better picture."

"Are you sure? You're not tired?"

Lucas shakes his head. "Not at all." He looks up at the sky. "It's a beautiful day. Would be a shame to waste it."

I nod and follow him toward a smaller boat in the dock. He helps me inside and I sit on the seat as he enters, holding onto the rims as the boat rocks with his weight. He grabs the paddles and rows us out into the middle of the river. "So, what questions do you need answered for your little blog?" he asks while I take a few close-up pictures of him.

I look at the display and smile at what I see. He really is handsome. "What got you into rowing?"

Lucas shrugs while he paddles. "It was just something to do. My parents are the fancy type. I wasn't really into polo or football. So I chose rowing." He turns toward me and smiles. "It relaxes me."

I nod. "Yeah, Seth said something similar about running."

Lucas halts his rowing and leans toward me. My breath hitches as he smirks down at me. He really is handsome. "So, what exactly is going on between you and Seth?"

I swallow. I have no clue how to answer that question, because I don't even know myself. "Nothing," I say, looking away and pulling my jacket closer around me.

"One minute the both of you are fighting and the next you're sharing photos as if you're besties."

I raise an eyebrow at him. "The same could be said about you."

Lucas scoffs. "Hardly."

"One minute you're mean to me and the next you're kissing me."

Lucas pokes my nose and says, "You mean you're kissing me."

I shrug. "Well, you weren't pushing me away."

Lucas chuckles and leans in closer, the paddles completely forgotten. "Would you push me away if I kiss you now?"

A part of me tells me to stop this. I just slept with Seth. I don't need to be playing around with Lucas. But then I hear Charlie in my head, her words echoing over and over again: *just enjoy your time with them and see where it goes. There's nothing wrong with having a little harem for yourself.* My eyes rake down Lucas's form, taking in his big strong arms, his built torso, and I wonder how it would feel to be in his arms. *Charlie really is a bad influence.*

I lean toward him, my nose lightly stroking his. "I don't think so," I whisper, my gaze dipping down to his lips.

It's slow at first. The soft press of lips against lips and it feels as if he's breathing me in. A hand comes to stroke my cheek while the other is pulling into him. I turn my head, my mouth opening. I moan as his tongue slips inside. My hands wrap around his neck, pulling him closer. He moans and pushes one leg open so I'm straddling his torso. I pull him down over me, moaning and gasping as the kiss grows with need. He strokes my arms, massaging my shoulders while I grind myself against him, igniting more moans from his lips. My hands play with his waistband while his travel underneath my shirt, sliding underneath my bra to fondle my breasts. My back arches and I gasp with wanton need.

I'm pulling at his shirt, but my gaze catches on the sky above me and I push myself up, suddenly very aware of where we are right now. I look around the river, wondering if anyone is watching us, but there are no other boats around.

"What is it?" Lucas breathes. He kisses my neck, mouthing it before raking his teeth down. His head nuzzles against me.

"I don't think—" He kisses me, swallowing whatever it is I'm about to say. His hands palm my back while his tongue continues stroking me, igniting dark desires whispering insidious thoughts into my head. *There's no one around. You could have a little fun out here...*

We are out in the open. What if someone sees us?

I break the kiss and press my fingers against Lucas's mouth when he goes to reclaim them. "I don't know if now is a good time," I say, my gaze dipping down and blushing at the obvious tent pitched in his shorts.

He kisses my fingers, sucking on the tips for a moment and I really wonder what that tongue can do in other places. *No, no, no!* "Lucas," I hiss, taking my fingers away from him.

He sighs and shakes his head. "Sorry, I'm just so turned on right now." He motions toward his pants and chuckles. "As you can see."

I bite my bottom lip and turn around, scooting my back closer toward him. I rub my ass against him and he stills, his head dropping into my shoulder. "That really isn't helping," he moans while his hands wrap around me and hold me against his chest.

"Do you think you can get off like this?" I ask, tilting my neck as he places hungry kisses on my neck.

"I think so," he murmurs. There's some shifting behind me and he takes my hand and presses his warm dick against my palm. Gripping his hard man flesh I blush and look around again, but no one is nearby. The angle is awkward, but it should be doable.

I stroke his tip, earning another hiss from him as he continues licking and sucking on my neck. It'll probably leave a hickey, but the pleasure he's giving me makes me not care about a love bite I can cover up easily. His hands rub against my groin, covered by my jeans.

I lean into him and toss my head back while his other hand slides under my shirt and toward my breasts. His fingers play with the underwire of my bra and I feel myself growing antsy as I wait for him to slip those fingers against my flesh. I hear a zipper and realize he has undone my jeans. His fingers press against my underwear and I moan, arching my back and needing more.

His lips find mine, silencing my moans as he continues stroking me up and down. I whimper as his other hand slides under my bra and against my nipple. He pinches and I gasp. I rub my ass fervently against his hard erection behind me while sliding my tongue against his. He moans and sucks his tongue while tugging on my nipple and I break away from the kiss, quickly looking around before turning my body toward him and straddling him.

Who cares if anyone sees us, I think while his fingers unbutton my jeans and pull them down, exposing my underwear to the world. I gasp when he slips inside my underwear and strokes my clit. His teeth tug up my shirt to mouth my breasts. In response, my strokes on his dick quicken. The boat rocks around us and I feel the light trickles of water splashing as he thrusts into my hand. I toss my head back as he continues ravishing my breasts with soft kisses. I nearly cry when his hand pulls away from my clit to pull down my bra, taking a nipple into his mouth to suck adamantly.

His dick throbs in my hand and as I gaze down at his dark hair, I wonder what it would feel like to have him deep inside me.

But I don't have any condoms.

I tap at his shoulder. "Lucas." I gasp when his finger circles around my clit. "Lucas," I breathe when he doesn't answer me. I bite back a moan as his finger slips inside me, going in and out before he slips in another. I rock against him, meeting each thrust of his fingers. But it's not enough. I want more.

I want him.

"Lucas," I say while pulling him away from me. He releases my nipple, pulled taut partly by him, partly by the chill in the air. He gazes up at me with pleasure drunk eyes.

"What?" he asks dazedly.

"Do you have a condom?"

Lucas grimaces and I realize sadly that I have my answer. "Sorry," he mutters. "I didn't really think that far ahead."

I nod and pull him to me, biting his lips and entangling my tongue with his. He moans as I kiss him slowly. I stroke my tongue against his. My hands stroke the back of his head and when he pulls away, I say, "It's fine." I stroke the tip of his cock and he stills. Precum leaks from his slit while I lean over him. "Next time then," I say while I take his mouth again and pump my hand up and down his long shaft.

Lucas moans, kissing me while slipping his fingers back inside. He thrusts his dick in my hand as I continue jerking him up and down, paying great attention to the sweet spot at his tip. I whimper as he continues pushing his fingers in and out of me, quickening with each thrust into my hand. His moans grow louder as his arm pulls me to him.

I hold onto him, meeting each thrust of his fingers and wanting more. Needing more. His thumb circles around my clit. The pleasure is so good I can feel myself getting there, nearing that peak; nearing that cliff dive into sweet bliss.

Lucas's lips slip away from mine and he tosses his head back, moaning as his body stills and his cock thrusts fervently into mine. With one last shout, echoing across the water around us, his body stills and I feel his cum smear all over my hand. He gasps, holding on to me as he attempts to catch his breath. His body shivers under me. His head lulls to the side and his body grows slack.

I pull away from him, washing the stickiness into the river and looking around to see if anyone heard us, but we are so far out. *Even if someone did see us, I doubt I would be able to see them.* A pleasurable shiver runs down my spine as Lucas's fingers continue toying with me. I gaze down at him with a smile while he strokes my clit slowly, adding more and more pleasure.

"Are you close?" he asks, pulling me back toward him and looking around as if he's just noticing we are outside and not anywhere private.

I shake my head. I had been close, but now I don't know if I could get off as easily as before. "Not at all. But its fine," I add quickly.

Lucas frowns. "No, it's not." He looks around again before pushing me down in the boat.

I chuckle and push myself up on my elbows so I am in a half sitting, half lying down position. Lucas is tugging my pants and underwear down while looking around like he's some sort of international spy. "Really, it's okay," I say. "I don't want us to get caught."

Lucas scoffs. "We're not going to get caught." He looks up at me, his mouth hovering above my womanhood. "Do you want me to get you off?"

I nod. "Yes, please." I cringe at how stupid I sound.

However, whatever worries I have about sounding stupid completely leave me as my thoughts are soon replaced by his mouth, licking and sucking on my clit. I lay back down in the boat and gaze up at the clouds. My hands stroke his hair while his tongue works wonders on me.

"You are so fucking sexy," he murmurs between kisses.

I groan, my legs trembling around him. His tongue continues stroking me while his fingers go in and out, slowly and deeply. He sucks me gently and my legs shiver as I try to keep myself from crying out. *He's bringing me closer,* I think while arching my back. *His tongue really knows what it's doing.*

"You like that?" he asks.

I grip fistfuls of his hair and nod. I can feel myself peaking and spiraling upwards toward release.

He pulls away from me and I gasp, lifting myself up to scowl at him. "I can't hear you," Lucas taunts while waggling his eyebrows.

I moan as he bites the inside of my thigh.

"I want to hear you, Rachel."

I moan when his tongue flicks against my clit. He does it again and I moan even louder, pulling him toward my womanhood.

"Do you like it?"

"Yes," I hiss.

Lucas chuckles and I swear I just might hit him. "I can't hear you."

"Yes," I shout and gasp as he takes me into his mouth, licking and sucking me. I fall back against the boat and moan while thrusting myself against him. He grabs my hips and pulls me closer toward him until my heels are digging into his back.

"Oh my God yes," I gasp as he thrusts several fingers deep inside me. I feel myself peaking again. My moans are getting louder and I try to cover my mouth. Lucas grabs my hands, pressing them back into the boat.

I try to wiggle out of his hold, but I feel as if my body has become muddy against his mouth and I'm unable to move as he continues sucking on me. My moans become shouts and I thrust myself against him as pleasure blossoms within me.

"Lucas!" I scream, clenching my thighs around him and gripping his hands as pleasure washes through me, leaving my body a shivering mess in the middle of the boat. I gasp while trying to regain control over myself, but I feel like a used up rag doll.

Lucas crawls toward me and places a kiss on my lips. "Good?" he asks while smiling down at me.

I try to nod, but my head lulls up and down as I stare up at him dreamily. "Very."

I should really listen to Charlie more often.

***

Maybe I shouldn't have listened to Charlie.

I sit at the cash register. It's a slow Saturday morning. Most likely everyone is hung over from last night's festivities. Or they're too busy at some sort of meet or game to come spend their money on athletic clothes and accessories. It wouldn't be all that bad, but Seth is hiding out in the back.

I'm beginning to suspect he's pretty mad at me for going to Lucas's meet last weekend. It doesn't help that the whole week after hanging out with Lucas and getting my rocks off in his boat, Seth has spent it avoiding my very presence. Like now.

I look up at the clock and groan. It's only been an hour. Three more to go. I sigh and push myself away from the desk. Maybe there's something I can clean around here.

I walk over to the cleaning supplies closet, which is near the back exit and kept separate from the stock room. Which is annoying, because I would give anything to just saunter in there and see what he's up to. Maybe say something along the lines of "How are you, Seth?" I cringe. Most likely he would answer something rude or mean and then I would have to go back to the cash register annoyed.

I grab a broom and begin sweeping at the imaginary dust. It gives me something to do while I obsess over my predicament. I scowl down at the shiny floor. It's not like I did anything wrong with Lucas. Seth and I aren't even dating. He's barely spoken to me since we hooked up and it's not my fault he's feeling all weird and awkward around me. I shouldn't feel guilty about Lucas and Hunter. They're always sharing their girls anyway.

I stop sweeping and stare up at the ceiling. Am I really one of their playmates that they toss around? It doesn't feel that way to me. It feels more like... things are on my terms. That I have a substantial say. Not to mention, Lucas and Hunter are rather sweet.

Hunter has kept up with the cleaning, which has been absolutely fantastic. And Lucas has been an amazing cuddle buddy. Seth... well Seth has been grumpy.

Maybe I sucked in bed. I recall his moans and the way he thrusted deep inside me, his gasps becoming whimpers as he gripped my thighs. It definitely didn't seem like he hated it. It's not like I don't have enough on my plate to worry about. I should be more focused on my photography project. Not obsessing over this nonsense. I don't need to choose between them and if Seth has a problem with it then it's his issue, not mine.

I glance over my shoulder and scowl at the door leading into the stock room. I just hate this silent treatment. It's so freaking annoying. I lean the broom against a shelf full of running belts and compression socks and go over to the store window. Looking back and forth, I see no one in the vicinity of the store and decide now is better than never. I stride toward the back room and slam open the door.

Seth glances up from steaming the new runner's shirts. He looks shocked at first, his gaze softening for a moment before he returns to his work. "What's up?" he asks. "Did a big group come in? Need my help?"

I rest my hands on my hips and stride toward him. *Just ask him, Rachel. You can do it. He's not so big and scary.* My shoulders slump as my courage deflates. He continues ignoring me while running the steamer over the clothes. *Maybe now isn't a good time.*

"I know I'm sexy as fuck, but do you really have to stare, Rachel?" Seth smirks. "I'm actually trying to work here."

Anger ignites through me again and I push my shoulders back, jutting out my chin. I'm tempted to take the shirt and throw it across the room, but that would be childish. "Why are you avoiding me?" Brilliant. Straight to the point.

Seth shakes his head. "I'm not avoiding you."

"You've been acting weird since... that night."

Seth scoffs. "Since we fucked?" He shrugs. "I'm not the type of guy to get all attached after one night." He glances up at me and smirks. "Thought you would realize that by now."

I scowl at him. "Well, if that's all it is then," I say. What else can I do? If all he wanted to do is have sex with me and then dump me, then I should have known better.

I turn on my heel and blink back the tears. I'm not going to let that asshole see me cry. I leave the stock room and inhale deeply while I stride over to the cash register. I look up at the clock. Just two and a half more hours. I can probably draw something while I wait for this terrible shift to end.

"Why do you even care?" I hear Seth ask and I turn around, seeing him following after me. He stares back at me with a dark look. Something else is hidden behind those eyes. Possibly worry, remorse? Although I doubt Seth has the capacity to feel remorseful over anything.

I grind my teeth to keep back whatever sob is threatening to boil. I have to appear strong. I have to appear unbreakable. "I don't." I sniff and inwardly groan. Whatever strength I was trying to exude, it was obviously broken by that.

Seth walks around to the other side of the cash register. "You went to that meet with Lucas," he says while pacing back and forth.

"So?" I shake my head, trying to figure out what exactly he is trying to say. "What does that have to do with anything?"

"You went to Lucas's meet!" Seth shouts while pointing at me.

"Seth—"

"Did anything happen?" Seth stops pacing and strides toward the cash register, his eyes wide and wild. "Did you—"

"Yes," I say. His face seems to break then, like he's about to cry or scream. I look away from him, not knowing what else I can say other than the truth. I can't lie to him. Not about this. "Yes, something happened between us."

Seth doubles over. I lean over the desk. His shoulders are shaking and I reach out to touch him, to provide whatever comfort he needs. I had no clue he would be so upset about this. But my hand pauses as I realize he's laughing. He grips the desk and continues laughing as he leans in close to me, wiping the tears from his eyes.

"What's so funny?" I whisper. Has he completely lost it?

"I guess you really want to leave us now, don't you?"

I step away from him, my ass bumping into the shelves behind me. "What?"

He inhales deeply. His gaze is cold, almost cruel as he stares back at me. "The agreement. You fuck all three of us and you can break the contract. That's what you wanted, wasn't it?"

I shake my head. I had completely forgotten about all that. Things had been nice since that day out. Actually, I was beginning to adjust to the whole bro household. "Seth, I don't want to—"

The bell rings and I straighten myself immediately. "Hi, welcome to—" I stop when I see it's just Hunter, looking around at the place.

Seth glances over his shoulder. "Hunter, what are—"

"Hi, Rachel," says Hunter, smiling while he strides toward me.

Seth barely has time to move out of the way as Hunter leans over the desk toward me. I cringe, feeling Seth's scowl without even having to look. I hear him walk back to the stock room, the door slamming shut.

"What is that all about?" asks Hunter, looking in the direction of the stock room.

I sigh and shake my head. "It's nothing," I say while rubbing my temples.

"I was actually wondering if you would be interested in dinner."

"Oh?" I glance at the stock room, wondering if Seth is hearing all this, but Hunter is speaking rather softly. "When?"

"Maybe tonight?"

I'm already shaking my head. "I have study group tonight."

"Then tomorrow," says Hunter quickly. "Or whenever you're available. Or not. I don't want—"

I chuckle and place my hand on his, instantly stopping him from saying anything else. Actually, I had been meaning to talk with Hunter about his extracurricular activities. His hand is now healed, but everything about him seems more sickly these days. I'm beginning to worry that it's not just football breaking his body down.

"I would love to get dinner with you, Hunter. Maybe tomorrow night?"

Hunter nods and squeezes my hand. "Great. I'll—"

The stock room door slams open and I see Seth wearing his varsity jacket, his backpack over one shoulder, nearly running toward the entrance door.

"Wait, where are you going?" I call after him.

Seth doesn't answer as he swings the door open and leaves.

Chapter 21

SETH

That fucking bitch.

I'm running home. Running as fast as I can. Probably even faster. Anything to get away from her. Rachel and Hunter. Oh, how wonderfully cute they looked. Him, leaning over the counter, gazing at her lovingly while she laughed and twirled her stupid hair.

And the worst thing of all, is that it's all my fault. I told her if she wanted to end the contract suddenly, all she had to do is fuck all three of us. I didn't think the bitch would actually go through with it.

I don't want her to go through with it. I shake my head. I can't think of Rachel. The more I think of her the more upset I get. Which means I'll have to admit something I really don't want to. I care about no one other than myself. Bros before hoes. That's our motto. And Rachel has the ability to destroy everything we stand for.

I slam the door to the apartment open and waltz inside, downing a large glass of water before I kick open my door and dump my backpack onto the floor. I whip out my phone, wondering if a good Millie-fucking is all I need to get Rachel out of my head. Millie with her huge breasts. Millie with her leg over her head. I close my eyes and try to imagine it, yet every time I think of Millie in bed, her face morphs into Rachel beckoning me toward her. Rachel with her head tossed back in sheer bliss. Rachel screaming her orgasm while her nails dig into my shoulders.

Rachel fucking Lucas after his rowing meet.

I grind my teeth to keep from shouting and instead kick the bed, instantly regretting it as pain explodes through my big toe, leaving me hopping up and down on one foot and cursing Rachel's very existence.

She has to go. She can't stay. Not when she's making me feel this way. And she's getting in the middle of me and the guys. I open the chat between Hunter and I and quickly type in: BRO MEETING. STAT.

I wait for a response. Lucas has seen it, but isn't replying while dots are next to Hunter's picture. I scowl down at the screen, just waiting for him to reply that he's too busy with psycho bitch to come.

He better fucking not text that.

Instead, he responds with: WHAT'S IT ABOUT?

My hand clenches around my phone. I type: YOU'LL SEE WHEN YOU GET HERE.

Lucas still hasn't responded and I don't even know if he's coming, which makes me even more pissed off. So he thinks he's too high and mighty to grace us with his presence, huh? I slam open my door. Rage brims through me, about to boil over as I stomp down the hallway toward Lucas's door. I don't even bother knocking as I slam it open, seeing him sitting on his bed while he writes inside his notebook. His phone lying next to him in bed.

"What the hell, man?" he says while pushing himself up, scowling back at me. "Don't you know how to knock?"

"Are you coming to the meeting or what?"

Lucas rolls his eyes. "You must be kidding me."

"Well, are you or what?"

Lucas closes his notebook and throws it onto his bed. "I don't know Seth. What is it about? You being a lying mother fucker or you being a fucking asshole?" I cringe, but Lucas doesn't back down as he strolls over toward me. "So, which is it Garcia?"

Before I can answer the apartment door opens. I peak around the corner, wondering if it's Rachel coming in to yell at me, but it's too soon. She should still be at work. I see Hunter's blond head bent over while he takes off his shoes and hold back the need to roll my eyes. Hunter, taking off his shoes at the door... just what the fuck has Rachel done to us?

"Alright, Seth, what is it?" asks Hunter. I ignore his grimace as he rubs his shoulder.

I give Lucas one last scowl before going into the living room. Lucas follows me and both him and Hunter sit down on the couch, gazing up at me as if I've completely lost it. Which in all honesty, is definitely a possibility. I haven't felt this on edge since my track meet senior year of high school which was supposed to decide if I was getting this scholarship or not.

I think my issues with Rachel have actually surpassed that amount of stress.

I inhale deeply to calm myself. "It's about Rachel," I say.

Lucas throws his hands up in the air. "Why am I not surprised?" He casts a dark scowl in my direction. "So, are you going to finally tell us you've been fucking her?"

Hunter's mouth opens, but nothing escapes. He glances between me and Lucas in shock. "What?" he breathes finally before settling his gaze on me. "You've been fucking Rachel?"

"Yeah, and he didn't even tell us," says Lucas while motioning toward me.

"Why?" asks Hunter. "I thought—"

"I'm sorry, okay," I say quickly. "I wasn't thinking. I should've told you, but I didn't."

"But you broke bro code rule number one," says Hunter.

Lucas crosses his arms while he nods. "Yeah, he did, Hunter. So Seth," Lucas tilts his head to the side, "you think you get to make up the rules and just break them? Somehow, you think you're better than us?"

I rub my head. "No, it's not that."

"Then what, asshole?" Lucas bounds up from the couch. "You're the one who made the rules," he says while pointing at me. "And now what? You can just break them whenever you feel like it?"

I scowl at Lucas. "Yet, that didn't stop you, now did it, Lucas?"

"What?" Hunter's voice is loud and he jumps up from the couch, sticking himself between me and Lucas. "You also fucked Rachel?" He throws his hands up in the air. "Am I the only one who hasn't fucked Rachel?"

Lucas smirks back at me. "I didn't get my dick wet, but things definitely happened." Lucas leans in. His face so close to mine I could headbutt him easily. I'm still thinking about headbutting him when he has the audacity to say, "So, Seth, what did you think?

Because I thought she tasted pretty good. Thinking up eating up that sweet pussy of hers tonight."

Something within me snaps and I lunge for Lucas, my hands going for his throat. He falls back against the couch, making it slide with a loud screech against the floor. I straddle Lucas, my hands fisting and ready to knock against that stupid face of his when he suddenly flips me over. I hold up my hands to block his punches as he lands blow after blow on me.

"Stop it!" Hunter shouts while grabbing Lucas under his arms and pulling him off me.

I wipe at my face, seeing blood on my hands while Lucas struggles against Hunter's hold. I touch my nose gently, wondering if it's broken, but it seems like I just bit my lip.

"Lucas, stop it!" Hunter shouts again, shaking Lucas slightly.

Lucas inhales deeply. "Fine," he mutters.

Hunter lets him go and Lucas shoves him away. He stares at me darkly, but doesn't move from his spot.

"We can't go on like this," I finally say after a moment of silence.

Lucas nods. "No, we can't."

"I'm sorry I broke the code. I didn't mean for it to happen. I just —"

"Didn't want to share," Lucas says bitterly. He smirks cruelly back at me, but I can't deny it. He's right, I didn't want to share.

I nod while rubbing the back of my head. "I think we need to get rid of her," I say. I don't look at the bros while the words come out, and the second they are out I want to take them back, but then what? We're fighting. Over a girl who should mean nothing to us. Our friendship is more important than this bitch we barely know.

"What?" Hunter asks.

"We need to kick her out," I say again, more firmly. "She's getting in the way. She's ruining our friendship."

"No," says Hunter, but I'm looking at Lucas.

He's not saying anything. He's not even looking at me. "Lucas?"

He shakes his head and turns away from me.

"Lucas," says Hunter, stepping toward him. "Come on. It's not her fault." He glances over his shoulder at me with a dark scowl. "You're such a fucking asshole." He strides toward me then and shoves his finger into my face. "Just so you know, I didn't even fuck her. All I did was kiss her. So are you going to be an asshole to me?"

I sigh and run my hands through my hair.

"We share girls all the fucking time. So why can't we share her?"

Once again that feeling goes through me. That feeling I don't want to admit resides deep inside. "She's..." I swallow the words down and decide to say, "she's just different, Hunter. If she stays, what's going to happen to our friendship?"

Hunter doesn't say anything.

"Fine," says Lucas from the hallway and I release a sigh in relief. "She doesn't have to stay."

I look at Hunter. "Two against one," I say while patting his shoulder. He smacks my hand away and stalks back to his room, slamming it behind him.

***

I stare at my watch. It's 9:00. Just when is she getting home? I want to get this done and over with as soon as possible. Hunter leans against the counter with his arms crossed in front of him. He hasn't said a word to either of us after the decision was made final. Lucas is leaning against the couch, also with arms crossed. Both look upset. But this is for the best. As soon as she's out of our lives, things can go back to normal. I can go back to fucking around and not caring. We can go back to sharing girls without me getting all weird.

Things will be better without Rachel in our lives.

I hear a click and glance at the door, rearranging myself on the couch while I wait for Rachel to walk in. She's carrying several bags and a to-go cup from The Cup. I hate to admit it, but she looks absolutely beautiful with her hair in her face and her mascara slightly smeared under her eyes. She looks exhausted. A part of me wants to bring her back to my room and apologize for the way I acted. Maybe even kiss her.

I grind my teeth. No. This is exactly why I need to get rid of her. She makes me all weird.

Rachel glances up at us, surprise written all over her face as she glances between all three. She chuckles nervously and pushes back her hair. "Wow," she says, "you guys look pretty upset. Did something bad happen?" She dumps her bags down next to her. "Hunter, is your mom okay?"

Hunter bobs his head, but he doesn't bother looking at Rachel. "Yeah, she's fine," he says solemnly.

"Then, what's going on?" She turns to me. "Seth?"

Lucas sighs and runs a hand through his hair. "Yeah, Seth. Do you want to tell her?"

I cringe. Not really. But Hunter won't and I can tell Lucas is about to change his mind about the whole thing. "So, we've been talking," I begin, pushing myself off the couch and walk casually toward her.

Rachel chuckles. "You actually do that?"

I stop the need to retort with something as equally flirty. "We believe you need to find someplace else to stay."

Rachel tilts her head. "Huh?"

"We're kicking you out."

She glances around the room once more. "Are you serious?"

Lucas nods. "Afraid so."

"But... why?"

I sigh. "That doesn't matter now, does it?" I refuse to look at her. Her eyes are filling with tears and if I continue staring at her I know I will take back my words. "It's not working out and you need to go."

"But the contract—"

"Fuck the contract!" I shout while throwing up my hands. "You have to find someplace else to stay. Isn't that what you wanted anyway?"

Rachel looks at Hunter and Lucas. "And you both agree to this?"

I watch my bros, wondering if they will go back on their word, but instead they both nod their heads solemnly.

Rachel inhales a deep, shuddering breath. "I see." She sniffs. "Okay. Fine. I'll have my things moved out tomorrow."

"I can help you," Hunter says quickly, taking a step toward her.

Rachel scoffs while she picks up her things and strides toward her bedroom door. "You can go fuck yourself, Hunter. You can all go fuck yourselves," she says before slamming her door.

Chapter 22

RACHEL

I blink my swollen eyes while I stare around my now empty room. I stayed up the whole night crying and after not being able to get to bed, I spent the rest of it packing up my things. To think I actually hated this room when I first moved in, and now all I want to do is throw a big hissy fit, fling myself into the bed and refuse to budge.

I release a shuddering sigh. I'm about to cry again, but I push it down. I need to leave this place with my dignity intact. I can't let Seth think that he won. That he finally broke me. I swallow a sob as I remember asking him: *are you still going to be mean to me after this?* A part of me feels like laughing at the foreshadowing. Of course he's going to be mean to me. It's Seth. He's always been cruel to me.

Looking back on last night, I actually feel a bit bad for Hunter. I don't think he actually wanted me to leave. The way I spoke to him was cruel. After all, he just wanted to help. I wasn't in any mood to accept help. I'm going to miss him.

And I hate to admit it. I think I'm actually going to miss all of them. Even Seth. Although I have no clue why.

I hear my phone buzz and see that it's Josh: HERE. WAITING FOR YOU OUTSIDE. I smile at the message before tucking my phone into my jean pocket. Amongst the crying and the packing I also messaged Charlie, Lauren, and Josh about the whole ordeal. Charlie was actually shocked I was being kicked out. Lauren felt so bad for me. Josh offered me his couch, which was actually a good start. After a couple more days of crying I can look for an apartment to move into. Hopefully an apartment with girls. Nice girls.

I drag my suitcase behind me and through the apartment, trying to ignore the doors I pass to get to the front. No one comes out to say anything. I shouldn't be surprised. It's not like we actually had anything. I leave my keys on the counter and open the door. The suitcase plops on each stair as I go down. Out of the corner of my eye I think I see Seth in the distance, running back to the apartment. Must be a training day for him.

Ignore it, I tell myself while smiling at Josh waiting for me on the sidewalk.

"You got everything?" he asks, taking one of my suitcases.

I nod. "I think so." I take one last look at the apartment, then turn and follow Josh down the sidewalk.

***

I groan as I shuffle in through the door. It's been a long week and sleeping on Josh's couch has felt like torture. I miss having a proper bed to roll around in. And some privacy. Josh's apartment is so small compared to my old place. And we have to share the key. Not to mention, his roommate recently broke up with his girlfriend and rather than going out and drinking until the early hours of morning, like the bros, all he's wanted to do is obsess over her previous text messages and try to understand what it all meant and if there were any hidden messages in the current ones. Because, you know, women are complex.

I drop my bag down next to the couch and plop myself into it. Women aren't that complex. Honestly, I don't think any of her messages had any secrecy written in between the lines. I think she just wanted to be rid of him, but how can I tell Josh's roommate that without sounding like a jerk? I had my own things to go through and relationship advice is not my strong suit.

I lean back against the cushions and sigh while staring up at the ceiling. It's Friday night and I wonder what the bros are getting up to. Not like it's any of my business. I wonder if they are passing Millie around. If they miss me at all or maybe they're just happy to be rid of me. Maybe they can move another bro in and have a big orgy. Maybe they're using my old room as the orgy room.

I push my hair away from my face. It's not my problem anymore. I take out my phone and wonder if I should message Charlie and Lauren. They invited me to a party earlier today. At the time, I wasn't interested. I was actually wanting to drown my sadness with some ice cream and old rom coms, but now that I'm back in this hell hole, I kinda want to escape.

I should be more grateful.

It's really nice that Josh is allowing me to stay here during all this. I'm sure it's a big hindrance to him as well since he can't use the living room and kitchen however he wants. I've been trying to look into apartments so I don't have to inconvenience him anymore, but everything is all taken. There's nothing available until at least January, and all those places look shady.

"Hey," says Josh while coming out of his room. "What are you up to? Did you just get home?"

I nod. "Yeah. Nothing much. Just worrying about life."

He chuckles and sits down next to me. "It's Friday night. Worry about life later."

I smile at him. "Are you up to anything tonight?"

He shrugs. "Roommate is gone so I want to take advantage of the silence."

I burst into laughter. "Yeah, I hear you there."

"Has he been going on about his girlfriend?"

I nod while laughing. "Way too much."

"Well, apparently he's at a party tonight. She's supposed to be there. He's on a mission to win her back."

I groan. "Oh no."

"Yeah, I think he'll fail, too."

"I guess it's just you and me tonight."

Josh smiles, bobbing his head as he holds my gaze. "I guess so. We could watch a movie if you want. Maybe have some drinks."

"Sounds nice," I say while watching him get up and walk over to the refrigerator. He opens the door, hitting it against the dinner table. Everything's pretty small in the apartment. Even my leg bumps against the table. There's hardly any space to cook, which is why the kitchen is so clean. I haven't cooked anything the whole week. Even getting a glass of water is annoying. Josh pulls out two bottles of tequila and I laugh. "You planning on drinking all that?" I ask while he falls back into the couch, handing me a bottle.

"Maybe just a bit," he says while taking the remote and switching on the tiny TV across from us. He switches the channels until he finds an old black and white version of Frankenstein.

"You into old horror?" Josh asks before taking a long swig from the bottle.

I shrug. "I can be." I hold the bottle my hands, but I don't take a swig. I'm just not in a drinking mood. I really haven't been since the tailgate party.

Josh moves closer toward me. His leg rubs against my thigh while his hand lightly strokes mine. I move my hand away from him. I don't know what's wrong with me. I should be loving every minute of this. I should be throwing myself into his arms, especially after what the bros did to me. But I guess it's just that. After what happened with the bros, I really don't want anything to do with romance. I just want to wallow in my self-pity and heal my aching heart. Maybe I can date next semester after I feel a bit better. Maybe it can be Josh.

But I'm just not in the mood now.

Josh puts his arm around my shoulder and it's hard to watch the movie, knowing that maybe this is going somewhere I don't want. I'm tempted to stop everything and tell him now is not the right time. But I could be reading into something that isn't even there. This could just be nothing.

"You're not drinking," says Josh.

I glance up and notice he's staring at me and not the TV. I open my mouth, but whatever I am about to say is swallowed by his mouth pressing against mine. I still in his arms while he moans against me. He tries to push his tongue into my mouth, but I keep my lips firmly close. I try to push him away. Tequila is emptying all over my clothes and the couch. I pat at his shoulder but he doesn't budge. His teeth nip at my bottom lip and I take that opportunity to quickly turn my head away.

"Josh, stop," I say while trying to shove him off me. For such a small man, he's actually quite strong. He takes my hands and pins them next to me as he climbs on top of me.

"Don't you want this?" he whispers.

I shake my head. "No, Josh," I say sternly. "I don't want this."

I try to lift my body off the cushions, but he uses his weight to force me down. "But I know you like me," he says while leering over me. "You used to look at me all the time." I cringe as he kisses my throat and try to wiggle myself out of his hold. "Why don't you want me now?"

"Because, Josh, I just don't!" I shout, hoping someone, anyone hears me. "Let me go!" I try to kick him, but he dodges me easily.

"Oh, come on, Rachel," he murmurs in my ear. "Everyone knows you've been fucking the bro hoes. Everyone knows you're a slut." I still when I feel his hand unbuttoning my jeans. His hand sliding inside my panties. I sob and try to shake out of his hold. "Why can't you just put out a little for me?"

I kick him again, slamming into his balls. He groans above me and I wiggle out of his hold, rolling onto the floor. I try to crawl into a standing position, but he grabs my leg and pulls me back. I scream while I grip one of the table legs.

"Stop being a pain in the ass, Rachel!" He shouts while turning me around and pulling my legs apart. His other hand unbuckles his pants and I try to kick him again. He falls over me and grips my arms, pain seeping through me as he shakes me. "Stop it!" he shouts.

I cry and try to push him away. Tears stream down my cheeks as I continue sobbing. I smack him and he grabs my hands, holding them tightly. "Stop it, Rachel!" I spit in his face and he flips me over, my cheek hitting the table leg. With another kick, I connect with something behind me and go as fast as I can to the door. I hear him running after me. I need to run faster. I fling the door open and run down the hall, my pants barely remaining up as I continue running.

"Come back here!" I hear him shout as I continue running down the staircase.

I can't stop running. My arms hurt. My eyes hurt. My face hurts. Everything hurts and I have no clue where I am going or whose apartment I am standing in front of. I knock on it frantically, shivering and rubbing my arms up and down. It's so cold. I don't have a coat. I knock again when there's no answer.

"I'm coming, I'm coming," I hear on the other side.

I glance over my shoulder, wondering if Josh is there. If he has followed me and will take me away. Light permeates behind me and I hear, "Rachel?"

I turn around, tears streaming down my cheeks as I hold back a sob. I see Lucas standing in the doorway with Seth and Hunter behind him. His eyes widen and I wonder if I look as terrible as I feel.

"Are you okay?" Lucas asks, his voice barely above a whisper.

He lifts a hand and I flinch, holding up my arms. Seth is coming up behind Lucas and he pushes him to the side. "Rachel," he says, wrapping a blanket around me and pulling me inside, "are you okay?"

I burst into tears, unable to stop myself from sobbing into his shoulder. He rubs my back while the door closes and leads me to the couch. Seth kisses the top of my head and strokes my hair away from my face. "It's okay now," he whispers in my ear. "Everything is going to be okay." He kisses my forehead again. "God, Rachel. I'm so sorry."

I close my eyes as I lean into his hold, wondering for a moment if this is all just a terrible dream.

Chapter 23

SETH

Black and purple bruises stain the side of her cheek and I see more going down the length of her arm. Her pants are unbuttoned and I have to stop myself from imagining what exactly took place. It will only piss me the fuck off more. Lucas is making some tea for her in the kitchen. The fact that we even have tea is another question I'll need answered. But later.

I hate to see her like this.

It doesn't help that the whole week she was gone I couldn't stop thinking about her; constantly wondering if she was okay or if she found a proper place to stay. Once I thought I saw her walking through the town square and I quickly hid. But it was only someone who looked like her. I even thought I would run into her at work. I spent all of Wednesday night wondering what I would say to her only to discover that she changed shifts with Susan.

I should have felt happy, knowing I wouldn't have to suffer through a whole four hours of her giving me the silent treatment.

Instead, I felt worse.

Before she even arrived at our doorstep I was considering having another bro meeting. Everyone has seemed so out of sorts lately. Ignoring each other. Not going to parties. As if we were mourning someone's death rather than some bitch who seemed to be getting in the middle of our friendship.

In the end, it really is all my fault.

I just didn't want to share. I was acting like a fucking toddler. Even now, I hate that Lucas knows exactly what to do. He hands Rachel a cup of tea while Hunter offers her another hug. Meanwhile, I'm just staring at her like some fucking idiot. I push myself off the couch and run my hands through my hair. I pace back and forth, wondering what's next, what we should do.

"Can you tell us what happened, Rachel?" asks Lucas.

Rachel is in the process of slurping her tea, but quickly stops. Hunter takes her mug and she sighs, leaning into the crook of his arm. Why can't I be like that for her? Something for her to hold onto during all this. Rachel pushes back her hair, releasing a shuddering sigh. "I've been staying over at Josh's place." She sniffs and her face crumples as if she's about to break all over the couch.

She dabs at her eyes with the blanket while Hunter asks, "Who's Josh?"

I also don't know who this Josh is, but Lucas's gaze has turned dark. Even for him, he looks like he's going to smash his fists into the TV. "Four-eyes," he mutters.

"What?" Hunter breathes.

I scowl down at the floor while I remember that wormy little bastard. I knew something wasn't right about him. I knew he was lurking around her too much. My hands fist at my side and I feel something boil deep within me as I imagine him smacking her, grabbing her legs and pulling her back to him as she screamed.

"We were watching some movie on TV," she says in a high-pitched voice before she swallows other sob. She's sniffing and dabbing at her eyes again. "And then he... he..."

Rachel doesn't say anymore and she doesn't have to. I already know exactly what he did.

"We should call the police," I hear Lucas, but I ignore him as I stomp over to the entranceway and shove on my shoes. Or maybe they're Hunter's. I don't care. I open the door and hear Hunter shouting, "Where are you going?"

I don't bother turning around as I say, "I'm going to beat that mother fucker's face in."

I slam the door and run down the stairs. I hear footsteps behind me.

"Seth," calls Lucas.

I don't stop. I can't stop. It's freezing and I was stupid enough to not grab my coat. Did Rachel run in this weather without her coat on? God. That mother fucking bastard is really going to eat my fist.

"Seth, stop!" Lucas shouts.

I feel something tugging at my shoulder and raise my fist, about to slam it into Lucas's face. Anyone's face. So long as it stops this feeling from surfacing. I see Hunter and not Lucas standing right behind me, tugging my shoulder. I can't be taking this anger out on my bros. They didn't do anything. I lower my hand with a sigh, my gaze going heavenward.

"Come back inside," says Hunter while tugging me back to Lucas, who is waiting on the sidewalk. "We'll figure it out together."

"I just can't stand it!" I shout while Lucas slings an arm around me. "That the mother—"

"I hate it, too," says Lucas calmly. "But we can't just go in there swinging our fists around. Four-eyes can say we attacked him and how will that help Rachel?"

My shoulders slump. "It won't."

"She can't go back," says Hunter while we walk up the steps.

"Well, obviously she's staying here," I say irritably. "Alone," I add while glancing between Lucas and Hunter.

Lucas scoffs. "I doubt she wants any male attention after tonight."

"We'll get her things tomorrow," says Hunter and before I can say anything the door swings open and I see Rachel cradling herself on the couch, sleeping soundly.

I stride toward her. Lucas and Hunter sidle up to me and we watch her sleep for a moment. My hand strokes the side of her face where the bruise is, and once again I am hit with that need to pummel four-eyes until he isn't recognizable.

"Yeah," I say. "We'll get her things tomorrow."

***

Josh's place is such a shit hole. I have no clue how she lived in this place for a week. It's teeny tiny with two bedrooms that remind me of closets and a living area that is pretty much unlivable. The so called couch she was sleeping on is really a crappy version of a futon with a blue blanket thrown over it in order to make it look more welcoming than it actually is.

Thankfully, the bastard doesn't put up much of a fight as all three of us bros plus Rachel enter inside the cramped space and begin grabbing her things. Even more wonderful is that she's been living out of her suitcase anyway so packing goes quickly and I don't have to stay around this mother fucker any longer than necessary.

Four-eyes watches us from his bedroom doorway with arms crossed as he leans against the frame. In particular, he watches Rachel with a dark look. I inhale deeply and count to ten. Don't punch him, I tell myself. He's not worth it.

I gaze back at Rachel, sitting on her suitcase while she zips it. Her bruises are darker than last night and she hangs her head, avoiding her attacker. I didn't want her to go. In fact I recommended highly against it. But I guess Rachel wanted to face her harasser as some sort of power move. I really wish she would go to the police about him. What if he does this to someone else? Someone sweet and innocent just like her who can't see through his good guy mask.

But Rachel doesn't think it would help.

I'm hoping I can convince her otherwise. Eventually.

She should at least warn her girlfriends.

"Is this it?" asks Lucas while carrying out a large bag filled with God knows what.

Rachel takes the bag and shoves it in the top of her other suitcase, which barely zips. How the hell did she get all this stuff here? "I guess so," she says while looking around. Her gaze lands on four-eyes and I watch her step toward him while I and Lucas grab her suitcases.

"Thank you for the couch," she says while looking down at her feet.

I can't believe she's fucking thanking him. For this place? It wouldn't have happened if you hadn't kicked her out, a voice whispers in the back of my head, making me feel immediately guilty.

It's my fault she had to go through this.

"I can't believe you are making a big deal out of nothing," says four-eyes, scowling down at her as if she were nothing more than a pesky little ant on his floor.

Rachel's gaze pops up and she scowls back at him with her hands on her hips. "What do you mean nothing? You tried to—"

Hunter laces his fingers with hers and pulls her back to him. "He's not worth it," he says while pushing her hair back behind her ear. I grind my teeth at her grimace as Hunter accidentally touches her bruised cheek. "Let's just go."

Rachel nods. "Okay," she says.

Lucas and I shuffle outside with the suitcases while Rachel leads the way. These bags are so heavy and so bulky. I can't believe she was able to get them on the plane.

"Enjoy your slut, boys," four-eyes calls while sticking his head out of the door. Rachel stills in the hallway, looking around at the other apartment doors. Her face blushes and I see in her prickling eyes she's about to break again. "Although, I'm sure her vagina is probably flapping in the wind with all the fucking around she does. Doubtful you'll be able to get off with it. Maybe try her a—"

Hunter's fist punches four-eyes right in the jaw and I watch as the wormy bastard grabs his face, crying in pain while he melts to the floor. The footballer towers over four eyes, his finger pointed in the other's face. "You ever fucking touch her again," he nearly growls, "I'll fucking kill you." With one last look, Hunter turns on his heel.

I throw my arm around Rachel's shoulders. "You ready to go home?" I ask while we walk down the stairs.

She smiles back at me. "Definitely."

We make it back to the apartment easily enough, and Rachel spends the rest of the Saturday afternoon unpacking her stuff. I should be getting ready for a party, or doing some day drinking, but I'm too on edge. Even though she's back and she's safe, I don't want things going back to the way they were.

I leave my bedroom and pace back and forth in the kitchen. Hunter and Lucas are playing Mario Kart. It's like nothing effects these two. Well, at least they're not thinking of the same things I am.

"Roommate meeting," I finally call.

Hunter groans. "Again?"

I see Lucas look up at the ceiling. "Please don't tell me you are already regretting having Rachel back."

Hunter turns around on the couch. "I'm not kicking her out again. I utterly refuse."

Lucas turns around and nods. "Definitely not doing that again."

I shake my head. "No, no, that's not what this is about."

The door opens and Rachel stands with her hands on her hips. "I am not moving out!" she shouts and stomps down the hall with her finger in my face. "Seth Garcia, you must be—"

"You're staying," I say with hands up. "But I can't have things going back to the way they were before."

Lucas nods while rubbing his chin. "You mean with the lying and the backstabbing."

I send Lucas a cold glare. "Yeah, Lucas. That."

Rachel rolls her eyes. "I don't understand what the problem is, Seth." She crosses her arms. "You share girls all the time."

I grab her hands, lacing my fingers with hers. "But I don't know if I can share you." I pause, those feelings bubbling up within me and I decide this time I won't push them down. "I.... I really like you, Rachel. Like really like you and I don't know if I can share you like the others."

"I think we can all admit, Seth, that we really like Rachel," says Lucas.

"But how do you feel about us?" asks Hunter while glancing between everyone.

She opens her mouth and I wonder how I will react when she says she chooses Lucas. Or Hunter. I try to steel myself, but I'm already feeling mushy and I think I will shatter into tiny Seth pieces if she tells me she doesn't like me in that way.

"I like all of you, too," she says.

That isn't what I was expecting.

"What do you mean?" I ask while pulling her toward me.

"I can't choose," she says while looking away and shrugging. "All of you are important to me. I can't choose." She shakes her head and her gaze meets mine, making me feel all warm and fuzzy inside. "I like you, too, Seth." She glances at Lucas and Hunter. "And I like Hunter and Lucas."

I nod, feeling giddy. She likes me. Well, she also likes Hunter and Lucas, but she also likes me. She won't choose anyone else over me. I feel her hand lace with mine and all the torment from the last week falls from my shoulders. I feel like I'm floating in whatever it is I'm feeling. I can't quite put a name to it.

She isn't tossing me to the curb and that's all that matters.

"So, you choose all of us, then?" I ask while nuzzling my nose against hers. I enjoy the way she feels against me; smooth and warm.

She smiles and nods and I can't help but kiss her. Her lips are soft against mine and she opens herself willingly to me. My tongue strokes against hers, tasting that fire which has always ignited something within me. And too soon the kiss is ending. She pulls away from me and I feel my heart melting all over again as she smiles up at me.

"I think I can deal with that," I breathe and glance over my shoulder, finding Lucas watching us with arms crossed. Hunter is rolling his eyes. "What about you boys?" I ask, knowing the answer already.

Lucas and Hunter look at each other for a moment and I watch as Lucas raises an eyebrow and Hunter smiles wickedly. I watch them, feeling uneasy, knowing through their telepathic conversation they have concocted some sort of scheme.

I don't have time to question as Hunter strides over and takes Rachel's hand in his. "I think," he says while tugging Rachel toward him. "That we have been talking way too much."

Rachel chuckles and opens her mouth to say something, but Hunter quickly silences whatever she is about to say with a kiss. A part of me instantly feels jealous, but Rachel's other hand in mine strokes my palm as reminder of her affections for me. Just that little movement calms me and I watch as Lucas comes up from behind her and kisses her neck.

This might take just a little bit of getting used to.

Rachel pulls away from Hunter and her lips are quickly taken by Lucas, who wraps a muscled arm around her waist and pulls her toward him. His other arm grabs her leg and holds it at his hip. She whimpers as he rubs himself against her.

I can't deny that I hardened just a twinge hearing her pleasure.

Lucas pulls away and Rachel stumbles back into my arms, gasping for breath. Her cheeks are tinged pink and she turns her glossy eyes back to me. She leans into me, nudging my hardening cock with her ass and I moan as I kiss a path up and down her neck.

I hear Lucas chuckling, but I dare not stop as I continue sucking and running my teeth along the sensitive flesh at her nape, enjoying her whimpers and her desperate need to get closer to me.

"I absolutely agree with Hunter," I hear Lucas say and when I look up, I see him waggling his eyebrows up and down.

I swallow. I'm finding it difficult to pay attention as Rachel continues rubbing my dick with her ass. My hands roam over her body, cupping her breasts before sliding down to stroke her groin through her jeans. Her ass presses against me even more and I hiss, finding standing very difficult at this point. I bury my face in her hair while my hands slide underneath her shirt. I'm just about to grab her breasts when Hunter pulls her away from me.

I moan in protest and I'm about to tell him to fuck off when I find both Lucas and Hunter leading Rachel down the hall to her room. Lucas smirks over his shoulder at me and before I can even think about how, why, or even if should I really be doing this, my feet are taking me down that hall and into that room.

I can't believe I'm doing this.

I lean against the door frame, not even bothering to shut the door as I watch Hunter press his lips against hers. I shiver as my hand runs down the length of my body, rubbing myself lightly as I watch Hunter tug up her shirt and throw it behind him. His hands grab her ass and I find myself already stripping out of my clothes and throwing them haphazardly around the room.

I look over and see Lucas copying me while Hunter continues making Rachel whimper and moan. A shiver runs down my spine as I reach for her, tugging her toward me and unclasping her bra. Her hands find my dick and she strokes me as I mouth her beautiful nipples.

Lucas kisses her throat from behind. His dick slides against her ass. I slightly complain when she releases my cock and strokes Lucas. I rub myself against her desperately, already missing the warmth of her hand. And I find I need more. This is not enough. I want her naked and begging for more. I want her whimpering and demanding to be filled.

My hand slides to her jeans, quickly unbuttoning and unzipping them. She shrugs out of them, kicking them down her legs while I slip my fingers inside her panties and search for her clit. I slide my thumb against it, feeling her twitch and hearing a soft moan in satisfaction. Her head lulls back and rests against Lucas's shoulder, giving the both of us easier access to mouth and graze our teeth against her flesh. She clings to me, her nails digging into my flesh which sends ripples of pain melded with pleasure through me.

Lucas's hands grab her breasts from behind and he pulls and pinches her nipples. She moans, her head lulling from side to side and her hands pull me closer, her hips thrusting into me. I slide my thumb down her clit, feeling her wet slick coating my fingers and she whimpers and thrusts against me again.

"More," she whimpers.

My hand slips out from her panties and she gasps, lifting her head from Lucas's and scowls back at me. She grabs my hand and pulls it back to her panties and I chuckle. "I said—"

I silence her with a kiss and pull her toward me as I step backward through her room. I release her and turn her around, pushing her back so she stumbles onto the bed. Lucas sidles up next to me and we look at each other. His face is heated. His lips are completely swollen. I'm sure I look the same.

I can't believe I was going to give up our friendship because of all this when there is such any easy solution to this mess.

I didn't have to make things so difficult.

I feel a kick and turn, seeing Rachel in a half laying half sitting position. She smiles at all of us and says in a lustful tone, "I'm waiting."

She grabs both Lucas and my hands and tugs us toward her onto the bed. I crawl toward her, not knowing exactly which position I should be taking or of I should ask the bros what they would prefer.

I grimace. What a way to end a wonderfully sexy situation: *Hey, bro, you want ass or vag? Or perhaps the mouth?*

It definitely isn't my first time sharing a girl, but that had always been with one other dude and with a girl I had no feelings for.

Three dudes, has the possibility of being a crowd.

Especially, when I kinda want all of her.

I look up, about to question the bros how we want to go about this when I see good ol' Hunter, now completely naked, kneeling between her spread legs. He pulls down her underwear and inserts a finger inside her, watching lustfully as Rachel whimpers arches her back in such a wonderfully sexy way it has my cock twitching in response, leaking with need and want. I watch him lean forward and stroke her clit with his tongue and I bite my lip to keep my moans to myself.

I bend over so I'm laying down and take one nipple into my mouth while my hand plays with her other. She bucks against me as I graze my teeth against her sensitive flesh. Her gasps encouraging me to suck and prod her nipples while her hands run through my hair. Sometimes tugging to keep me in a specific place.

Lucas claims her mouth and she writhes under us as we continue worshipping her body. Her gasps of pleasure get louder as her grip on my head tightens and I feel her twitch, knowing she is about to orgasm. I glance down and see her thighs tense around Hunter's face. Her whole body seems to be trembling. I thrust myself against her leg, aching with need and wanting to join her in her orgasm. Her moans heighten and her heels dig into Hunter's shoulders until finally she wrenches her mouth away from Lucas and screams her release.

I release her nipple and kiss her lips gently. Her head lulls from side to side while her hands stroke up and down my back. Her whole body lies limp in the bed as she gasps and stares up at the ceiling while trying to regain her breath.

But I'm not done.

And neither are the boys.

I glance over my shoulder and see Hunter fumbling with his jeans on the floor, grabbing several packs of condoms and throwing them at the bed. Lucas quickly wraps himself while I stroke my dick, watching Rachel's splayed body. Her breasts move with each gasp she takes, and I find myself leaking in my hands, unable to stop myself from stroking my sensitive tip.

Hunter, his dick wrapped and ready to go, rolls Rachel over until she's on all fours. She shivers as he leans over her. His dick presses into her ass. "Do you want more?" he whispers in her ear.

I watch her head lull up and down before taking Hunter's fingers and sucking on them.

He moans and nuzzles her neck. She grinds her ass against his hard dick and I find my hand moving faster as I stroke myself; completely turned on at this point and needing my release. Lucas lays down on the bed, his hard cock twitching. Hunter nudges her toward him.

Rachel stumbles toward Lucas and her legs go on either side of him. She moans as she slides her clit against his dick and her whole body seems to spasm in need. Lucas moans, his hands gripping her hips, his cock seeking for her entrance as he continues rubbing himself on her little button of pleasure.

Rachel grabs him, slowly jerking his taut flesh. Her finger plays with his slit. Lucas whimpers and lies limply on the bed, becoming a slave to the slow and pleasurable torment. She angles him at her entrance. I moan, unable to hold myself back while I jerk myself, watching as she lowers herself on his cock and takes him all in.

Lucas shudders and grips the bed. He bites his bottom lip while Rachel continues to ride him. Hoarse whimpers escape his lips while Rachel leans forward on the bed, her mouth mere inches away from my cock. She licks her lips seductively and I edge toward her. I'm so close to begging. She opens her mouth, but doesn't bother moving any closer. Lucas's moans underneath her have me whimpering and trembling as I edge even closer toward her.

I whimper as she licks my tip, tasting the pre-cum leaking out of me. I thrust toward her, but she dodges me. Another whimper escapes me and I feel like I have become her next sex slave, completely in her control. She strokes the length of me with one finger and I edge toward her even more, wanting her to take all of me in that sweet mouth of hers. My hands slide against her cheeks, stroking her as her tongue licks my shaft before sliding against my slit. She sucks my tip into her mouth, as if it's a lollipop she's truly enjoying. I groan as she sucks on it, one hand cupping my balls while she balances on the other. I feel my balls tightening. I feel myself getting close. I thrust into her mouth and she takes me fully in. I moan and thrust into her again. I'm just about to explode everything into her mouth. All of it.

Nearly there.

I cry out as she lets go, leaving me near release as she bends over and kisses Lucas. She thrusts against him harder and as she releases him he grabs her breasts, sucking on her nipples while she tosses back her head in ecstasy. I look up and watch Hunter massaging her ass. A finger currently pushing in and out of her other hole.

"Hunter," Rachel whimpers. I groan when she takes my cock into her mouth once more, but the pleasure is short lived when she releases it quickly with a pop. "I want your dick. I want your dick inside me."

Hunter groans and angles himself at her other entrance. "I'm working on it," he says in a hoarse voice.

"I want to be filled."

We moan in unison. Shudders ripple down my back at the implication behind her words and she takes my dick again, going deeper until I'm completely inside her. She bobs her head against me before releasing me quickly. Her hands grasp mine tightly and she gasps when Hunter thrusts inside her, her body jerking from the response.

"So good," she moans while Lucas and Hunter continue thrusting inside her.

Rachel grabs my dick and continues sucking wonderfully on it. Her tongue wraps around me. She takes me deep several times before focusing her attentions on my sensitive tip. I'm about to come. I'm nearly about to come all over her face. And she better not fucking release me again this time.

I glance down and see Lucas writhing under her. His moans are coming out shriller. I know he's getting close. Hunter's pace has sped up. Rachel is whimpering while she continues taking my dick deep.

I groan. My hips are moving on their own. I can't stop them. I feel it build within me, deep in my balls. I try to hold myself back, knowing I should last longer than this. I want Rachel to come with me. But it doesn't help that Hunter and Lucas are also moaning, making me unable to concentrate.

I can't fucking concentrate.

"Fuck, Rachel!" I shout and with one last thrust into her mouth I come, unable to hold back my cries of pleasure.

Rachel takes all of it, licking every last drop from my dick. I pull away from her, inhaling deeply as I lay back on the bed next to the threesome. I grab my head while pleasure racks my body, making me tremble in absolute satisfaction. I look over and see Hunter grunting behind Rachel, pushing in and out of her desperately while his hands grip her hips.

Lucas is gasping underneath Rachel and I know he's close. I bite my lip as Rachel continues moaning. The shrill in her voice making it known she's going to come again. Hunter's moans pick up and I watch his pace grow as he smacks himself deep into her ass. With one last grunt, Hunter thrusts deep into Rachel, emptying himself into her.

Hunter leans over her, massaging her ass while the pleasure shakes through him. He nuzzles her back while Lucas continues thrusting inside her. Slowly, Hunter pulls himself out of her and kneels on the floor, pressing his forehead into the bed.

Lucas grabs Rachel's hips and rolls her over onto the bed. He climbs on top of her, quickly grabbing her legs and throwing them over his shoulders before pounding deep inside her maniacally.

Rachel screams, her hands gripping the sheets as Lucas continues thrusting into her.

Rachel's fingers rub against her clit and I lean over, batting them away and replace them with my own. Hunter crawls onto the bed and sidles up next to her. He grabs her breasts and rubs his thumbs over her nipples. She arches her back, her legs trembling as she thrusts against Lucas's cock.

"So good!" she cries while smacking the bed. She cries out, grabbing both me and Hunter as she thrusts one final time, her body stilling while her nails dig into my skin.

Lucas shouts as he thrusts into her deep. His hands hold her hips still as he comes inside her. Rachel goes limp and falls back onto the bed. Her hands stroke through my hair while Hunter places kisses along her shoulder. Lucas topples over her, moaning before rolling over between Rachel and Hunter.

We all lie in bed for what feels like hours. Our gasps being the only sound as we try to calm our breathing. Maybe it has been hours. Just staring up at the ceiling; all of us sharing the same bed. Rachel laces her fingers with mine while I stroke her hair, unable to stop myself from touching her while I recall previous events and I find myself already wanting to do it again.

She turns to me and her lips twitch upwards into a mischievous grin.

I think I can get used to this.

Chapter 24

RACHEL

I stare at the mess in front of me. Snow lingers by the windowsill while the chill air frosts the sides, making it difficult to even see out the tiny window and look for Lucas and his car. I can't believe the semester is already over. What I originally thought was going to be complete and utter torture actually turned out to be amazing.

And I really hate to leave it all behind.

Not for long, I tell myself. *It's only for the holidays. I'll be back for next term.*

In the same house.

I smile while folding a sweater and stuffing it into my already overstuffed suitcase. Some of the stuff I am bringing back to New York to leave, since there are clothes I never use. Since running with Seth and working at the running store, I find myself pretty much in jeans and yoga pants. The nice stuff I only wear for going out, which isn't every day. I nearly laugh, thinking about what Seth is going to say when he sees this giant suitcase.

He definitely won't be happy. He'll probably go on and on and on about how I need to pack lighter. It's not necessarily my fault. I don't know where the closest Goodwill is and none of my friends wanted them.

I did offer it to Charlie, but unfortunately we have different styles.

I grimace, remembering Josh in all this. After the whole event, I still had to deal with him being in my photography class. Thankfully, he stayed away from me and I stayed away from him. But I didn't have the guts to tell Charlie and Lauren about the whole event. I haven't told anyone. Not the police. Not my mom.

I'm still wondering if I should.

At least I got an A on my photography project. I honestly could not believe it. It makes me wonder what else I can achieve if I just put my mind to it, and I'm excited to see what I can create with my newfound talents.

"There," I mutter to myself, having finished with the packing. I frown at the lid, noticing how it's definitely going to be a pain in the butt to close. I sigh and sit on it before pulling on the zipper. *I really, really hope it doesn't break,* I think while tugging on it.

"Let's go!" Seth calls from the living room.

"Give me a minute!" I shout back. The zipper is halfway there. It just needs to get through the difficult bit and then it should be okay. Hopefully.

"If you don't leave now you are going to be late!" I hear Seth.

"Perfect," says Hunter and I choke back a laugh. Out of all the bros, Hunter has definitely vocalized his disdain at my leaving for the holidays. *He even asked Lucas to have his parents fly my family out here.* I chuckle at the memory. *"People go home for the holidays,"* Seth had said, although he also seemed pretty bummed. Lucas did seem pretty keen on the idea, he probably would've gone through it if Seth hadn't stopped him. I sigh. I really am going to miss them.

All of them.

With one last tug, my suitcase closes. I wipe the imaginary sweat from my forehead and stand.

"Done!" I look down at the gigantic thing. "Can someone please help me?"

Seth comes to my bedroom door, standing in the threshold with his hands on his hips. He looks down at my suitcase and makes a face. "You must be kidding me?"

I hold back my giggles, knowing it's just going to upset him more.

"I thought I told you to pack lightly."

I shrug. "Too late to repack now," I say. He opens his mouth and I quickly add, "Just a moment ago you said we were running late."

A horn beeps behind us, only emphasizing my point. It's most likely Lucas with the car, I assume. Seth goes to my window, opening it and looking outside with a scowl.

"Lucas?" I ask.

Seth slams the window shut and stomps toward me. "You do realize you won't have any of us there at transfer to help you lug this thing around the airport, right?"

I chuckle. "I know, I know. Just down the stairs? Please?"

Seth frowns and I can tell he's not upset with me, but the fact I'm leaving. *Two weeks isn't a long time,* I tell myself. I'm tempted to tell Seth, but I know he'll never admit to missing me.

Some things never change.

"Fine," he mutters while shoving past me. "Hunter!" he calls. "Rachel needs help with her suitcase!"

I fight the need to shoot him a glare. It's so typical he makes his bros do the heavy, dirty work for him. But then again, Hunter is pretty strong. I'm sure my suitcase would be like carrying nothing.

Hunter strides inside and sweeps me a mocking bow. "At your service," he says in a terrible British accent, before grabbing my suitcase and pulling it behind him like he is pulling a small toy wagon.

"What the fuck is taking so long?!" shouts Lucas while slamming open the door. His car keys jingle in his hand while he scowls at all three of us.

"Sorry," I say hesitantly. "It's my fault."

His gaze softens. "You're going to miss your flight at this rate."

"Perfect!" Hunter calls while lugging my suitcase down the apartment steps.

"Be careful you don't slip," I call after him. Last thing he needs is to slip and fall. He's still dealing with his shoulder pain.

"Alright," says Seth while wrapping an arm around my shoulder and pulling me toward him. "Let's get this done and over with."

I smile and allow him to lead us down the staircase and into Lucas's car.

"Alright, you have our numbers?" asks Seth while Lucas drives away from the sidewalk.

"Yes," I say, trying not to laugh at how fatherly he sounds. "I promise to text."

I stare out the window, watching the snow-covered houses and the beautiful mountains behind them pass us by. I wonder if New York is just as snowy right now. We drive to the airport in silence. I glance over to Seth, seeing him watching me. His hand laces with mine and he gives me a gentle squeeze. I peak over Hunter's shoulder and see the airport in the distance, knowing soon we will be parting ways. I sigh. *I really wish I could stay. At least a bit longer.*

"Seth, did you ask her about the thing?" Lucas says as we pull into the airport parking lot.

"What thing?" I ask. My gaze meets Seth's again and I can see that he's blushing.

"It's kinda last minute but... we're all meeting up for a New Year's ski trip," says Seth quickly as Lucas comes to the sidewalk in front of the airport. "You can always join us. If you want that is."

"My parents have a cottage in the mountains around this area," adds Lucas while unbuckling his seatbelt and turning around in his seat. "I can help with the plane ticket."

"But only if you're not too busy," says Hunter while also unbuckling and turning around.

I chuckle, glancing between all three boys. "Sounds like fun," I say. "I'll be there."

Continue reading in Life in the Brohouse Book 2 - Roommates!

Other Titles by Carmen Black

Life in the Brohouse
- Bully, Enemies to Lovers, College, Reverse Harem -

RoomHates

RoomMates

FlatMates

Another Roommate

Seth

The Princes of Powell
- Bully, Enemies to Lovers, College, Reverse Harem -

Revenge

Recover

Printed in Great Britain
by Amazon